A Just

The First Fall

A SEAL Stories
Steph Austin Mystery

By Brett Hanson

Hanson Education Services Publishing
Sturgeon Bay, WI 54235

Cover Design by Seth Hanson
All images are property of Brett Hanson.

Printed in the United States of America

ISBN: 9798408208739
Imprint: Independently published

The First Fall: A SEAL Stories Mystery
p. cm.
I. Mystery II. Military III. Crime Fiction

To purchase additional copies of The First Fall or other SEAL Stories books, or learn more about the author, please visit hansoneducationservices.com

DEDICATION

To everyone who ever tried to do the right thing.

A Just Cause Excerpt: Coming in 2023

CONTENTS

A Just Cause Excerpt: Coming in 2023

ACKNOWLEDGMENTS

Although this is a fictional story, many of the events, dilemmas and resolutions are based on real events, ones I didn't experience alone. So a specific thanks to all my brothers from SEAL Team Four's Alpha Platoon in the early 1990's. Thank you for challenging me, supporting me, and helping me on my quest to become a better man.

A Just Cause Excerpt: Coming in 2023

1 - LOS AMAZONAS

"Five minutes!" yelled Denilson, his voice cracking a little in his feeble attempt to overcome the immensity of the river, the jungle, and the pervasive blackness that seemed to absorb everything but the millions of stars spread across the dome above them. El Madre de Dios at night is like most Bolivian rivers in Los Amazonas: overwhelming, absorbing, dangerous, and exhilarating. The two US Navy riverine patrol boats flew across the murky water as if they had every right to cut, sever, and search el peligroso Amazonas quickly and purposefully. But no matter how strong and powerful they looked and felt, they were not part of this ancient river. They were foreign and unwanted, as if their wake and every trace of their path was devoured as quickly as it was created. Some people might still think modern explorers can actually find ancient treasures hidden in such amazing places with modern technology and months or years of preparation, but Los Amazonas does not give up her mysteries easily.

Fortunately, these Americans weren't searching for anything mysterious, but something concrete. They didn't actually care about El Madre de Dios. The SBU drivers knew exactly, to the longitudinal minute and latitudinal second, where they were going. Their boats exuded power through reinforced, rubberized hulls, high gunwales for additional security, and twin 440 outboard engines that could drive a PB through almost anything. At least, that's what they thought. Los Amazonas knew differently. In truth, the loud, violent machines were no more than black specks on a dark river that has snaked its way through the densest ecosystem in the world under the vastest sky for the longest time imaginable.

The first PB, screaming along the eastern boundary of the river, dangerously close to the unpredictable amber colored clay bank, was actually just a decoy, carrying only the two SBU drivers who would navigate their boat to random fake insertion points. Slowing rapidly, the pilot would turn hard toward the riverbank and slam the bow up onto the muddy, slick earth, wait approximately 30 seconds –hoping nothing would happen– then pull the expensive, modern war-boat off the bank and fall in behind the main boat, taking the centerline position as the main PB slowly edged toward the same eastern shore, waiting its turn. In stealth mode, with low light dials, a hi-tech light-absorbing material covering the entire boat, and a streamline design, the PBs could barely be seen by human eyes, even indigenous ones that might be watching the river as they had for centuries, but they could be heard by anyone and everything for miles in every direction. This SEAL insertion would not be stealthy. But there are many ways to hide the obvious in plain sight. Hiding the obvious has always been a valuable skill for these men, and one of the many reasons they have accomplished such difficult missions in such dangerous places.

The main PB carried one SEAL squad from SEAL Team 4's Alpha platoon, stationed in Virginia Beach, Virginia but deployed out of Panama City, Panama. In 1989, the U.S. still legally controlled the Panama Canal Zone under the Torrijos-Carter treaties, so ST4 launched most of its missions through SOCOM. A few of the eight highly trained SEALs crouching below the gunwales had been there and done that. But most of the newbies never would have guessed a couple years ago, as American teenagers playing football on manicured fields of grass under Friday night lights or trying to persuade pretty girls to trust them more than they should, that one particular night very soon they'd be leaping out of a small black boat into an incomprehensibly dark jungle for the country they loved —no questions asked.— These men, some of the world's best spec-ops soldiers, had theoretically trained for anything: silent insertions, jungle navigation, sniper assassinations, riverine ambushes, clandestine explosives, HALO insertions, intelligence reconnaissance, hand-to-hand combat. You name it, these men were trained to endure and survive it, to kill whenever necessary, and —perhaps most importantly— follow orders, no matter what!

One of the SEALs, a newly promoted 3rd class petty officer serving as the platoon's newly installed intelligence rep, was different. He wasn't focusing, as he should have been, on the threats detailed in the mission plan or his specific responsibilities. Petty Officer 3rd Class Stephen F. Austin should have been organizing pertinent intelligence in his memory, checking the safety on his Car-15, ensuring his gear was not securely fastened (in case they ended up in deep water) making sure he remembered the radio frequencies — primary and secondary— since he was the backup comm guy as well as intel rep. Or he should have been imagining the terrain he'd studied on the Bolivian maps, the distances between the insertion and each checkpoint, the approximate location of towns, and the river's layout in relation to their route. He should have been imagining what could go wrong, especially in the case of an emergency land exfiltration: how the indigenous people might react to a squad of intimidating Americans carrying big guns and asking for help, how to properly set up the UHF radio antennae in a jungle denser than any forest back in Virginia, where to find line-of-sight for the new sat radio (if it worked at all), what to do if the unreliable cellular technology couldn't find a signal when they most needed it (which it wouldn't in a third-world country in the world's densest jungle). He should have been preparing himself for the realities of a dangerous mission in a foreign jungle in an unknown country, but he wasn't. He was stargazing.

After leaving the relatively safe city of Riberalta, just northeast of where El Beni pours itself into El Madre de Dios, the river and jungle slowly absorbed everything except for sound and stars. Few Americans know real darkness. It was so black on El Madre de Dios, even with a sky full of stars, that their own bodies didn't seem real anymore. If not for the sweat streaming down their backs and the consistent collisions between the hard boat and the unforgiving river, Steph could have forgotten himself in the stars. A fascinating unknown, a night sky so dark that the stars looked more like softly pulsing, spontaneous surges than distant sources of light and heat. The longer he stared, the more colors seemed to emanate along the brightest strands of galaxies, like the blue veins and arteries along the inside of pale, cold forearms. So many stars slowly pulsed above him, bringing the universe to life, that they made Los Amazonas seem even darker, even more thrilling. The sky didn't seem to move at all; it felt like the river and stars and even he himself were all flowing together, slowly revealing a connection that has always existed. Steph couldn't put the idea into words, but he felt it. Occasionally, he'd turn his head just enough to glimpse the edge of a tree branch, and the divisions of river, jungle, and universe would re-establish themselves. But the longer he gazed and the more he noticed the deep color of midnight jungle stars, the more connected he felt, and the more distracted he became. As wonderful as it was, he longed for even more.

Austin's patrol buddy and best friend Petty Officer 3rd Class Steenmeister tapped him on the boot. Steen was behind him with the squad's M-60, a one-man killing machine that could lay down approximately five hundred 7.62 rounds per minute at an effective distance of 1200 yards. Of course, that meant little in Los Amazonas because nothing existed 1200 yards away in the jungle. Everything lived right on top of you or it didn't seem to exist, especially at night. But the 60 could still wreak havoc and destruction, while making a hell of a lot of noise. And it was the noise that would most likely save them. Carrying the 60 sucked because it and its ammo weighed so much more than a little Car-15 or M-16, and Steen loved to remind Steph about his burden. But that's not why he tapped him. Steph looked back at his best friend, his roommate and SEAL brother, whose confident, supportive eyes wrinkled at the corners, revealing an awkward smile within the carefully painted camo paint intended to hide his softer features and help him flip the switch.

The Switch. Every spec-ops soldier understands flipping the switch because sometimes they have to do the undoable, the unimaginable. And this paradox would one day soon save Steph's life. But flipping the switch also meant simply focusing. Lose your focus in Los Amazonas and something bad will happen, almost every time. Steen tapped his temple with his forefinger. He knew his friend was a bit of a dreamer, a deep thinker, a little lost at times, and sometimes a little too smart for his own damn good. Steph nodded, turned onto his side a little, and took a deep breath. He closed his eyes, —*Get your shit together! Focus!*— But the stars were still there, calling like a distant brook or a childhood memory, out of sight but not forgotten. He whispered aloud to himself, "Focus."

"Two minutes!" Denilson yelled as the decoy PB finished another false insertion, continuing the leapfrog procession down the river. Each boat had done it many times already. Whenever the boat slowed to hit the bank, Steph marveled at the great black wall separating the water and the jungle. He'd trained in the jungles of Puerto Rico and Panama many times, but Los Amazonas was different. It thrilled him in a way he hadn't expected, scaring him in a way he'd never admit… a good way. Sometimes the wall seemed to shoot right out of the water, as if wall and water worked together to warn people. But warn us of what? El Madre de Dios or los Amazonas? This river the locals had called the Mother of God for centuries, or the dangers of the greatest jungle in the world? It didn't matter to Steph. It was all thrilling, and, as he would soon learn, it was all the same.

As PO2 Breckendae moved toward the PB's broad bow, the LT looked over his shoulder to make sure everyone was ready. Breck, the point man, would be the first to breach the wall, and the first to secure their perimeter. The insertion point was in the northeast corner of La Reserva Nacional Manupiri Heath, so the chances of danger during the insertion were minimal, but better safe than sorry. The LT leaned back, whispering something into the radio that sat on PO3 Smith's back, and Steph suddenly realized he'd forgotten the radio frequencies, their destination, and whether he'd ever been told the particulars of their target. He remembered their basic purpose: surveillance, reconnaissance, and intelligence gathering, but he couldn't remember where they were actually going or why. He knew they would patrol through the Manupiri Heath for a while before leaving the reserve and heading toward their hard target. He thought to himself, *Shouldn't I know where we're going, and why? Shouldn't I remember more about this spectacular place? What am I missing?*

The LT looked back at everyone again, ensuring they were ready and knew the severity of the moment. Breck, the LT, and Smith would go first, with Steph and Steen behind them from the right side of the boat and Chief Wendley, Simpson, and Ensign Walker following from the left side. If all went well, the PB would slam into the bank, high and dry, so all eight SEALs could easily leap from the high, protruding bow right into the jungle, or at least onto dry ground, minimizing exposure time in case of an ambush and keeping all their gear clean and dry. "Clean gear is happy gear," and a pipe dream in the jungle. This would also allow the PB to depart in thirty seconds or less, maintaining the fake insertion pattern and maximizing everyone's safety. But as Murphy knows, nothing ever goes as planned.

Denilson whisper-yelled "Ten seconds," which seemed ridiculous to Steph. *Why whisper anything with these giant engines waking every living thing for miles, and we don't really need to be told 10 seconds since we can all see the jungle right there; besides, the guy in front of me is getting up. When he goes, I go.* But Steph, who didn't want to admit to himself he was nervous, remembered that Denilson was doing his damn best to be the best damn SBU driver he could be. Everyone knew he aspired to more, a SEAL wannabe. So, he deserved a break, right? Besides, protocol always has a purpose. Who was Petty Officer Austin to question protocols put in place by the best Special Warfare Riverine Craft drivers in the world? They didn't tell him how to be a SEAL, so he shouldn't tell them how to deliver SEALs to the insertion point. He tried to focus on the mission ahead, reminding himself again,

Get focused.

Stay sharp.

Flip the switch.

But as the dark wall of jungle towered over him, becoming more real the closer the PB got to the bank, he grew intensely excited, almost giddy, to finally see the heart of the matter, to finally go dark. That which he had read about and dreamed about for so long was finally becoming real.

As the bow rose, it seemed they might actually be able to leap straight into the jungle, but once again, nothing ever goes to plan. The boat slid up the bank for another second and then just stopped, as if the river refused to let go or the jungle refused to open up. Petty Officer First Class Renton, the LPO of the PB, accelerated more but then yelled, "That's it. Go! Go! Go!"

The clay bank would not give way, so Breck and the LT jumped down to the bank and then clambered up the slick, reddish, moist clay. Breck clawed at the muddy earth with both hands like an angry lizard with an M-14 sniper rifle slung over his shoulder. The point man for each SEAL squad is usually a graduate of the best military sniper school in the country, maybe the world. He can neutralize a target, whether a human, vehicle, or control device, at incredible distances with one of many high-tech sniper assault rifles, from a small modified M-16 firing a 5.56 round to the new monstrous 50 cal., which can fire incendiary or explosive rounds capable of extraordinary violence. But in Los Amazonas, nature dictates everything. A hand-crafted, precision model, compactable sniper rifle would be unreliable after a few hours in the bush, much less a few days. A good old-fashioned M-14 accurately fires a large 7.62 round that cuts through vegetation, but more importantly has sufficient clearance in its mechanics, the firing chamber and the trigger mechanism, to still fire after getting in and out of the water and crawling through all the vegetation, jungle rot, and insects. The Colt 45 on his hip might have been a little overkill for this mission, but so was Breck.

With his light load, he was up the bank relatively quickly, especially since the LT pushed him from below. The high bank and wet clay together were formidable, but once Breck was up, he reached back to pull the LT over the crest, then disappeared into the bush. His most important job at the moment was to secure their position in case of an ambush or chance encounter. He pulled his M-14 off his back as he went deeper into the dark, settling quietly on a spot twenty or thirty yards from the river to acclimate his eyes. It's amazing how quickly light seems to dissolve, but even more amazing when your eyes acclimate, allowing you to see in deep darkness. It would take quite a while for everyone to acclimate to the sounds of the jungle. Roaring outboard engines leave a ringing that can't be washed clean in a few minutes. As soon as possible, the rest of the squad would settle into a half-circle perimeter and then quietly wait for the PB to continue its fake insertion pattern down the river. This was the most dangerous moment of the mission, at least that's what Steph had been taught.

The LT reached down to grab Smith's hand while Steph tried to help from below, but the clay was already much slicker, smoothing a bit more with every frantic step, and a radio and its batteries weigh a lot more than an M-14. Steph was relatively light, both in gear and build, so it would have been easy for him to leap up to the ridge with the LT's help, but he didn't want to look anxious. He tried to sling his CAR-15 onto his back so he could use both hands to push Smith up into the jungle, but the weapon swung back down in front of him, jamming the barrel into the moist bank. The LT glared at Smith, as if anger could force him up the bank faster. Steph was now pushing with both hands, and Smith finally made it over the edge, but not smoothly.

The LT hissed, "Steen, get that 60 up here, now!" and disappeared into the black-green jungle. Steph's front was coated in clay, and he hadn't realized his barrel was packed with a little clay plug. He turned to help Steen up the bank, which was even slicker than before, but that wasn't the main problem. PO3 Steenmeister was perfectly suited to carry the 60 through the jungle, but he wasn't a lizard. At 5'11" and 210 pounds without the 60, which weighed 23 pounds without ammunition, Steen was bottlenecking the insertion. Steph turned his knee into a step. Once Steen was partially up the bank, Steph and PO3 Simpson, the squad's corpsman and resident smartass, tried to push Steen's slightly bigger ass up the bank, literally. Unfortunately, the 60 barrel was stuck on a root, so while Steph and Simpson were pushing, Steen was trying to maneuver himself back down the bank enough to unhook it.

He finally whisper-yelled, "Quit!"

Which Simpson was happy to do, replying a bit too loudly "Fine, get your own fat..."

But Chief, appearing just in time, cut him off, "Simpson, shut it. Steen, get up there. NOW! It's not Bunker Fucking Hill!"

PO1 Renton, the SBU captain, was getting anxious. He had a mission to do and the dangerous part was almost over. Every second he stayed on the bank was another second that something could go wrong. "Let's go, let's go." he kept saying, mostly to himself.

Denilson turned toward him, "They're doing their best. You try it." Renton gave him a hard stare, yet said nothing else. But Renton was right. A PB grinding up on a river bank is an easy target and an accurate identifier of the real insertion point. Usually a PB waits until everyone is safely inserted, but Chief Wendley, knowing darkness was their friend and noise their enemy, gave Renton the signal to pull off while four SEALs were still exposed on the bank. Ensign Walker, who had just recently finished STT (SEAL Tactical Training) and been attached to Alpha platoon to gain experience, had found another way up the bank and maneuvered into position to help pull Steen over the small ridge.

Chief and Simpson, still unaware the barrel was caught on the root, were still pushing him up the bank as the LT popped out of the dark, hissing "What the hell?"

Steen whispered, "Sir, my barrel's stuck on something."

By now, they had pushed his entire body around the lodged weapon, which was still connected to Steen by the sling, so he had to detach the sling, push the stock down and slide it from the root. As soon as possible he reattached his sling, ran to his station in the perimeter, and hoped the LT had a short memory. Steph and Simpson, both young, lean, and motivated by the LT's anger, leapt onto the small ridge and pulled the not-so-lean Chief, the last exposed SEAL, to safety. Chief always insisted on being last.

After everyone disappeared into the dark foliage and the LT returned to his position, Chief walked up to Steen and whispered in his ear: "When we get back to VA-Beach, you're on a fat-free diet, fat ass."

Steen shot back, "Look who's talking."

Chief and Steen had teased each other about their non-stereotypical SEAL physiques since the platoon formed, but both of them could run for days, swim for hours, and do whatever it took to protect their teammates. They just liked to eat more food and drink beer, lots of beer. They smiled at each other as Chief walked to his assigned position in the perimeter, patting and rubbing his belly like a mercenary Winnie the Pooh. The LT, who somehow kept an eye on everything, didn't think it was funny. The LT's intensity seemed to give his eyes extra color when he was mad, a pulsing fire-blue. As he silently walked the perimeter, he put a very rigid, very vertical finger over his dark green lips while looking sternly into everyone's eyes, even tapping Steen, who was busy checking the M-60 barrel and his sling, to make sure he knew the deal. The LT wanted everyone to understand his intentions. If looks could kill, his wouldn't have been deadly but more like a thin sharp blade across the cheek, reminding everyone of their place and purpose: Follow orders, his orders! The LT wasn't that much older than Steph or Steen, maybe twenty-five or twenty-six, but for him, life was all about ambition, the opportunity to climb the ladder, whatever ladder you happen to be on. Steph couldn't help but wonder, on many occasions, if he wasn't a high functioning sociopath. He never seemed to run out of energy or focus, like a nuclear power plant constantly on the edge, but never melting down. Even after the PB was far enough upriver that the twin 440's had started to fade into the constant insect hum of Los Amazonas, Steph felt like he could still hear the LT's ambitious mind working. Steph's mind worked overtime too, but not that way.

For the next few minutes, they acclimated themselves to the nighttime jungle, ensuring their position wasn't compromised, and giving everyone a chance to flip the switch, or at least reset it. Most SEALs are notoriously sarcastic and rebellious, but also programmed to excel. From the moment they report to basic SEAL training in Coronado, California, candidates are taught that weakness and errors are unacceptable. SEAL Team Four's grinder and training areas were covered in signs reminding everyone that "Failure is Never an Option," "The Only Easy Day Was Yesterday," and "Pain Is Only Weakness Leaving the Body." It's motivating and helpful on the grinder when you're doing pushups, pull ups, and dips or preparing for a night dive in the Chesapeake Bay in March, but reality doesn't read posters. In Los Amazonas, failure is always an option. And in the bush, a lack of focus or an error in judgement can quickly lead to death.

Some guys, like Petty Officer Breckendae, seemed to be flipped on constantly, which isn't healthy. Once, on a live-fire training mission on Viegas island off the coast of Puerto Rico, he'd started yelling down an ambush line as the plastic targets (simulating enemy troops) were only halfway into the kill zone, and then opened fire early, at a dangerous angle –directly violating the LT's orders.– The OPS Master Chief, one of only two remaining Vietnam SEALs at ST4, asked him, "What da fuck happen'd, kid?" Breck, usually very respectful to the older SEALs, blamed everyone else, yelling about a return signal that everyone must have forgotten. Finally, the LT gave Chief a stern look and walked away. Chief Wendley subtly took Breck's weapon from him, checked the safety, and calmed him down while everyone else returned to the beach camp for a few beers. At first Breck refused to acknowledge his mistake, but Chief handled him, as he always did. Everyone had learned a lot from Chief, but he had a way with Breck that was clearly turning him into an excellent SEAL. As much as Steph secretly disliked Breck, he admired his skills as a soldier. He was the real deal.

But Chief was also the real deal, as a SEAL, mentor, and role model. He knew how to reach everyone, when to pull rank, and when to sit and listen. He always seemed to know what was wrong and how to deal with the situation, like a bush psychologist with one iron fist and another holding a free beer. Rumor had it that he really should have been a senior chief by now, but Navy politics had screwed him. When his guys asked him about it, he refused to disrespect the Navy. He'd just say, "Shit happens. I'm okay with it.

The Navy's been good to me. Where else can I get paid to drink beer all over the world while hanging out with studs like you?" Someone said he punched the Ops Officer. Someone else suggested he smuggled something for some kid's surgery. Smith said he refused a promotion "so he could stay with his guys." Steph couldn't count how many times Chief had said, "Yea, I love the Navy and America, but I'll do anything for the Brotherhood... no matter what."

Steph was very different than Chief, and almost the opposite of Breck. It was difficult for him to flip the switch, and even harder to stay flipped, especially in amazing places like Los Amazonas. As the PB's foreign, metallic whine finally faded, Steph realized the subtle but rising sounds of the jungle, as if it was slowly unmuting itself. Birds were calling out, probably identifying the nearby threat. They caw-called and whistled, rattling back and forth like slightly broken musical instruments sounding ancient hymns of life and struggle and survival. From a distance, somewhere deep in the darkness, a louder whistle-and-flutter broke through the other sounds. Steph wished he had the bird book he bought in Riberalta, Aves de Bolivia. The distant whistle-and-flutter had a physical shape, color, plumage, beauty, meaning, and he wanted to know it, at least as much as it could be known by a Norte Americano. As the squad sat quietly, the rising subtlety shifted to a soft normalcy, at least in his ear. Angry birds squawked at them less and at each other more, as if fighting over a branch or piece of fruit hidden in the dark. He imagined large toucans or brightly colored parrots, but then remembered that most birds in the area were smaller than expected, but that didn't make them quieter.

A frog, or more likely a large group of small frogs, squawked and croaked in patterns he knew he could remember if he had enough time to give the sound shape and find a place in his memory palace. He wondered if they were glass frogs or clown frogs, or maybe even the tiger monkey tree frog. The thought of seeing one of these beautifully colored amphibians in the jungle at night tinged his throat with adrenaline. *Could I actually see one in the jungle at night? Is it physically possible for the human eye, even if it is right in front of me?* Somewhere far away, a monkey, maybe a spider monkey or a black howler, was calling to its brothers and sisters.

But the croaks were closer, and the bird calls crisper and more colorful.

Yet, the most prevalent sound of all, inescapably the most powerful sound on the planet, was the hum of trillions and trillions of insects living and breathing, dying and seething an incomprehensible reality that permeates all life and death, growth and decomposition, the history of Earth as we know it. Steph thought it must be something like that distant microwave hum that supposedly proves the Big Bang theory, the one only astrophysicists understand, or at least claim to understand. Somehow, deep below the words, he knew the two sounds, so seemingly distant, are somehow related. The birds, more comfortable now, quieted a little as the insects sang what seemed to Steph a song reminiscent of the beginning of time.

By now their eyes were mostly acclimated, which allowed Steph to see a little farther into the tangled jungle. Near the river, the ground canopy is usually thicker because light and river moisture penetrate from the side. He assumed it would become easier to see more of the jungle as they went deeper into it, like in Panama. Steph hoped to actually see some of the birds, frogs, or monkeys that he could hear all around them. Yet, he thought to himself, *In a sense I am seeing, or at least experiencing, these animals. So close… so amazing!* But he still hoped for more. He slapped his neck, killing another bug. He didn't need hope to experience the insects because they were crawling all over his exposed skin. No matter what you wear or how hard you try, you'll never avoid insects in the jungle. No, he didn't want to see them, but he would endure all the bug bites in the world to see what he wanted more than anything else, a puma. The elusive mountain lion of Bolivia and Peru, the panther of Los Amazonas and Los Andes. El puma concolor! Whatever we call it, it's the same animal, the same mysterious American cat, the majestic predator, the guardian of the jungle and time and...

When Simpson kicked him, Steph hadn't even noticed they were moving. Breck, the LT, and Smith had already broken the perimeter, and Steph hadn't heard any of it. He quickly rose to his feet, grabbing a handful of soil and rotting vegetation. He lifted the ground toward his face and breathed deeply, solidifying the memory. He self-consciously let the earth, filled with immeasurable living and dying insects of all sizes and shapes, fall through his fingers. As it fell, he looked over his shoulder and saw Chief watching him. Steen, standing between them, was pulling something from his shirt pocket, probably a granola bar or some beef jerky, so he didn't notice the exchange. Steph self-consciously stopped smelling the soil and rubbed his fingers on his pants as he tried to look stern and serious, focused and cruel, like the carefully painted camo-mask on his face. But his Chief smiled and shook his head, as if saying *Damn, Austin, I don't know what's wrong with you, but I've got your back, no matter what?* Steph smiled too, although he instantly wished he hadn't, and then quick-stepped past Simpson to correct his distance from Smith, to maintain the integrity of his squad, to fulfill his duty to his Team and country, to be a dangerous man in a dangerous world. But he couldn't resist the temptation to smell his empty hand again, connecting the color of the birds' calls, the shape of the frogs' croaks, the palpable hum of insects and screaming monkeys, and the literal possibility of seeing a puma. As much as he tried not to, he couldn't resist smiling again, revealing a little bit of teeth, white and reflective, exposed and vulnerable. When he turned his head forward, he instantly saw the LT on one knee, checking the squad, seeing him, his teeth, and his vulnerability. He wasn't smiling.

∞

There are certain fundamental requirements in special warfare. The first is to always know where you are. It's impossible to plot a reliable course to any destination or request emergency evacuation or call in fire support if you don't know where you are. In the late 1980's, GPS technology was new and therefore unreliable, especially in the jungles of Northeast Bolivia. Cell phones existed, but Bolivia didn't have a network of towers, and sat-com required line of sight with satellites. Since there is no line of sight in the jungle, the squad had to rely on Breck and the LT to always know their location and trust they were navigating the planned insertion route. Ideally, Ensign Walker, the last man in the patrol, would also know their location, basically navigating from the back in case the point man is killed or injured. But Mr. Walker was a newbie, so nobody expected much from him. The most difficult terrain to navigate is the jungle because the only fixed reference points are rivers, which are everywhere and therefore easily confused, and towns big enough to be on the map, which are few and far between in northeast Bolivia. Since the squad's insertion route took them through the farthest northeast section of La Reserva Nacional Manupiri Heath toward Federic Roman, most of their humping would be boring, difficult, hot, and blind.

They'd taken breaks only when necessary, drinking and eating, resting and watching, neither talking nor expecting anything in particular. SEALs should always be ready, not for something, but for anything. If you expect something, a specific threat or event, you will act in a pre-planned manner instead of reacting instinctively. But in order to react instinctively, you must stay focused. After a while, it seemed like every imaginable sound distracted Steph from his vow to stay focused, but he hadn't seen anything but green jungle and hadn't felt anything but annoying insects. He hadn't seen any threats or birds; no danger, but also no frogs or monkeys. He hadn't seen any enemies, but also no pumas or tapirs. They were all tired, sweaty, itchy, bored, and annoyed.

The squad humped slowly up small rises, down wet ravines, around gigantic, fallen trees, and over and through all the vines and tanglers Los Amazonas had to offer. They humped slowly and then quickly, waited patiently and irritably, took more breaks, drank more water, ate MRE's, rested and watched, without talking or expecting anything. They humped and searched for what seemed like the longest day of Steph's life because no matter how hard he wanted something to happen, something to become seen, something to change, it didn't. He tried to stay prepared, but it didn't seem to matter. They just humped and humped, and then did it all again the next night and the next day.

When they started humping again on the third day, Steph was exhausted. He'd never been able to sleep in the bush, whether jungle or forest. The incessant bugs and inconsistent sounds distracted him, kept him thinking, rejecting sleep. His body was tired, deep into his bones, the type of tired that BUDS prepared them for. His body was exhausted but supple. His focus wasn't sharper, but his mind was tuned to the surroundings in a relaxed way. At some point in the middle of the day, without any conscious thought, he realized that he felt strangely different, but it wasn't just him. The environment seemed to be changing. Los Amazonas, instead of attacking him, encouraged him. He felt the air tighten his skin a little, without actually constricting it. He looked at Smith's rucksack, about ten yards in front of him. It looked heavy. He glanced over his shoulder at Simpson and Steen and saw even deeper exhaustion. He could barely see the Ensign, his movement admirably smooth and camouflaged, but still heavy. They all looked tired and resigned to the reality of humping, except for Chief. His face had changed at some point in the previous night. The soft was gone, replaced by sharp angles, as if he knew something the others didn't. Steph wondered if the LT knew or sensed it? Did Breck? It was as if Los Amazonas was speaking to them, not warning but whispering. And then Steph heard it, or to be more accurate, didn't hear it.

No bird calls. No frogs or monkeys. It was quieter than it had been since they started the mission. Steph's skin tightened a little more, but he felt no fear. His blood warmed a little. He forgot his aching back. He took a deep breath, unclicked the safety on his Car-15, and, surprisingly, forgot his thoughts too. Everything was different, like nobody and everything had been wrapped up together, and had gone still, very still. He no longer had to remind himself to stay focused. No thought, no predetermined action, just reaction, just instinct. Yes, he unknowingly, unintentionally felt prepared for anything, but nothing could prepare him for what was over the next rise.

2 – THE FIRST FALL

The squad had just crossed yet another small rise in the never-ending series of small rises, dropping one by one into a ravine deeper than all the rest, a unique convergence where the air changed dramatically. Everyone must have noticed the cool, refreshing stillness, the oasis of lighter, softer air without any breeze or movement. It cut the humidity clinging to their sweaty bodies. You see, after so much humping in Los Amazonas, even the slightest relief feels exaggerated, but this relief went straight to Steph's core. With every downward step he felt calmer as well as cooler, reassured as well as relaxed. Elemental forces seemed to rebel all around them as the final SEAL, Ensign Walker, dropped into the strange botanical oasis hidden in a bowl of resistant green. It wasn't that Los Amazonas didn't want them there, but more that they were obviously foreign, and thus naturally repelled. Steph sensed it. His skin, already tingling, seemed more attuned, and he wondered if his Brothers could feel it. He could see all his buddies around him, but couldn't shake the feeling that they didn't sense it, that he was experiencing this moment alone, or at least differently than them. And then it happened.

The first one shocked him, even though nobody heard it. Steph could see it like a laser beam spiraling in slow motion. It wasn't red or green, but white with touches of lavender and blue, like the translucency of skin in sunlight. The first petal seemed to carve a groove through the air, to descend forever, until a second petal, and then a third, followed suit, appearing out of nowhere. As the first dissolved into the ground vegetation, other petals took up the revolution, turning and carving, reinforcing the effort of the first, building momentum, which in turn seemed to pull yet more petals from the jungle. Soon, dozens of petals were falling and spinning, like tiny, twirling dervishes indifferent to their fate. Very little sunlight reaches the jungle floor, but as more petals fell from above, some of them caught the precious sunbeams, reflecting and refracting throughout the cool oasis. Steph looked left and right, up and down, trying to absorb the moment, completely unaware of the threats that could be all around him, still unaware of the clay plug stuck in the barrel of his weapon, unaware of the rest of his squad or what he was doing so deep in the jungle, so far from his safe, well-known, American life.

The petals poured like silent rain. Blue, white, and lavender petals fell onto his sweaty camos, his weary face, and his green hands. It was only after looking at his hands that he really remembered his Brothers: Steen, Smith, Chief. He looked at Smith's rucksack again, which was a little farther away this time. It seemed the same, except for the petals. He looked back at Steen and Chief. Steen's head hung toward the ground, as if too heavy to pay attention to anything but humping. Chief was looking to the left of the squad, toward a very dark area up the rise, totally engrossed in the shadows. They didn't seem to realize the immensity, the beauty, of the moment. For Steph it would always be the moment he experienced and thus believed in Relativity, even if he didn't understand it. His mind instinctively flashed to the room in his memory palace where he kept memories of Einstein and his theories. He saw an old smiling face with two kind eyes surrounded by electrified white hair, an old train station with an observer on a wooden platform pointing to his watch as two old trains approached from different directions at different speeds, a warping transparent field of graph paper stretched across space while Earth, like a glass marble, rolled across it, leaning precariously toward the sun.

He had been tired, insecure, and a little hopeless just a moment ago, but something had changed. And then, as suddenly as the silent shower started, it stopped. A few rogue petals twirled toward the jungle floor where they would inevitably sink into the earth, quickly decomposing. Steph wanted to reach down, grab some petals, smell them, and then hide them in his pocket to prove they existed, that it had happened, but he didn't dare after the last time. He simply blinked, and then blinked again. That was it. Except for the petals clinging to their sweaty clothes, it was over.

It's difficult to see altitude in the jungle, but easy to feel, especially for tired legs. As he rose out of the botanical bowl, a unique Eden he knew he'd never forget, Steph looked over his shoulder again. Smith looked tired, but he could really see Steen's exhaustion. He had pushed his camo hat back enough to let the coolness touch his forehead, and a few petals had stuck to the sweaty camo paint around his eyes and cheeks, softening their hard reality. And behind him, Chief's face, also slightly adorned with petals, beamed a child-like smile. He was pointing with two fingers, first at his own eyes and then toward the shadows to the left. Steph thought he was telling him to stay alert, to look for threats, so he nodded. But Chief smiled and did it again. So, Steph looked toward the shadows, but saw nothing but shades of green and colorful petals because he couldn't stop thinking about what had just happened. He was too much in his own head now, and he'd deeply regret it soon.

He turned to pick up the pace and thought, *Maybe it was a botanical anomaly. We accidentally stumbled into a very sensitive ecosystem, changing the core temperature at just the right time to cause rare and sensitive jungle flowers to drop their petals simultaneously. Or maybe Los Amazonas is not rejecting us, but reassuring us. Maybe this amazing jungle is reassuring us, to keep searching, to believe in something new and amazing in the middle of a harsh and dangerous world.* Either way, Steph would never forget it. Just as he would never forget what Chief said to him after scurrying past Simpson and Steen, breaking protocol and creating unnecessary noise.

He smiled as he whispered into Steph's ear, "Did you see it?"

Steph nodded his head up and down while holding a few petals in his hand. "Yea. They're beautiful, aren't they?"

Chief looked at his hand and laughed at him, "No. Not the fucking flowers!" Steph suddenly realized that the two-fingered gesture wasn't a warning, but an invitation to look at something.

"Up on the rise behind us, to the left, in those really dark shadows. I swear to God... a puma. I saw a fuckin' puma!" Chief pointed backward and to the left, toward a tree near the highest part of the rise, like a kid convincing his friends that he'd seen bigfoot or a ghost.

Steph looked at Chief as if he told him he was his father. "Bullshit!"

Chief just smiled and whispered, "No shit... I saw it. Never thought I'd see something like that, all this time in the jungle. But hell, walk around long enough and you're bound to walk into something amazing, right?" Chief just smiled and shook his head, a petal smeared with sweaty camo fell off his forehead toward the ground.

Steph didn't know what to say. He just looked along the rise where Chief had pointed, hoping for a glimpse. He didn't know why, but he believed Chief completely, and it showed on his face.

Chief smiled again and then whispered, "It just goes to show, be prepared is a great motto, but nothing can prepare you for this place. Nothing." He patted Steph on the shoulder. "Let's go. Don't want to keep the LT waiting."

Steph would later wonder if Chief's comment was a premonition or just a coincidence, especially after all the deaths. But then, as he turned to continue the monotonous humping toward a target he'd basically forgotten, he became angry with himself, disappointed that he hadn't been more attentive. He glanced back at the ridge a few times as they settled back into their tedious routine, but he didn't want to seem distracted. He would have given every flower in the world, even if Einstein himself had cut them into secret universal theories, to see a puma in Los Amazonas.

Damn!

Another regret.

Another lost moment.

3 – BE PATIENT… THERE WILL BE DEATH

"Austin! You okay?"

The light filled the space subtly, no dramatic beams or revelations. Just light. And he knew it was just light. In that moment Steph wasn't thinking about the light or how the jungle tinted everything green, as if through a soft green filter. He wasn't thinking about the pain filling his neck and shoulders, in both waves and pulses, or why he was in this predicament. To be honest, he didn't seem aware of much, so he didn't hear Petty Officer Simpson.

"Hey! Are you okay? The LT wants to talk to you… if you're up to it."

Steph was looking the other way, through the high window near the edge of the room, lost in the vast green canopy that filled the small, rectangular pane of glass. In any other part of the world, except maybe Southeast Asia, if a wounded soldier looked out such a high window while lying so low in a grunt-like, makeshift hammock, he'd probably see fluffy white cumulus clouds or web-like cirrus striations or maybe stormy dark clouds or a metallic grey blanket of clouds, or maybe just open skies. But in this part of Los Amazonas he'd have to either be in town or the middle of the river lying flat on his back in a boat to see pure open sky. Jungle green dominated everything.

Austin thought to himself, *In this cement hut, on this backwoods-ass base, the jungle literally towers over you. It's overwhelming! How does any civilization survive here? How can people survive in this place? God, I fucking hate it... How deep can one particular color go, or I guess here you would say grow, even in a place like this, a relentlessly alive place that eats everything as fast as everything that's been eaten grows into something else that will in turn eat whatever it can? How long would it take to eat, say, this cement shithole we've been living in, with its tin can roof? I mean, it can't be more difficult to devour than the jungle. I wonder which would take longer to eat, this aluminum foil barracks with its loose tile floors, rusty pipes, moldy wood, and dilapidated head or a large part of the jungle? What about just the insects, how long would it take for just the insects to eat this barracks, not including humidity, gravity, animal claws, and hairy, deadly caterpillars?*

He shook his head, tried to scratch his wound, then thought, *That's stupid... the meds must be messing with me.... But, really, what about this shitcan versus, say, an ancient civilization? I mean, could the Mayans handle it down here, or the Aztecs? Not for a day or two, but for real, for ever! I remember reading about that explorer who thought there was a great civilization in the Amazon... what was his name... ? He was British, I think, but he disappeared with his son and his son's friend, and then all those idiots went looking for him. Yea, he was British. Only the British. Only dumbass Brits and dumb Americans! They had no idea what they were getting into. What was his name... I can't remember... It's in here somewhere.*

He closed his eyes and imagined the book room in his palace, the shelf shaped like an S, South America, and the book that turned into a river shaped like a Z... *That's it! The Lost City of Z... Percy dumbass Fawcett. That's him. He died down here, probably eaten by a herd of giant caterpillars that laughed the entire time they ate him. I wonder what he looked like? Did he drink tea while trekking through Bolivia, or did he trek through Peru? No, I think it was Bolivia. But really, could the Mayans do it? Because I've been there, seen that... and this place, this pervasive, relentless green consumption and organic destruction blows everything in Central America and the highlands of Peru and the strongest winds of the hottest deserts, Atacama or Gobi, away. I mean, way out of the way. Ughhh, man! I can feel the poison coursing through my neck, just eating away at my flesh. God, I hate this fucking place!*

Austin reached up and scratched around the bandage again, and then ran his fingers along its ridge. The gauze and tape felt like mummy skin, or at least what he thought mummy skin would feel like. It wavered and rippled due to the humidity, like everything else, making the tape kind of slick and inevitably loose. His skin outside the edges of the bandage was not at all loose, but hot and tight and itchy and smooth. The wound was very small; he couldn't even remember where it was now due to all the swelling and bandages. He remembered that at first Simpson, the Alpha platoon corpsman, didn't know why Austin had stopped and kneeled down, hissing through his teeth and reaching toward the back of his neck. You see, nobody had seen the attack coming because it's so easy to miss the obvious when it's hidden in plain sight, especially if it's also unexpected.

Simpson, still standing next to him in the barracks, asked him again, "Dude, ARE... YOU... OKAY?" He gestured with his hands as he said each word slowly, as if speaking slower and louder would make him easier to understand. "DID... YOU... HEAR... ME?"

"What?" replied Steph.

"What do you mean what? For such a smart guy, you're a fucking idiot. It figures you'd be the one to get your ass kicked by a damn bug."

"Shut up, Simpson!"

"They're going to put it on your tombstone, which by the way, will probably be somewhere over there, next to the shit pile." Simpson shivered as he gestured toward the river, near the site where he'd been, as he so eloquently put it, "shitted by some little brown shitter who needed to learn to use a proper shit hole." After the squad first settled into the barracks, Simpson was helping Smith put up the long distance HF antenna, which is really just a wire pointed in the right direction at the right angle. As he was gathering the throw-line so Smith could try again, he smelled feces, wrinkled his entire face, smelled his hands, and then gradually but emphatically freaked out. Chief tried to convince him that it was probably from a dog, which seemed less nasty to everyone, but Simpson wouldn't hear it. He immediately used the incident as another racist excuse to degrade the Bolivians.

He popped a fresh dip into his lip without even thinking about it and went on, "They'll bury you next to your little brown friends. And then you can all shit all over each other until judgement day for all I care. Damn shitters!"

"What are you talking about?" Steph was still thinking about the deep green and Percy Fawcett and the Mayans, so hadn't really been listening at all.

"I don't know. I'm just in a bad mood. This place is on my nerves. It doesn't seem that hot, but it's so humid and it stinks, ya know? like... poor people... and mud. I want to go back to Panama City, or even better, Cartagena. At least there they dress like Americans."

Simpson certainly wasn't the only racist in the squad, or even the most virulent, but he talked a lot and never seemed to realize how offensive he was. Steph had learned not to debate racism with anybody but Chief or Steen. First, it didn't do any good. Second, and more importantly, he learned from Chief that it eroded the guys' trust, in general and in him. It was the late 1980's, and they were probably all racists, but the difference was that Steph questioned it, like everything else, and knew it wasn't natural or logical. And he knew he didn't like it. He remembered reading, in a book he speed-read at Fort Benning after a strange interview with an Army captain, about the three main types of racism: ideological, behavioral, and institutional. The photos were almost all African-Americans and from the 60's and 70's. Maybe a couple Asians, but no Latinos. There was no doubt in his mind that most of his buddies, as white American men with big guns and lots of money usually do, believed they were better than the people they worked with and theoretically served.

"Yea, I bet you wish that it had sucked you instead of bit you."

Steph looked up, surprised, "Man, Simpson, you are one weird dude!" smiling as if joking, but serious at the same time.

"Me? You're the one moaning in the jungle in the middle of a night patrol. Man, I thought the LT was gonna shoot your ass." Simpson raised an eyebrow a bit and spoke a little softer, "Ivy or no Ivy, that dude is wrapped way too tight, man."

"Yea. He was pissed. Did you see his eyes?"

Simpson had, but he didn't like life to get too serious, so he digressed. "Yea, but I'll never forget yours either, dude." Simpson contorted his face to look like a constipated Shirley Temple pretending to suffer the pangs of death while batting her eyes uncontrollably and then moaned his best impression of an invalid with a speech impediment, "Ohh my neck. Pwease help me. Pwease, pwease help me."

Steph just smiled as he remembered what really happened two nights ago.

∞

It was dark, darker than the insertion night. The kind of darkness that only happens at night in the jungle during the rainy season. The clouds had blocked all the celestial light, and since there was almost no man-made light in the jungle, their eyes were on their own. Steph had gotten a charge from the jungle shower of petals and the puma Chief had seen. Even though he hadn't seen it, he believed his Chief, so there was no doubt in his mind that a puma had been watching them. It never occurred to him Chief would have just plain lied about something like that. He joked with his guys, but he was more like a surrogate dad than a big brother. As far as Steph was concerned, something had been there. The weird thing about the jungle shower was that nobody said anything afterward. —Never!— Neither in Bolivia nor back in Panama or Virginia. But then again, bigger events would soon become much more memorable, much more dangerous. Murder tends to do that.

They'd been humping for what seemed like Biblical times, and everyone was dead-tired. After too many days in dense jungle, your focus starts to falter and people make mistakes, but Steph couldn't think of anything he'd done wrong. His mind was a little soft. He'd drifted quite a few times, but that doesn't affect gravity. And it wasn't as if somebody had intentionally dropped the furry little bastard on his neck. Living, crawling things fall or crawl or slither on soldiers in the jungle all the time. So it wasn't that the caterpillar was on him, but that it bit him, and literally, put... him... down.

"Oww! Shit!" whispered Steph, stopping for a minute and reaching back on his neck. He'd actually felt something which he

Steph, trying to get his canteen from his belt, finally understood the question. "Where is what?"

"The caterpillar?" Simpson's smirk, only visible because of the white of his teeth, hinted what was coming next, but Steph wasn't looking at him so didn't get it. "We might need to interrogate it or send it to the lab for samples, or, who knows, I might need to inspect it for poison... You might want to press charges." Simpson kneeled down next to him. "Do you think the UCMJ has anything about caterpillars?" Simpson's mock sincerity, the kind that well-seasoned sailors and soldiers are almost obliged to master and appreciate, floated in the air like pollen. "Wait, maybe it wasn't a caterpillar at all. Maybe it was a blow dart!"

Austin looked at Simpson, contemplating whether the UCMJ, and more importantly the LT, would consider him stabbing Simpson in the face with a stick an unreasonable response.

The LT walked up and hissed, "Quiet!" He looked at each of them separately, and then said, "What?" which clearly meant *Why have you two stopped walking? Why are you talking in the middle of this op? What is wrong with you?* and, perhaps a little less directly but equally forcefully, *Do you understand that I am in charge and I can destroy you?*

Simpson replied first, quietly, in his best baby voice "Austin got bit by a wittle catepiwwer" pouting his lips for effect.

"What?" the LT asked, sincerely surprised.

Austin, partially to make sure Simpson didn't make the situation worse, whispered, "Sir, something —I think it was an insect, maybe a caterpillar— landed on my neck. When I reached back to pull it off, it bit me, or stabbed me, or something. Now, my neck stings like crazy. It burns, sir." Immediately he knew what was coming from the LT, but it was too late, and he wasn't ready for the intensity of the response.

The LT leaned in close to Steph's face, his green, black, and grey camo paint subtly streaked with tracks of sweat and small green and brown bits of the jungle. His face shimmered like hot oil, exaggerating his startlingly white eyes which widened and flexed like a muscle, until he simply said, "Shut... up! Get moving."

"Yes, sir." was all Austin said, gritting his teeth.

As the LT walked away, Simpson quickly smeared some cream on Austin's neck, realized that the swelling had already started, and handed him two pills. Steph swallowed them without question, stood up, poured water on his neck and motioned to Simpson to rub it with the stick, and fell back into his patrolling position. Simpson, since he'd never been taught to rub insect bites with a jungle stick, threw it into the bush. The burning on Steph's neck didn't stop —it was bad— but the burning in his mind was worse, a mix of anger, shame, irritation, bad luck, and a little injustice. He thought, *Yea, I know the deal. The LT has a job to do, but he doesn't have to be such a prick about it.*

The rest of the night was awful, no other way to put it. They walked through the jungle as Austin's neck burned and swelled, swelled and burned, and he consistently felt worse and worse. At the next perimeter, Simpson smeared some more cream on it and realized how much the site had ballooned since the last application and how much warmer the skin had become. He told Chief. Steph just closed his eyes, cursed nature, and humped on as the burning got worse. He realized that he couldn't turn his head, but he only needed to see the radio pack in front of him to do his duty. As dawn started to filter into the lower canopy, Steph started stumbling and felt strangely prickly on the inside of his skin, like heat stroke and a bad fever combined with delirium and exhaustion. The burning in his mind was gone now; his ego didn't care anymore. All the pain was in his neck and shoulder, demanding, pulsing, consuming, expanding, devouring. The next time they stopped, after kneeling on the ground as Breck and the LT checked their location, he didn't stand up again when everyone else did. He didn't fall, but he didn't get up either. He leaned toward the earth, pushing his right palm into the leaves and dirt. A few ants started crawling across his hand immediately, as if staking their claim. Chief looked at his neck and told the LT they had to stop, that they'd have to head straight for El Madre de Dios and call in the PB's.

∞

Chief Wendley, looking annoyed and surprised, stepped into the space. "Hey, dumbass! didn't you hear me. What are you doing?"

Simpson gave Chief his dopey, what-me face. "We were just reminiscing about… The Attack!"

"Don't call it that, you twit." But Chief said it with a smile. "Isn't it almost time for a radio check? If not, go rewrap some bandages or rub oil on your rod. Uncle Sam's paying you top dollar down here. You don't want to cheat the taxpayers by not doing your duty, do you? Never mind, don't answer. You wouldn't know your duty if it was tattooed on your ass."

"Well, no Chief, remember. You told me yesterday that I couldn't find my ass with both hands." Simpson starting grabbing himself everywhere but his ass. "Besides, taxes are a scam and a lie, I mean, that we have to pay them. You see…" Simpson was about to start one of his tirades about taxes. Austin had tried to force him to acknowledge that taxes pay for everything they do in the SEAL Teams, including get a paycheck, but Simpson had a special gift for self-imposed ignorance and denial.

Chief had also heard it all before, and didn't want to hear it again. "Simpson?"

"Yea, Chief?"

"Get out!"

"Don't you want to hear my five point plan to eliminate all taxes?" Chief just raised his eyebrows and nodded toward the door. "You're the boss." Simpson said as he left, grabbing an MRE from

Steph's box on the way out.

Chief looked at Steph and said, "The LT still wants to see you. He's already pissed that he has to stay out of the field to work this out, and we've got to go into town this afternoon, too. So, you better not make him wait too long." He paused for a minute, and then asked, "How ya feelin'?"

Chief was tough, but out of the bush, cleaned up and wearing his Teva's with green army issue socks sticking out, you'd never guess he was a SEAL. He looked more like a 5 foot 9 inch, slightly plump, 195 pound baker who should be selling donuts and Easter cakes. None of his muscles could be seen, with or without a shirt on, and no amount of running seemed to penetrate his second chin (in all fairness, it wasn't fatty, but a more genetic inevitability). He had a smile that always seemed to sneak out from behind the mandatory Navy chief grimace.

"How's the neck doing? How are ya feeling?" He asked again.

"It's a little better." Steph said, looking out the window again. "Chief, have you ever noticed how intense the green is down here? I mean it's almost more than a color. How does one describe this kind of green, this pervasiveness, in words? I mean, if you were, say, writing a letter to someone."

Chief raised his eyebrows, "First of all, who the hell says "How does one describe?" And second, are you writing a letter to someone?"

"No." answered Steph.

"Then why do you care?"

Austin couldn't see the expression on Chief's face, so he bent down to put on his sandals, securing the velcro around the back. His neck was still so swollen that he couldn't turn his head more than a few inches left or right, and only tilt it a little more up or down. He had to reposition his entire body to look most places.

Chief shook his head, sighed, and said again, probably for the fiftieth time, "Austin, are you sure you're in the right place?" It had become a running joke between them.

Chief Wendley had known Steph since he got to the team as an E3 waiting to get into STT, desperate for his Trident, and still wet behind the ears and everywhere else. On his third day at SEAL Team 4, Chief had helped haze Steph in the morning, driven him to housing and pulled some strings to get his VHA/BAQ stamp for extra money to live off base in the afternoon, and then took him to the strip club that night for beers and wings. Steph listened to Chief talk about his wife and kids adoringly as he kindly slipped dollar bills into one of the young girls' g-strings as if he was giving his kids quarters for the vending machines. Then he'd look at Steph and say, "They gotta make a living." For him, everything was about doing it the right way... the SEAL way. He explained to Steph how it's all part of the Brotherhood pact: Do your part, and they'll be there for you, no matter what. It became his catch-phrase: *No matter what.*

Chief had always been there for Austin, even though he was... well, different.

First, Austin always seemed to have a book with him. It didn't matter if they were flying from Panama to French Guiana after a brutal going-away party (way too much rum, not enough fruit juice) on a tiny C2 with more wind and propeller noise than anyone wants to hear above the Atlantic, or if they were riding a CPB, Coastal Patrol Boat, through rough waves from SOCOM to Cartagena, Columbia, Austin always seemed to be reading or thinking about stuff most of his teammates just didn't care about. He read some of what a typical sailor or soldier would read, Tom Clancy and John Grisham, but he also read history books, biographies, nature publications, country reports on all the countries of Central and South America, and —whenever possible— the great literature of whichever country they were in or headed to. He tried to convince Steen, the LT, the JG, and even Chief Wendley, to read *One Hundred Years of Solitude* by Gabriel Garcia-Marquez, *Elementary Odes* by Pablo Neruda, *The Night* by Jaime Saenz, or *Gabriela, Clove and Cinnamon*, by Jorge Amado. You see, Steph wasn't always an avid reader and thinker, just as he hadn't always wanted to be a Navy SEAL, traveling the world to serve his country and the American ideals of democracy and justice. At different points in his life, he'd been homeless and depressed, a drunk and a druggie, a lost soul without a purpose. But now he felt like he had a purpose, and wanted to hone whatever skills and knowledge might help him fulfill his duty. He had just recently started considering that in addition to fulfilling his SEAL and

American responsibilities, he also had a duty to be a good person. As he would soon learn, doing all three simultaneously is sometimes much harder than it should be.

Second, he endeavored to be honest, or as he called it, sincere. He told the truth whenever possible, which caused a lot of problems, especially for a young SEAL. Almost all his Team Brothers thought honesty was a stupid virtue. One of the many mottos they lived by was "Admit nothing, deny everything, and make counter accusations." He tried, but Steph hated being false, especially for petty reasons. He wouldn't lie to get laid, avoid punishment in BUDS, or to hide his weaknesses. He simply hated the feeling lying left hanging around his throat, just above his heart. Basically, he told the truth or kept his mouth shut unless it was absolutely necessary. But as Chief ironically pointed out to Steph, "Aristotle knew the deal: 'We are what we repeatedly do.' So you will shoot the way you usually shoot, endure the way you usually endure, and manipulate people the way you usually manipulate people. Good or bad, you must do what's best for the Team." Steph knew Chief meant well, but he believed deeply in sincerity, honesty, and self-reliance. *To this iron string be true.*

After watching Steph strap on his TEVAs, Chief said "Well, wherever you're supposed to be, here you are. So, I got your back." Chief smiled at him, smirked, and gestured toward the door. "The LT…"

"Yea, I'm going."

The First Fall

4 – THE LT

Steph didn't know what to expect when he walked into the makeshift office/command center. The LT was on the phone, sitting at a small desk with a plastic filing crate next to him. He held up one finger to Steph, not looking away from his papers, while speaking Spanish into the phone. Steph understood Spanish much better than he led on, but wasn't confident enough to assume a role as a squad translator, so he kept his quickly growing skill to himself. Technically, he was just beginning to study it, but he learned new systems quickly. When he realized he'd have to wait, he looked nonchalantly around the room. It was small, with a desk, a couple chairs, a small filing crate, a fireproof briefcase safe, and a burn bag. A closed closet hid in the corner, and a high window, like the one in their bunk room, let in light and air. A wisp of cloud floated slowly through the small rectangle, so he watched it, identifying its type and trying to decide if it meant more or less humidity. He intentionally ignored the LT's conversation. It seemed rude to listen. When he heard the phone click down, he looked at the LT and said, "You wanted to see me, Sir?"

The LT looked straight at Steph, leaning back in his chair. He was a good looking, well groomed, intelligent WASP with Grecian lines and athletic shoulders. Steph thought Simpson was probably right, the LT had probably graduated from some Ivy school, Harvard or Brown, Yale maybe, but since he didn't have an accent, Steph assumed he was probably from Baltimore, maybe D.C. Either way, it was obvious that the LT was on his way somewhere important, and being a SEAL was just a step toward something else. He gestured to the small chair, "Sit down, Austin."

Steph didn't reply, just pulled the seat around so he could keep the desk between himself and the LT and sat down.

"I'm sorry I went off on you out there. We were all tired."

"That's okay, sir. Shit don't stick, so..." Right after saying it, he wished he hadn't. Some officers liked to feel closer to the enlisted guys, using their expressions, their slang and profanity, but Steph assumed the LT wasn't one of them, and he'd be better served staying professional.

"Yes... well, how's the shoulder?" The LT tried his best to look concerned.

"It's mostly my neck sir, and it's better. I still can't turn my head, but there's less pain and the swelling hasn't gotten any worse."

The LT looked at him closely. Steph knew the LT was trying to solve something but didn't know exactly how to go about it. He needed to know unequivocally if Steph wanted to be shipped back to Panama, but didn't want to ask him. He needed to be in charge, but at the same time didn't want the blame for any health or safety mistakes. Simpson, the squad's corpsman, had been really nervous after they got back to the Bolivian base. The skin was strangely colored and the swelling was immense, but the real concern was

Steph's fever, pain, strange behavior, and, most surprisingly, his hands. The knuckles had swollen a little, but the fingertips looked filled with white air and seemed to glow. Steph resisted answering their questions, or really saying anything at first, but when he did, he spoke deliriously about birds, predators, time, and gravity. One of the Bolivian soldiers told them los campesinos sometimes died from la polilla gigante del gusano de seda, which Simpson assumed meant big fat caterpillar but was really a type of giant silkworm moth. The soldier added that it occurred mostly in Brazil and that the moths had become harder and harder to find. Apparently, the bush people used them for a variety of reasons.

Breck couldn't believe it. "We're not considering canceling our mission because of a fucking caterpillar, are we? ... Bullshit!" The LT agreed with Breck, but Chief and Simpson said they shouldn't risk Austin's health. They thought the LT should at least consider medevacing him back to Panama, to a military hospital with American doctors. Finally they decided to wait a day, two at the most. So far, they had only canceled a reconnaissance mission to quietly gather intel while getting much needed jungle experience. Chief suggested that, since they hadn't been compromised, they could still go back if their training time allowed. Their role was technically to train and advise, but if they also learned something helpful in the jungle, all the better. Once back at the base, the LT decided to send everyone else to the jungle training camp just northeast of Riberalta, which meant Breck would be in charge of training the Bolivians on basic special warfare tactics. Breck wasn't happy they'd canceled the op for an insect bite, but he was excited to be in charge of so many men with guns.

Finally, the LT leaned back and asked Steph directly, "Do you think you need to go back to Panama?"

Steph knew the LT wanted him to say no. It's true that just a few minutes ago he'd wanted to leave, to return to U.S. air conditioning, U.S. breakfasts in the mess hall, and U.S. doctors, but for some reason he changed his mind. Suddenly, he wanted to stay. This trip, his first full deployment out of the U.S. controlled Canal Zone, had been a shock even before the attack. At first he hated how dirty everything was, the incessant bugs, the sad weight of poverty along the river, the oppressive humidity, and the apparently unfriendly Bolivians. They seemed different than the Panamanians, which, of course, they were, but Steph felt a sense of disappointment that he couldn't pin down. He'd never tell his buddies, but he usually wanted to like people, and be liked in return. Yet, this wasn't the real reason he wanted to stay.

He thought to himself, *Something's changed, or I've changed, and it seemed to happen after the attack. No, that's wrong. It probably started at the insertion... and I definitely felt it during the jungle shower. Something important has changed... Los Amazonas, the real Los Amazonas seems a little easier on me now, but it's more than comfort and ease. I feel something subtle changing. Something wonderful here.*

He couldn't quite put his finger on it, but he believed that if he stayed, he might learn something really important, that he was close to understanding something mysterious. Also, on a more practical note, he knew that every SEAL judges and remembers everything you do. The Brotherhood keeps everyone informed of everybody's loyalty and dedication to the Teams. To quit was one of the worst sins a SEAL could commit, even worse than dying, but not as bad as betraying a fellow SEAL. He wasn't a quitter. He always finished what he started.

"No. I don't want to go back to Panama... Sir."

"I didn't ask what you want, but what you think you need. There will be more deployments. We're not talking about sending you back to Virginia, just Panama." The LT had heard what he needed to hear, so now he was covering all his bases. Now that he knew he wouldn't have to arrange a medevac or end the trip early, he could do his due diligence. If something unfortunate happened now, he would be able to honestly say he'd followed procedures and warned PO3 Austin of the risks. The OIC (officer-in-charge) is always responsible, but now he had justification to keep Austin in Bolivia.

"I don't need to go back. The swelling will go down; in fact I think it already has. It doesn't hurt much anymore. Besides, we're only one squad here, so I really feel needed. Isn't that what it's all about? I'm good, sir." Steph had never been a good liar, but he wasn't really lying. He meant what he said, but at the same time he couldn't tell the LT he really wanted to stay because he didn't want to leave the jungle and the river. But it didn't matter. People don't care if you lie when they don't want to hear the truth.

The LT looked pensive. "Okay, as long as Chief Wendell okay's it, we'll hold off on the medevac. But I've found an American doctor who's volunteering with MSF. He's going to check you out as soon as he can get here, hopefully this afternoon. He has experience with this." He looked down at his papers, but Steph noticed that he didn't seem to be looking for anything specific, just shuffling his eyes around. Steph assumed he should say something, since he wasn't dismissed.

"What's MSF?"

"What?" The LT, looked up as if surprised Steph was still there.

"You said he was with MSF. What's MSF?"

He looked Steph in the eye. "His name is Sean Lukely. If he says you go back to Panama, you go. Got it?"

"Yes, sir."

"Go rest; he'll be here soon."

Steph realized two important things. First, the LT hadn't answered his question about MSF, as if he didn't want to talk about anything relating to the situation... or maybe he didn't want to talk about the doctor. Second, the LT had somehow turned the situation into a favor he was doing Steph as opposed to a decision that would minimize his paperwork and the chance of a failed mission, or at least an unsuccessful one. In the Teams, there's little difference. No officer wants to explain to the Commodore that one of his SEALs had to be medevaced from northeast Bolivia to Howard Air Force base in Panama because of a caterpillar, no matter how hairy.

The First Fall

1 – THE DOC

Steph was reading in his hammock, trying to keep pressure off his neck and shoulders. Chief also told him to rest and take advantage of his down time, then went to do a radio check with the squad and see if he could reach SOCOM via the UHF, and maybe SEAL Team 4 back in Virginia via the new SatComm. Chief stayed on top of everything, especially the little things most people wouldn't even notice. He made sure everything was right as rain so the rest of the squad could teach their Bolivian colleagues the tricks of the special warfare trade necessary to take the fight to one of America's most pernicious enemies: drug cartels.

After Nancy Reagan declared war on drugs in the early 1980's, the drug war became more of a priority in Central and South America, but U.S. military personnel were not legally allowed to interfere directly, only train and advise. So that's what SOCOM's Spec Ops soldiers theoretically did, but not too much. The platoon and operations officers carefully explained that SEALs needed to create a productive, diplomatic, respectful balance between their current mission and their future needs. In other words, teach them – but not too much, nor too well– because an ally today might be your enemy tomorrow. Chief added another important priority: Don't get dead!

These Bolivian special forces soldiers had apparently never seen a claymore mine or military grade C4, and rarely got to shoot their weapons, never with the type of abundance and consistency of a

55

SEAL, so they hadn't internalized basic U.S. military safety protocols. They didn't follow general SEAL safety guidelines with weapons and explosives, so, according to Chief, they were never to be fully trusted, especially not on the range. "Always back them up, way back!" Which meant stand and stay as far behind them as possible. And then there was the language barrier. Other than the LT, none of the SEALs in their squad spoke fluent Spanish (Steph's language skills were still secret) and almost none of the Bolivians spoke English. Ultimately, these issues, all valid, were often used to reinforce SEALs' superior attitude, and when added to Americans' overt and subconscious racist and Eurocentric political and social views, it led to a poorly hidden disdain, especially from Simpson and Breck.

Steph heard someone come into the room, looked up from his book, and saw a tall, handsome, fair skinned blonde man looking at him from the doorway. His first thought, *Wow, he looks like the LT's older, better looking, Nordic cousin.* They didn't actually look that similar, but they carried themselves alike. Dr. Sean Lukely also screamed privileged American upbringing, somebody who'd decided after years of expensive private schooling to forego the economic prosperity and comfort of the economic boom of the 1980's for public service. The only obvious difference was that this WASP was smiling, like a buddhist monk with a full head of hair who'd found not only enlightenment but another needy body to feed, heal, or comfort. Steph had already decided he would dislike the LT's doctor, but it just wouldn't take. His face was reddish tan and his hair long enough to be hip but not hippy. His black backpack was slung over one shoulder as if he was running late for class across the quad. Again, Steph realized two things immediately: First, he was genuine and kind. Second, the LT knew him better than he'd let on.

"You must be Petty Officer Austin. I'm Sean." He walked toward Steph, who was still holding his book awkwardly in front of his face. He turned his head a little to better see the cover and asked, "What are you reading?"

Steph, finally acknowledging he should get up, struggled to his right side in order to avoid his swollen neck while trying not to lose his place in the book and not fall out of his nylon pocket hammock. The doctor deftly grabbed the book, without embarrassing anyone by offering to help a SEAL get out of a hammock. Steph finally managed to escape the hammock, stood up, and looked Dr. Sean Lukely in the eye. He was still smiling and knew better than to look at the title of the book. His manners were instinctive, as if learned consistently from a young age. Steph didn't know what to say. This guy wasn't an officer or a SEAL, so he owed him nothing, but he still emanated authority, confidence, and kindness. Steph finally just said, "Hi."

"Hi." He held up the book, suggesting he'd like to look it over. Steph nodded. Dr. Lukely looked at the cover of the book, raising his eyebrows. "Los Leyendes del Pumapunku... Hmmm."

"What?" Steph didn't mean to sound confrontational, it just came out that way. —Habits die hard.— Challenges, even imaginary ones, were like threats, and all threats needed to be met, if not aggressively at least confidently. He instantly wished he hadn't said it that way, but it didn't seem to affect Dr. Lukely. Steph couldn't help but notice how similar he was to the LT.

"Oh, nothing. It just seems an odd choice... Do you read Spanish?"

"A little."

"A little? You're reading about the Bolivian legend of the beginning of the world, studied at one of the most remarkable archaeological sites in South America..." He raised his eyebrows again. "You read... a little Spanish, and you're studying the Door of the Puma?" He shared an open face, still smiling.

"Reading."

"What?" the Doc asked.

"I'm reading, not studying..." He didn't know why he was arguing with this stranger. Steph felt surprisingly comfortable, considering he usually didn't like talking about his books with anybody. His buddies, except for Steen, loved to tease him about books, especially the nonfiction ones unrelated to weapons. Thick skin is helpful in life, but it has consequences. He finally looked away, not ashamed, but more to think for a moment. And then he added, "Yea, it was kind of a mistake."

"What do you mean?"

Steph looked back at him again, feigning ignorance. "What?" He asked, hoping he'd give it up.

Dr. Lukely seemed to know Steph was stalling, hoping something or someone else would change the direction of the conversation. He smiled and asked, "A mistake? Seriously, how does a Navy SEAL mistakenly acquire a book on an ancient Bolivian creation myth of the beginning of the world?"

Steph looked up through the window toward the dense, green jungle, then decided he would trust this guy he'd just met, which was very odd since he really didn't like trusting anyone. He didn't even like thinking about trusting people. Easier to just not do it. He looked back at Sean, "I wanted a book on pumas. You know the cats? So it was a mistake."

"Where'd you get it?"

"At that weird little shop along the main street."

"Yea, Adolphos. As far as I know, it's the only place to buy this type of book in Riberalta." Then, he looked away as well, strangely, as if he'd misspoken or misstepped. "But, actually, I don't spend that much time here. I'm sure somebody can find you some more books." It sounded like an invitation as he handed the book back to Steph. "Is it good?"

"What?"

"Los Leyendes del Pumapunku, is it any good?"

Steph smiled, "Well, I'm not really sure. The vocabulary is a little above my abilities."

"Did you study Spanish in school?"

"No, they sent me to Antigua for a three week immersion."

"Guatemala? Did you like it?"

"Did I miss something? Are we on some kind of date? Are you

gonna ask me my astrological sign soon?" Steph said it as if he was talking to Steen or Chief. He didn't intend to be rude to this volunteer doctor who'd come to check out his injury for free. In the teams, they were never supposed to take anything personally, but civilians are different. He was happy to see Dr. Lukely smiling, and that there didn't seem to be much chance of offending him.

"No. Sorry. My sister always said I asked too many questions." He looked down into his backpack, as if looking for something specific but not being able to remember what is was, and then changed the topic. "I guess I should look at your wound, hunh?" He moved toward the only table in the room and set down the already opened bag, pulled over a chair, and said, "This'll do. Take off your shirt and have a seat."

Steph slipped his right arm out of his Navy issue green T-shirt, carefully slid it over his head, and pulled it over the other arm as he sat down on the chair.

"No, turn around the other way, so I can see your whole back. Go ahead, lean forward."

Steph did as he was told, thinking about how much power doctors have over their patients. He'd only known this guy for a few minutes, and he was already giving him complete physical control of the room and his body. *But that's what we do, isn't it? We give up control and power when someone has convinced us we should, and then fight for it like beasts when we've given up too much. Just for a second, the craziest thought popped into Steph's head: He could kill me, and nobody would know. Give me a shot of something, and that's it. But then again, every doctor could do that. Who was that guy, the former Marine who became a doctor and killed like 60 people? Swingle or Swango. Or that British guy, who apparently killed 250 people with morphine, no, what was it called... diamorphine... God, how do I remember this shit? Oh, yeah. It's hard to turn it off once you turn it on. Besides, the real question is why I remember this stuff, not how. How is much easier.*

Steph blurted out, "You're not going to give me any morphine, are you, Doc?"

"No. Why, are you in a lot of pain?"

"No, just curious."

"We don't really prescribe morphine if we can avoid it. Besides, that's not the issue here."

Steph's suspicions seemed ridiculous, but once aroused, it was hard to suppress them. "I guess I should have asked you some questions. Like, where did you get your medical degree? Why are you here? I mean, what are you doing here in Bolivia? How much will I owe you?"

"Well, I got my medical degree from the University of Michigan and now work for MSF, which you probably know as Doctors Without Borders. We are trying to mitigate, even cure if possible, Chagas. It's a parasitic infection, spread mostly by insects, known as Triatominae. MSF has been in Bolivia working on this since about 1986."

Steph's crazy memory kicked in again, "Yea, I know what it is. I thought it was caused by kissing bugs? Don't people swell up and then get a crazy, dangerous fever? It especially messes up kids, doesn't it?"

"Yes. You really do read a lot, don't you? Triatominae are also known as kissing bugs. Well, I'm working on it with some other doctors."

Steph thought Dr. Lukely left his explanation a little short, so he asked "Anything else?"

Dr. Lukely paused for a second, "What do you mean?"

"Are you doing anything else down here? Shipping toucans or bananas home in your luggage, or looting ancient burial sites? I could assume that you're shipping drugs home, but that'd be too obvious."

Dr. Lukely laughed softly, "You really don't miss much do you? Yes…"

Steph turned his head quickly, too quickly. "Oww! Holy shit, I was kidding. You work for the cartels! Does the LT know?" Steph switched to a serious, deep voice as he turned to face the back of the chair. "I'm sorry Doc, but you are under arrest for violating U.S. laws and doing really, really bad shit with really mean people." It didn't sound as funny as he thought it would.

"No, not like that. The good kind of drugs. In addition to my Chagas work, I'm also doing some research on other drugs. I have some pharmaceutical connections. That's part of the reason I was so interested when Andy called me."

"Andy? Who's Andy?" asked Steph.

"Oh, I mean Lieutenant Hensen."

Steph blurted out, "I knew it. You two know each other, personally. Don't you? Did you sail schooners off Cape Cod as children? Or, wait, you were partners in Adolescent Advocates for the Better Business Bureau?"

"Actually, we went to college together."

"Wait, don't tell me… Duke?"

Dr. Lukely stood up straight and looked right at the back of Steph's head. "How the hell did you know that? Did Andy tell you?"

Steph didn't answer, just raised his eyebrows and shrugged his shoulders a bit because he really didn't know how he knew. Maybe the LT said something about Duke, but he never really said anything personal to them, just Chief. He finally said, "I don't know... Maybe it was just a lucky guess. I mean Duke is one of the easiest elitist colleges to despise." He paused, picking at the bars on the back of his chair. "The truth is, sometimes I just sort of remember things, or connect things, or something like that. I think that's why they made me intel rep. That and nobody else wanted it."

"Is this your first, uhm... your first trip?" He asked sheepishly, the first hint of hesitation Steph had heard.

"Yea. Sort of." Steph hesitated a little... Something didn't seem right. Dr. Lukely seemed to be stumbling toward a conversation he'd already planned, asking questions as if he realized he shouldn't ask, but still did, while trying to make it seem nonchalant. Steph paused for another second, and then decided to change the direction of the conversation, mainly because he didn't want to feel managed. "So, what happened to your sister?"

"What?" Dr. Lukely didn't seem ready for this question.

"Your sister. You spoke of her in the past tense, with a touch of nostalgia."

He paused for a moment, and then admitted, "Yea... she died."

Steph couldn't explain this to Dr. Lukely, but SEALs talk about death in two ways, disdain and denial. Don't go too deep, or just don't go there at all if you can avoid it. So Steph decided not to go there. "That sucks."

"Yea..." Sean didn't want to go there either, so he continued his examination, inspecting Steph's neck, the swelling and the skin, and then walked around to examine his fingers. The silence created an awkward moment, a tension that bothered Steph a bit, but at the same time felt empowering. He looked directly at Dr. Lukely, almost daring him to make eye contact. Remembering his sister's death had obviously affected Dr. Lukely. Steph felt bad, so looked away. He would learn in the future that silence and the resulting tension can become weapons, like a small indiscrete knife or a shockingly explosive claymore mine hidden in the bushes. But on that day, in that cement shithole that didn't stand a chance of surviving Los Amazonas, he didn't understand many of the things that would have helped him prevent what seemed inevitable, so he released some of the tension.

"It's not a trip."

"What?"

Steph repeated, "It's not a trip. We don't call it a trip. Our time in Bolivia is called a deployment, and the entire time out of country is called a cruise... I'm sorry about your sister."

"Even though you don't spend any time on a ship, it's still called a cruise?"

"Yea." Steph knew for certain that Dr. Lukely was hiding something. How did he know they wouldn't spend any time on a ship? And, he knew to call it a ship, not a boat. Minor perhaps, but interesting.

Or was Steph just being paranoid? Either way, it didn't matter. Once started, he couldn't stop deducing.

Dr. Lukely changed the topic. "Well, let's look more carefully at this bite." By now he'd pulled on his rubber gloves and laid out a series of empty and partially filled vials. "Can you turn your neck?"

"Only a little, but more than yesterday. I'm certain the swelling is going down. I'll be able to get back into the bush in a day or two."

"We'll see... Can you feel this?" He was lightly poking Steph in the neck with a sharp needle.

"No."

"What about now?" He inserted the needle lightly through the skin and pulled it out as pinkish fluid oozed out of the hole."

"Nope."

"Can you feel any pressure or pain."

"No." Steph had a high tolerance for pain, but he didn't need it because he couldn't feel anything. He wondered if Dr. Lukely was messing with him.

"What about now?" He'd inserted the needle deeper, an inch or more from the bites, which had looked just like two small needle wounds but were now almost invisible, mainly because of all the redness, swelling, and stretched skin.

"Nothing... are you messing with me, Doc?" he stopped picking at the chair and stared at nothing as if staring confidently in the doctor's eyes.

He continued pushing the needle deeper, amazed at how numb the flesh was. "And now?"

"No." Steph was a little annoyed, wondering if he was teasing him, but a second later, as the needle passed through the paralyzed flesh, he felt it. "Aaaww, Fuuuck!" Steph's shoulders tightened, he grabbed the chair back, grit his teeth, and instinctively tried not to show any more pain.

Pain is just weakness leaving the body. Pain is just weakness leaving the body. Control. Control it. Control is always the best answer. Shift focus; It could be worse. It can always be worse. Imagine something worse… Steph didn't realize he was hissing while he was breathing and thinking through his pain mantra.

"Okay," the doctor stopped inserting and slowly drew the needle out a bit. "Sorry about that."

Steph instantly felt relief, but the pain lingered. He tried to shrug it off, "That's alright. Pain is just weakness leaving the body. It's part of the deal."

"What do you mean?"

"Well… which part?"

"That it's part of the deal?"

"Life is hard and filled with pain. If you want to do cool stuff, like being a SEAL or exploring the jungle or, well, whatever… it's part of the deal."

"I'm not sure most people would agree with that. Most people will go to great lengths and pay a lot of money to avoid pain."

"I actually think it's necessary. I mean, if I didn't feel any pain, you could do almost anything you wanted to me back there. Who wants that? Pain tells us when we're nearing our limits, physically and mentally, when we need to stop and fix something, and when we need to avoid things. Like crazy-assed caterpillars. Pain is a lesson in smart living."

"Yea, I agree, but I still don't think most people will."

"Is it out?"

"What's that?"

"The needle, is it out? I don't feel it anymore."

"Almost." Doc said. He worked quickly because he worried Steph would catch a glimpse of how far the needle had entered his flesh. He was done with the most important part of the examination. Pain.

"So, Doc, am I going to die?" Steph asked with a smile.

"Yes, but not today, or any time soon if I can help it." Dr. Lukely had finished bandaging the wound after taking samples of tissue, blood, local fluid, photographing the area, and cleaning it thoroughly.

Steph noticed that he didn't rub any ointment on it or say anything about antibiotics, but didn't want to seem nervous, so he didn't ask. He could feel Dr. Lukely tracing or writing something on his back, then the sensation would be lost when it approached his wound. He'd feel it again after a few seconds. "Are you writing a prescription back there?"

"No. Just… some indicators for swelling and…" He didn't finish, but Steph didn't really care. After less than a minute of diagramming, he applied a simple bandage with a lot of tape and said, "You're all set."

"So, do I have to go back?" Steph asked, getting up from the chair.

"No, but I do want to check it regularly, so I'm going to tell Andy, I mean Lieutenant Hensen, that you need to stay out of the jungle for at least a few days, preferably a week. Also, I don't want anybody else removing the bandage or dressing the wound. You got that?"

Steph never liked being told what to do, but since he didn't really care about his bandage or the wound, he turned directly toward Dr. Lukely, looked him in the eye for a long moment, ignored his question and smiled, "How much do I owe you, Doc?"

Dr. Lukely smiled back. "Nothing. But maybe you can do me a favor someday."

"I don't know. I don't like owing people favors... How about I just give you twenty bucks?"

"Is that all my services are worth?"

"I wouldn't know. Oh, I should also warn you. Simpson's probably going to be pissed that he can't, you know, doctor me up."

"Who is Simpson?"

"Our corpsman. He acts like a clown, but he takes his medical duties seriously." Steph couldn't resist the urge to scratch at the bandage.

"Don't do that. Tell him I know what I'm doing. And if he has any problems, to check with... with the LT, as you call him." Dr. Lukely could be very assertive while not seeming assertive. "I'm writing some simple instructions you must follow." He handed a small piece of paper to Steph.

"Doc, you write like a 3rd grader. I thought doctors were supposed to write in illegible cursive script. Isn't it required?"

"No, I've never liked script, too pretentious for a doctor, and I had enough to remember in the 3rd grade."

"Well, you can write in simple print as much as you want as long as I can stay."

"Right. Do what I say and you can stay, and you'll heal up fine. I'm sure your medic does a good job, but he's not a doctor." raising his brows and looking Steph in the eye for a second before putting his gear and samples in his specially designed backpack.

"We don't call them medics. That's only in the army or the movies."

"What do you call them?"

"I told you, corpsmen. But it doesn't really matter what we call them because we trust them. No matter what, they watch our backs."

"Well, as your doctor, so will I."

Steph could tell from the sincere look on his face that Dr. Lukely meant it, but he couldn't help but smirk as he picked up his shirt, and said, "Yea... whatever, Doc. You didn't get it."

"Get what?"

"They watch our backs. Get it, watch my BACK."

"Steph, you talk a lot about trust... Well, trust me when I tell you that's so dumb it's the opposite of funny, definitely un-impressive." he said, grinning as he shook his head. "But that other bit was..."

"What?" Steph replied as he struggled to pull on his shirt.

"About my sister." He secured the last zipper, slung his bag over his shoulder, and then stopped at the door. "I think there might be more to you than meets the eye."

Steph stared at him for a second. "Ditto, Doc."

6 – RIBERALTA

A few minutes after Dr. Lukely left to talk to the LT, Chief came in like a sudsing beer, all over the place. "Man, I don't trust civilian doctors. They're in it for the money and don't give a shit. What'd he say? Don't tell me, Take two and call me in the morning. That'll be a hundred bucks." Chief used the same haughty tone for every civilian professional he ridiculed. For non-professional civilians he drawled a slow voice that tried to imitate a midwestern farm boy who'd never graduated eighth grade. "What did he say? No, don't tell me. Man! Civilian doctors, never again!"

Steph was surprised that his first instinct was to defend Dr. Lukely, so he didn't say anything. He knew not to contradict Chief or argue with any SEAL truism, in this case: They might be right, but we're always righter! So, he just smiled and asked, "When was the last time you went to a civilian doctor, Chief? I can't even imagine it. First, you'd have to leave the base."

The running joke with Chief was his three types of people: 1. SEALs 2. The rest of the military. 3. Civilians. He loved to describe his hierarchy as a simple way to relate to the world, always reminding everyone that civilians were last for a reason. Although simple, it offered an apparently never-ending series of life lessons. For example, since his two highest orders of beings populated military bases, and, according to him, you could find anything you really needed on a military base, wisdom seemed to suggest you should stay on base, and when you can't, such as when you need to go to the strip club or out to dinner with your boys, stay as close to base as possible.

"Don't get me started on that, Austin. Especially considering that I'm gonna take you off base right now. Get your civies on."

"Off base? I didn't even know this collection of tin cans was a base. It's just a few buildings lost in a lot of tall grass that really wants to be jungle near a river that wants everything to be jungle. Does it even have a name?" Steph asked, changing his green T-shirt to a comfortable Smashing Pumpkins T-shirt.

"Damn! You look like the hunchback of Notre Dame." Chief exclaimed, exaggerating the hunchback part part while he let out a little puff of air.

"Yea, I know. Crazy thing is it's better now." Most SEALs hated when people drew attention to their weaknesses and loved every opportunity to do it to their buddies. He finished putting on his T-shirt and slipped on his faded black baseball cap. He'd had it so long and worn it so much it looked more brown than black.

"Does it itch?"

"What?" Steph asked, surprised.

"Itch, does it itch? I got bit by a nasty little screaming somethin' or other in Colombia a few years ago. Man! It swelled, itched, swelled and itched. Nearly drove me crazy. Let's go. Denilson's waiting in the truck." He held the door for Steph, who was wondering if he should change to his running shoes. "Forget the shoes, let's go. We're just getting some dinner and running a little errand in town."

"Okay. Who's buying?"

"You, you little shit. I've got three kids and a wife at home on the base. Your paychecks are all going straight into your bank account while mine are going straight to the commissary. Get out some of those

Bolivianos. I'm hungry... and thirsty."

"Alright. Wait, I forgot my wallet." Steph walked back through the main passageway to the room where he kept his cruise box, pulled out his wallet, and headed back. As he approached the slightly open door to the LT's office, he heard the LT and Dr. Lukely heatedly arguing. Usually, he wouldn't have stopped, but something about how they were angrily whispering at each other intrigued him. He didn't intentionally eavesdrop, he just stopped near the door.

"Let it go... it's been ages..."

"No, it only seems like ages to you. For me it seems like yesterday."

"It wasn't your fault. People die... "

"You don't have to tell me they die... don't you think I know that? Look at what I do for a living."

The two men's voices were so alike, especially while whispering, that Steph couldn't tell who was who. And sometimes he couldn't understand what either of them was saying. He knew they were still talking, he just couldn't decipher some of the words. He started feeling sneaky, guilty, and was about to join Chief when someone said louder, "He was young, for Christ's sake...."

"A life's a life... does it really matter how old..."

"You don't believe that... if you do, you don't know what you're talking about. Sometimes, we are responsible... I'm responsible for..." The sound of a sliding chair banging into something covered the rest of the sentence.

Steph's curiosity leaned him toward the door a little more, almost all his weight on his right foot, his head angled to hear better. Even more than what one of them was responsible for, he wanted to know who felt responsible. Steph also felt the moral weight of responsibility and wanted to connect with one of them. Suddenly, he heard a crisp, close footstep, and slowly twisted his torso which finally turned his head until he saw the LT's penetrating stare. Steph didn't move or say a word, just stared back. The LT glared at him, and then quietly closed the door.

∞

All three of them sat in the front bench seat of one of the two big pickup trucks the SBU guys had flown down with their boats. Denilson drove, with Steph in the middle and Chief hanging his arm and part of his head out the window like a happy teenager, hand carving the wind, hair fluttering as much as a neat and trim could flutter. Steph felt awkward because he couldn't lean back on his shoulder. It wouldn't have mattered, except that Denilson kept asking Chief questions about the Teams and becoming a SEAL. Steph felt a little sorry for Denilson, but he was still annoying. More importantly to Steph, he wasn't watching the road. The Bolivians drove mostly motorcycles in and around Riberalta, and they usually drove them badly.

"So, Chief, how much should I be running for BUDS?" Denilson asked.

Nobody thought Denilson had what it takes to be a SEAL, but Chief was a nice guy so didn't discourage him. It wasn't because his shoulders sloped when he wasn't paying attention, which they did, or because he wasn't very strong, which he wasn't, it was mainly because he lacked confidence, swagger. Other than being comfortable during difficult moments in the water and having a high tolerance for pain and bullshit, the only measurable characteristic that a SEAL wannabe has to have is self-confidence. BUDs instructors might be a little better than the average person at sensing fear, but they can definitely see self-doubt better than any living creature. Doubt leads to hesitation, which leads to failure, which leads to death. Denilson glanced at Steph, suggesting he could answer as well if he wanted to, but all Steph could think about were the families on motorcycles right next to the six thousand pound truck Denilson was drifting all over the dirt road.

"Denilson, why would you want to change your designation now that you're moving up in SBU? Hey, you should consider SWiCC." Chief avoided Denilson's original question, still looking out the window. "I've seen you on the river. You've got talent, and we need good SBU and SWiCC captains." He looked over at him, having to lean forward to see him around Steph, "We need guys like you, son."

Steph interrupted, "What's swik?"

Denilson answered, "It's a new designation for SBU guys."

"It's going to be more than that, Denilson. SBU is going to become more like the Teams, more hands on, in both training and live action. Many of the OP's officers are already calling you SWiCCs instead of SBU guys. I just can't break the habit. You'll always be "dirty boat guys" to me.

Denilson looked past Steph and said "Thanks, Chief, but I want..."

"Dude! Watch what you're doing!" Steph yelled. As the truck veered a little, a motorcycle appeared out of nowhere with what looked like an entire extended family and a couple of extra neighbor kids hanging on like dusty circus performers. Denilson didn't brake at all, he just swerved to

75

the left as he accelerated to pass, not even looking back at them.

He yelled out the window, "What the hell, you little..." flinging his arm and middle finger high in the air as he drove faster, creating even more dust from the dry, dirt packed road. Steph scowled at him. He almost ran over an entire family. Although it would have been partially their fault, Denilson was driving a huge, camouflaged U.S. pickup truck while they were clinging to a dirt bike in flip flops and hand-me-down shorts. Steph was about to tell Denilson to be more careful, but Chief beat him to it.

"Denilson, remember that you represent the United States Navy. They might not know all your English, but they know the universal arm gesture you shared. Besides, if you run some of these people over, it won't help your career. Got it, son?" He looked out the window again, hinting that a response wasn't necessary. "Man these little people really love their motorcycles."

Denilson felt that something wonderful had just happened. Chief's advice proved that he cared about Denilson and his career. He somehow ignored and forgot the warning about their mission, which was obviously more important to Chief Wendley, and focused more on the advice about his career.

"Got it, Chief." He somehow interpreted it as encouragement toward pursuing his dream of becoming a SEAL, not avoiding an international incident or killing innocent poor people out of simple neglect.

Steph, on the other hand, couldn't shake the image of the motorcycle family being crushed beneath the giant, green truck, children bleeding and dead on the side of the road, flip flops abandoned in the dirt. He also noticed that Chief had called them "these little people" in an odd way. It was the kind of thing that bothered him: Not the comment, but his noticing and worrying about it. *What difference does it make? They are kind of little compared to us. He probably just meant that... and even if he didn't, so what? I don't know them, so I don't owe them... Right?*

He tried to force it out of his mind as he watched the squatty, unpainted shacks lining the road, sometimes built further back and surrounded by dirty children chasing mangy little dogs or playing with pieces of trash. He didn't want to think too much about people he didn't know, people he didn't have an agreement with. *I signed up to serve our country, which includes "We The People," but that doesn't include these people. Where does it end? What can I do for them anyway? It's their country, their poverty, their problems.*

But poverty in Bolivia was like no poverty Steph had ever seen, and as much as he hated to admit it, he felt sorry for them, especially the kids. In America, poverty is tragically connected to crime, domestic violence, and a grinding cycle of more poverty, crime, and more violence, but third world poor people were literally dirt poor. The dirt physically and mentally covered them and their children, some of them never seemed to get away from it. Poverty weighs people down everywhere, but in places like Bolivia, it crushes.

While he was struggling with international economic disparity, they'd arrived in the main part of town. Steph could tell because the dirt road had become a dusty brick road, and the streets were packed with even more motorcycles. People of all shapes and sizes darted in and out of traffic, crossing intersections like fish darting through a coral reef. A few small kids were driving huge motorcycles alone, while poorer families putted through the main square with everyone calmly clinging to their spot. It was miraculous more people weren't hit, but then again, there were only a few cars and trucks, and very few as big and awkward as their Navy SBU trucks. Denilson was asking Chief a different set of questions now, hoping flattery might help his cause.

"Shouldn't you be a senior by now, Chief?" inquiring in a way that suggested he already knew the answer.

Chief shrugged it off, "Nah, don't worry about that. I've got a great life, and the Navy's done right by me. My time will come. Besides, senior chiefs don't get to deploy; they either run an Ops division or transition into outright administrators. And there's only one level of hell worse than administration in the Navy: political operatives."

Denilson doubled down, "Well, I think it's wrong."

Chief just smiled at him, and then at Steph who was looking toward the passenger window, trying not to embarrass Denilson with a shut-up-you-kiss-ass look. Chief smiled at him too, and just said, "Thanks, Denilson. But I'd rather just stay right here and keep an eye on my guys." And then he pointed to San Jose Mercado, "That's where you two will go on the way back, to get some things for the LT. Here's the list."

He handed it to Steph, who'd been watching Denilson's reaction to Chief's explanation. He knew Denilson thought he was talking about him too. He didn't have the heart to slam him by reminding him that he was not one of the guys. So instead, he asked Chief, "What, you got a date or something?" He was surprised they were splitting up since hanging out in town alone was a direct violation of protocol and the other truck was in the bush, but he was even more surprised that Chief ignored the question.

Chief just said, "There's the restaurant. Denilson, watch out for that bike! Damn, they're a bunch of crazy little drivers… Pull around back.

No need to advertise our presence."

Steph wondered, What's he doing by himself in Riberalta? And why is it a secret?

∞

They parked behind the only restaurant in town they knew served really cold bottled water, which was unusual in Bolivia back then. You could find a cold Coca-Cola on every street corner, in a machine or from a vendor, but not cold bottled water. Steph had read an article, probably in the Atlantic or Time, that explained Coca-Cola's monopoly on drinks in South America, especially in rural communities, and its detrimental effect on people's health. Coca-Cola was easier to get than milk or clean water. Once again he wondered, *Why do I care if they can get Coca-Cola easier than they can get milk? I don't even like milk... but kids do.* He couldn't stop thinking about the kids he'd seen on the back of the motorcycles. His conscience took him and his crazy ideas down all kinds of irrelevant paths, regardless of what he wanted to think about. Why can't I control my own mind, just turn it off?

They walked through a dark hallway into a slightly lighter room with scattered tables and loud campesino music blaring through speakers which had long ago blown their woofers. The walls were covered in advertisement posters illustrating mostly naked women holding a beer or a Coca-Cola or a glass of whiskey, as if most women outside Riberalta walked around in high heels and a bikini drinking scotch all day. They walked straight through the main part of the restaurant, which was mostly empty this time of day, out onto the patio, and sat at the table farthest from the door. Chief waved a hand and yelled across the room at the waiter, "Tres cervesas, Real... tipo de Real, pour favor... Rapido, 'migo... and chips."

"Chief, your Spanish is really getting better. How many years have you been down here?" Steph said with a smirk.

"Shut up, Austin. I get by." He was looking at the menu already.

Steph turned to Denilson, "If you want to help yourself out, Denilson, learn Spanish. People love it when you try to learn their language, and Ops loves soldiers who can communicate and translate."

"I tried in high school, hated it. I think we should do the opposite."

"What do you mean?" asked Steph.

"Well, English will soon be the world language everyone uses, so they should learn English. It will help them become more like us and have a better chance at a good life. Besides, English is easier."

"First of all, we're in their country, where people speak Spanish. Second, Spanish is a lot easier to learn than English, which has a million crazy rules. And third, you're more likely to get extra deployments if you can speak Spanish, Denilson. Nobody gives a shit what you think, only what you can do."

"I guess that's more politically correct, but it just doesn't seem right." Denilson said, ignoring Steph's stare while looking at the menu as if he was reading the Federalist papers.

Steph really didn't want to get into it with Denilson. Breck would have smacked him in the head for suggesting he was politically correct, but Steph ignored it. He wanted to drink enough beer to forget about his neck, but he was curious about the second comment. "What doesn't seem right?"

"Damn, Austin, you ask a lot of questions." Chief interjected.

"What can I say, I'm curious." He looked back at Denilson. "What doesn't seem right, Denilson?"

Denilson spoke while squinting at the menu. "Well, my grandma really didn't want me to study Spanish. She lived her entire life in Texas, and... well, she just didn't like it." He set the menu down.

"Ah, the beer's here. Enough talking about talking. Enjoy." Chief tipped his bottle toward the center of the table, where everyone clinked, and then he tilted it back to just the right angle to let a third of his beer slide smoothly down his throat. The waiter also set a basket of tortilla chips on the table with a small bowl of unusual pico. Steph swigged his beer, ate a chip and looked at the Bolivians in the street.

Late afternoon was starting to settle in, filling the square from the side with a different light, so the patio was the most comfortable place to sit and do as the locals did, watch the never-ending circling of motorcycles. The social hierarchy of Riberalta could easily be determined by motorbikes. The poorest people had none, and worked and saved to buy one so the family could prosper and socialize in the square. Many of the motorcycles were basic dirt bikes, most of which probably wouldn't be street legal in the U.S., but were ridden like the family mule with pop driving, mom on the back, usually sitting sideways with a baby or two on her lap and another kid hanging on the remaining two inches of seat. Sometimes a young person was riding with a brother or a friend, happy to be free from the family. You could immediately tell if someone was in the middle class because they wore newer clothes and had their own motorcycle. Finally, the rich kids were on bikes way too big and powerful for them. One of these kids was showing off right in front of the restaurant, holding the clutch while revving the bike, as if about to kick up a plume. He was a long-limbed, lean handsome boy of maybe fourteen or fifteen on a motorcycle that was certainly too big and powerful for him. He didn't seem cocky, just a little spoiled. He reminded Steph of many of the slightly spoiled American kids back home.

Every once in awhile, a wealthy person would drive by in a truck, which was very expensive compared to a motorcycle, thus owned mainly by landowners, transporters, and the government. Most people didn't want a car or truck because nobody would see you, so what was the point of spending all that money when you couldn't race and people couldn't see you? And since the temperature ranged from seventy to ninety degrees all year, nobody needed to worry about the cold. Besides, you couldn't run a truck at the races. Riberalta was famous for its bike races and beauty pageants on the beach along the shore of El Madre de Dios. The locals said the river, the mother of God, kept her most beautiful daughters nearby, and that's why they had the best beauty pageants in Northeast Bolivia.

The waiter showed up with three plates of food. "I didn't order this?" Denilson said.

"I did. Eat up, it's good." Chief said, already eating. "We've all got things to do, so eat."

"What is it?"

"Don't worry about it, Denilson. Just eat. That's an order… Besides, it's delicious."

So they ate quietly for a minute. Steph because he liked Bolivian food. Denilson because Chief told him to eat. "Is it… fish."

"Why do you care? If it tastes good, enjoy it. If not, just eat it because I said so."

"What's the hurry, Chief?" Steph looked at him, waiting for a response.

"Never mind." He put another forkful of deep fried fish and some unknown fried vegetables into his mouth, little bits of rice falling out while one or two stuck to his lips. "You don't need to know everything, Austin, Petty Officer 3rd Class Austin." He looked at Steph with a mischievous, pregnant smile. Steph couldn't explain it then, but he felt like Chief was warning him about something.

As they ate, the sounds were all clearly Bolivian: local salsa-like campesino music blaring through bad speakers, dishes clashing and people laughing in the kitchen, and the endless hum and vroom of motorcycles circling the plaza. But Steph could hear another persistent sound beneath and around the obvious ones. Even near the center of town in the middle of so many Bolivian noises, he could still hear the faint hum of insects. He wondered if it was his imagination.

After eating his entire meal, Chief stretched, finished his beer, and rubbed his belly while laughing loudly, lightening the mood instantly. "Okay. Austin, make sure you pay the bill; I'll get the next one. I'll see you back at the base." He got up and walked out the front door. Steph was a little surprised at how quickly he'd left, and wanted to go after him. They were never supposed to go places without a buddy. If it were up to the LT, nobody would go into town at all, but Chief had talked him down, persuading him to let the boys –including himself– have liberty in town. He'd argued, "For Christ's sake LT, were not squids!" But this was different. He seemed to be hiding something, as if working on the side. But in an instant, it was too late. He was gone.

"I don't like it either," said Denilson.

Steph had almost forgotten he was there. He wanted to ask Denilson if he knew where Chief was going, but didn't think he'd know and didn't want to admit that Denilson might know more about his Chief's motives than he did. Steph had tried to like Denilson since they started preparing for this trip. He was a hard working, dedicated sailor, trying to improve his situation, and he loved his country. But no matter how hard he tried, he just couldn't. Something about Denilson gave Steph the creeps.

"Are you done?" Steph asked.

"Yea. Let's go." Denilson got up, sipped his beer, and said, "Don't forget to pay."

If anyone in his platoon would have said that, Steph wouldn't have even noticed, but in an instant he wanted to punch Denilson in the teeth. They were the same rank, but Steph's SEAL superiority complex didn't like Denilson telling him what to do. He weighed the moment, and decided to ignore him, again. The last thing they needed was an incident in the middle of town as evening was falling and more and more motorcycles were pouring into the square. But still, something about Denilson bothered Steph.

7 – THE PALACE

Steph had been practicing his palace drills for at least an hour when he heard a truck skid to a stop outside. His neck itched like mad, but he didn't want to make it worse by scratching. The Doc had been very clear about the importance of letting the medicine do its work and that permanent scarring and more pain was possible if he scratched it. But then he remembered that Dr. Lukely hadn't actually given him any medicine, just took samples and did pain tests. Steph was taking the ibuprofen Simpson gave him for both the swelling and pain. He remembered Doc suggesting things could get worse if he didn't follow his instructions to the letter, but wouldn't explain. According to the him, Steph's main job was to try to keep his mind off the pain while resting and doing as he was told.

Steph's memory drills helped a lot because they focused his mind deeply into a difficult task, almost navigating around the pain. After Denilson had dropped him at the door, he'd given the LT his two bags of supplies from the store, found a quiet spot, and started his mental drills with a reinforcing tour through his memory palace in order to place grounding events from the day. He planned to finish by creating a new shelf to remember the new birds from his Bolivian bird book, including names, calls, and essential identifying characteristics. His memory palace was demanding (especially at first) and Steph wasn't sure other memory practitioners felt the same weight, but it had also had become a place of refuge.

Every memory palace is as subtly unique as its creator, but they all depend on a few fundamental ideas first explained by the Greek poet Simonides. First, the palace must be created from a familiar place, such as a well-known building with lots of rooms or a museum or park. Second, specific locations, called loci, (a chair in a specific room, a desk, a series of paintings or drawings along a wall, bookshelves, etc.) should be pinned or identified along a permanent path or paths so ideas, details, and events can be attached to something already remembered. And third, the visual memory should be as shocking, fascinating, or unusual as possible because the mind rejects the mundane. Then, you simply imagine walking along a specific path in your palace, attaching new memories to preexisting *loci* by visualizing the detail (bird sound, insertion coordinates, historical names, military facts) in a strange way. The Greeks, knowing young men as they did, suggested they use sex or violence when creating their memory paths. As one's memory improves, the details spring to mind easier, often leading to other relevant details not already intentionally connected. At least, Steph assumed everyone subconsciously connected relevant ideas. He didn't really know anyone else who kept a memory palace.

Steph's main palace was his grandparents' home. He loved spending time there as a kid, so in addition to improving his memory and enhancing his mind, he enjoyed tagging items and moments into his favorite childhood rooms. At first, he was uncomfortable imagining nude women on his grandmother's kitchen table or violent acts in his grandpa's study, but he was used to it by now. And he knew from experience that if he struggled to remember something, say whether Jefferson was the third of fourth president, all he had to do was add a little sex or violence. Steph imagined President Jefferson screwing a naked Sally Hemmings, his mistress slave, but she has three breasts. Third president.

He was cataloguing the types of basic events an intelligence rep ought to remember, so he walked an easy, very familiar path, adding as many details as possible to each loci. He'd invented the modification the moment they made him intel rep. Someday, he would be expected to share important intelligence on the spot, so he needed to practice remembering daily as well as historical details. He could never have guessed all the opportunities and trouble it would cause him in the years to come. His basic detail path started in his grandparents' driveway because he could write number and word details in colored chalk on the driveway (a game he played as a kid) or enter the gate and plant important images, labeling them with plant tags, in his Grandma's garden (which he weeded for pocket money), or go into the garage to build structural memories on his Grandpa's workbench (a place he'd never forget). If he needed tastes and smells to solidify sensory details, he could go into the house and up the four stairs to the kitchen. Or, if the situation called for locations, and the details that go with them, he could go down the stairs to his grandpa's library with the maps. He especially loved creating memories in his grandpa's library. After closing his eyes, he could literally smell the slightly musty aroma of the books and see the beautifully sanded, slightly waxed pine shelves glowing a soft sturdy light, emanating reliability, just like his Grandpa. And of course, maps were ideal for his job as an intel rep. His grandpa had picked up a map table at a library auction, and they loved talking about all the places they might go some day. In one of his oldest memories, Steph was small enough to kneel on the edge of the table and watch his Grandpa's sturdy, worn hands turn the old, hinged plastic sleeves, which seemed huge to him. Most of the time Steph knew the memory was unreliable, but what did it hurt for him to add one or two to the archive. He loved his Grandpa deeply, and never wanted to disappoint him.

After labeling the bird details under imaginary flowers that looked just like Bolivian birds, he started a new path, closed his eyes, and went down into the library and straight to the maps' table. He wanted to remember the details of Riberalta before finishing for the day, before his Brothers returned from the jungle. As he turned the first sleeve, a blank map appeared in his mind with the general shape of El Madre de Dios, at the top, slowly transforming into a brown snake, which came to life in different ways, but always returned to its geographical shape. Avenida Beni Mamore ran east-west across the northern part of town, spontaneously becoming the top of a gleaming cross, as if the roadside had sprouted small gems, while another avenue (he couldn't remember the name, he'd ask Chief) ran north and south, slanting toward the southwest, creating the almost vertical part of the cross. The airport, named after Capitán Lopez, slashed up the northwestern side of town. The visual cross was important because a Catholic church hid quietly on the southwest side of the airport, just in case they needed a safe-house. He'd chosen the hospital and the park in front of the restaurant as possible rendezvous spots because they were at or near the center of his imaginary cross. Now, all he had to do was solidify the memory by mentally walking it a few times and then share the details with his squad.

He started with the brown snake of the river, which rose from the beach and transformed itself into a mythological creature: half snake, half Bolivian beauty queen. Riberalta claimed to have the most beautiful women in the world at their beach beauty contests. The queen-snake was nude and wore a glowing cross on a light chain between its large, brown breasts. The top right part of the cross grew longer and changed into an airport, slanting northwest as it grew. An airplane took off and dropped little men under parachutes at the church that grew out of the creature's right hip. Its left hand pointed to the center of the growing cross, while one of the gems turned into a merry-go-round and another a red cross sign. The hand held up all five fingers, the number of miles from the hospital to the airport.

This was when he heard the SBU truck skid up to the building, breaking his concentration. But he didn't want to stop creating the safehouse memory, so he kept his eyes closed. The imaginary creature had mostly disappeared, but one faint hand drew a green line that became more and more snake-like as it traced the best route from their small base in the northeast corner of Riberalta to the boat launch on the river. Steph was trying to will a natural image to remember other emergency egress routes with R's and L's at some of the intersections when Denilson burst frantically into the building.

Steph opened his eyes.

Something was wrong.

Denilson was white as a ghost, even considering his military tan, and breathing rapidly. His hands were shaking and his eyes were wide open. "Where's Chief?"

"I don't know."

"He's not back yet?"

"No... I don't think so. Check with the LT." Yes, something was definitely wrong, but it wasn't Steph's problem yet, so he didn't want to know too much.

Denilson muttered to himself, "No... not yet. Gotta find Chief... I don't know what..." and then he turned to leave.

"What happened?" Steph asked. Denilson ignored him and went back out to the truck. Steph followed him to the door, his curiosity fully aroused. "Hey, where are you going?"

Denilson was already sitting in the truck with the door ajar, muttering to himself, looking like he was going to cry. Everything else looked normal at first, and then Steph saw that the front right fender was dented, and it hadn't been dented at the restaurant.

Steph called out to Denilson, "Hey, man. What happened to the truck?" Denilson looked at him for a moment, his face even whiter, and he calmly pulled his leg in and closed the truck door.

"It's got a dent in it now." Steph pointed at it.

Denilson started the truck and backed out slowly, not looking at Steph. He arced around the dirt area toward the dilapidated gate and drove off toward town.

It all seemed odd, but so was Denilson. He'd probably hit a tree or car and didn't want to tell the LT, so he was looking for Chief. It was getting a little darker now, and Steph started wondering why Chief wasn't back yet. *What can he be doing in Riberalta, off-base? I shouldn't have let him go alone, but what could I do? He could be with a hooker, but it doesn't seem like his style. Maybe…*

But that would have to wait because just a few minutes after Denilson pulled out and before Steph could make any sense of Chief's disappearance, the other truck pulled in with a mad band of SEALs hanging all over it. The boys were back.

8 – THE BOYS

PO1 Renton, the lead petty officer and SBU guy driving the second truck, looked relieved as he parked and killed the ignition. He got out and started walking around the building toward the side door where the SBU guys had access to a separate part of the building. Breck, Steen, and Smith jumped from the back of the truck, starting to unload their gear enthusiastically, while Ensign Walker climbed out of the cab. Breck whistled, held up his hand, and yelled, "Renton..." as if nothing else had to be said. Mr. Walker headed toward Renton, smiling. Renton stopped, ignored Breck who was only a 2nd class petty officer, and argued respectfully with Mr. Walker. After a few minutes, he handed over the keys and walked away.

Breck said something under his breath, causing Smith to shake his head a little, smirk, and laugh a slightly sinister chuckle. As Mr. Walker tossed Breck the keys, he looked annoyed and a little indecisive, probably wondering if he should try to put Breck in his place. As a young, inexperienced officer, he knew that insubordination shouldn't be tolerated, but he was tired. Trying to figure out how to be a good SEAL officer while managing "the boys" would exhaust any young ensign, especially with Breck in the pack. But he also knew how rumors can paint an officer into a certain type of leader, an undesirable leader, and as much as he hated to admit it, experience and connections are currency in the Teams. Better to not take the chance

"Thanks, sir." Breck pocketed the keys and grabbed the sniper rifles out of the back of the truck, then ran up the stairs, past Steph without a word, and into their secure room.

Steph walked down to the second step. "It's good to see you guys. How'd it go?"

"Great! Just great!" Steen yelled as he walked toward the stairs with two M60's and his rucksack on his back. "The fuckers almost shot me!"

"What?"

"Yea, Breck was teaching them how to adjust for wind on a long shot, and one of them dropped his gun or fell, or some other crazy shit…" He'd stopped at the stairs. "The M14! Well, it went off, and with my luck it wizzed right by me. Right fucking bye me!" He started to gesture with his arm, apparently forgetting the M60's, and so finished with his shoulder and head. "Right by my head!"

"Quit whining, and hurry up. I want to take a quick shower before we go." Breck jumped the stairs and grabbed some more gear from the truck.

Steen stopped at the top stair and whispered as he walked by Steph, "Right by my head."

"Where are you guys going?" Steph asked.

Smith walked toward him carrying a bunch of radio gear. "The races, down on the beach."

"What do they race, and on what beach? The jungle literally sinks into the river."

"Motorcycles, of course. The Bolivians told us about it. It's supposed to be a big deal, crashes, betting, and beautiful women all over the place."

Steph gave him a disbelieving eye, "Every weekend?"

Breck walked by again. "It's true. They have Riberalta beauty contests all the time. They wear bikinis and I'm getting me some of that." He looked right at Steph, tilted his head a little, and said, "Help unload, or are you too tired?" The sad eyes and pouting were unnecessary. All the effective sarcasm was in Breck's tone.

He pushed past Steph, who followed him to the truck and told Simpson, "Give me something to carry."

Simpson was looking for something in his med bag. Without looking up, "How's the neck?"

"It's better. I'm staying. Give me something to carry before Breck shoots me for being empty handed."

"No. I don't want you carrying anything heavy." He'd found what he was looking for and slung his bag on one shoulder. He jumped off the back of the truck, grabbed his M16 and another bag. "Here, you can carry this." He handed him a garbage bag.

Steph took it and jammed it into the garbage cans on the side of the building, lifting his right arm to test his flexibility. He could raise his arm a lot higher than before, and he realized his strength was mostly there, just not much flexibility. He hadn't really thought about if the venom had decreased his strength until now. He walked back toward the truck, yelling toward Simpson, who was on his way to the control room. "I'm fine. Steen, slide me the MRE boxes."

"Cool." He slid the two remaining cases of ready-to-eat meals toward Steph, who carried them inside and dropped them in one of the bunk rooms. Steph sat on a metal cruise box, feeling out of place because he wasn't filthy and sweaty.

Steen pulled his civies out of his cruise box. "Dude, grab my wallet out of there and make sure it's locked. I'm going to take a shower." He stopped at the door. "Hey, are you coming with us? It's our only chance for some action in this dump."

"I gotta check with the LT."

"Why? He said we could hit the town."

"I think the Doc said I should take it easy... I'm sick of taking it easy!"

"Simpson said you can't party? I don't believe it." Steen looked truly stunned.

Smith walked in, already clean and combing his hair. "Sucks to be you, dude."

"Simpson will change his mind... You can drink YooHoos... or fruit juice or something. Hey, designated driver!"

"No. The LT brought in a real doctor. Some wanker he knows from college."

"He can't tell you what to do. He's a civilian." Steen couldn't fathom not being able to go out for beers.

"No, but the LT can."

Smith, intending to make a joke, walked up to Steph and set his hands on his shoulders. "Too bad... Holy shit!" He pulled his hand back like he'd touched a leper. "Your shoulder is hot and lumpy. Let me see that? Take off your shirt!"

"Fuck off." Steph pushed his hands away.

"Dude," backing up a bit and dramatically wiping his hands on his pants, "you're like the elephant man or something." He contorted his face as best he could, looking more confused than swollen.

Steph smiled, "Well at least my abnormalities are temporary."

"Dude, we all know I'm the best looking stud in Alpha platoon. And tonight I'll be the best looking stud in all of Riberalta." He combed his hair slowly, pretending to look in a mirror, joking, but at the same time believing the joke.

Steph smiled again, "Yeah, that's not the kind of abnormality I was talking about."

Steen laughed like an idiot, pointing at Smith. "Ha ha… you're an abnormality."

"Austin!" The LT startled everyone, as if they'd forgotten he existed. "Get in here."

Steph followed him into his little command room where small stacks of paper, a couple of maps, and manila file folders covered the table. The burn bag still sat on the floor next to the chair. The LT stood in the middle of the room, staring at Steph expectantly. "Are you going into town with everyone?"

"I wasn't sure if I'm allowed. I mean, the Doc said,"

"Don't worry about him. You deserve a break. Besides, somebody has to drive and get everyone back by curfew. 11 o'clock –no later.– Everyone back, no fights, no cops, semi-sober. Got it?"

Once again Steph felt like the LT had hidden an assignment inside a favor. But this time, instead of keeping him around, he seemed to be getting rid of him. "You're dismissed."

Steph almost thanked him, but then just said, "Yes, sir."

Smith was still combing his hair, Steen was heading to the shower with a way-too-small towel. "What'd he want?"

"I can go." Steph sat down on a cruise box and kept his suspicions to himself. It wasn't unusual for him to keep his deeper thoughts to himself, but this was different. He felt like he was navigating in a very dark room, while other people in the room could see him but not each other. As if he were one fixed point in a series of connections nobody understood yet. LT and Chief were definitely in the room, probably Dr. Lukely, and maybe Denilson. But what about Breck? Simpson, maybe? Not Steen or Smith. Steph couldn't shake the feeling that someone, or some people, were trying to understand something through him, something he inadvertently knew. He thought, *But what the hell do I know?*

It might seem impossible to sort complex ideas while sitting on a cruise box in the middle of a squad of horny, hyper, soldiers listening to loud music and preparing to party, but he didn't need much effort to sort ideas, to let go of control and let his mind arrange and rearrange, stack and sift, sometimes float and sometimes focus on pertinent details as the irrelevant ones faded. This type of thinking differed from calculations or logical deductions, which usually started with a debatable position or hypothesis. The only real problem was how Steph became oblivious to what was going on around him, unobservant and therefore vulnerable. But he didn't need to worry about that now. He never felt safer than with his SEAL Brothers.

His eyes usually stayed slightly open, angled toward the ground, like a monk meditating. The first image that rose into his imagination was the smiling face of Dr. Lukely; Steph could see him arranging and rearranging his test tubes filled with different colored fluids, most of which looked like blood. The Doc would look at the tubes, then straight ahead as a smile bloomed across his face. But when he looked over his shoulder, a heaviness settled across his entire demeanor, draining the color from everything but the test tubes. The vision repeated itself, slowly fading each time. Next, the LT's face slowly appeared, as if floating up from behind Dr. Lukely, which seemed obvious considering their relationship was clearly more complicated than either of them wanted to admit. The LT's face looked as it usually did, although slightly unfocused around the edges. It didn't smile, didn't turn, didn't change, but Steph sensed a sadness behind the stern SEAL mask. Chief's face didn't actually appear, but he was there, as if he'd always be there even though nobody noticed, always around, sometimes in the light, sometimes in the shadows, keeping an eye on everything. Steph tried to understand why he knew Chief was there, but he couldn't figure it out.

Something else was rising, another idea, another image. He could feel it willing itself into his mind, but like Chief it wouldn't come into focus. He closed his eyes firmly, which acted almost like a circuit breaker or switch, in order to push back the everyday memories, the ones we usually call real. Steph had already begun to question this dichotomy. *Why are the images and memories made and kept accidentally more real than the ones created intentionally?*

But this wasn't the time for debate, so he mentally drifted back to the images. While sitting on that cruise box in their tin can barracks, he imagined lying in the bottom of the PB as they flew down El Madre de Dios, marveling at the stars and jungle at night. Then he flew into the green-black wall of Los Amazonas and the bird calls and frog songs. He saw the flower petals falling on dangerous men, and a black hole in the jungle where a puma might have watched them. And there it was.

He opened his eyes just a little, unfocused on the floor, and the Doc, the LT, and the hints of Chief Wendley reappeared in his mind. But now they were highlighted by a faint image of a beautiful V-shaped green moth with four yellow and black circles sitting on fibrous wings, like eyes watching and warning predators. At the bottom of the V, small wing-like protrusions that looked like feathery feet pointed outward in opposite directions, as if the wings themselves were the creature. Its actual body, another V made of golden, sun yellow fur, could only be seen near the top of the larger V, under the antennae. Around the wings, a blood red vein separated the beautiful creature from everything else, like an outline drawn at the last second, just to make sure. A final warning. It seemed the longer Steph focused on the moth, the more real it became. It didn't seem to breath, but pulse. Subtly, it started to reverse metamorphosize, folding its wings onto itself, then into itself; its light and furry parts pupated into flesh and fluid as the moth shrank back into a worm shape and eventually into a caterpillar. It wriggled in midair, like any smooth, green caterpillar found anywhere in the world, except that its back was lined with brightly colored orange, yellow, and blue balls and rounded spikes, all with tiny black protuberances on them.

Steph felt his blood quicken. The other images, of powerful men, hadn't changed as the caterpillar completed its transformation. Then it faded until it was almost transparent. Steph suddenly felt like he was being watched instead of watching, by someone or something just behind him, just over his shoulder, just out of sight. In his vision, as in real life, he couldn't turn to see who or what was behind him.

"Dude! What are you doing?"

Steph had no idea how long Steen had been standing next to him. He blinked his eyes a couple times. "What?"

"What are you doing? Are you okay?"

"Yea. Why?" Steph replied, putting one foot on the cruise box.

"You looked freaky, like you were in a trance or something."

"No, I was just thinking."

"Well, stop thinking. It's time to party."

As Steph followed Steen out of the room, he couldn't help twisting his torso to look over his shoulder, just in case. But no matter how hard he tried, he couldn't see who or what was behind everything.

9 – TROUBLE IN TOWN

According to their Bolivian hosts, Las Carreras was the place to be, and today's races were the best of the year because today's beauty contest had a larger prize, drawing women from farther away. Other than Las Carreras, Riberalta had local bars, a couple small discos (which only got going later at night) and some social events that didn't meet their needs. The races apparently started early in the day and went into the night. They'd soon find out the serious races and the beauty contest were earlier because there wasn't enough outdoor lighting to have them at night. But, unfortunately for them, most of the young guys stayed late, drinking cheap beer and watching los locos race in the dark.

Breck drove recklessly, worse than Denilson, which made Steph anxious. They knew they should head towards Avenida Máximo Henicke and then follow the people toward the beach. It was getting dark, and the streets were packed with families on their motorcycles. They were nicely dressed and happy to be on the move, happy to be part of Riberalta's social scene, and many of them were going to the same races the SEALs were trying to find. The rule of assertive mass seemed to dictate the simple driving regulations: Big and aggressive has the right of way, try not to kill anyone, and most importantly, don't fall in the street.

"Breck, slow down. You're not going to get laid in jail." Steph felt irritable.

"Yea, at least not the way you want." Simpson snickered.

"Shut up, both of you. I know how to drive... and get laid."

Simpson went on, "We have to be back by 11. Not even Smith has a chance to get laid in two and a half hours. Let's just get some beers and set something up for next time."

"What are you talking about?" Breck interrupted. "We probably won't have a next time. I can't believe the LT let us out tonight, especially without Chief."

Steph had forgotten he hadn't seen Chief since the restaurant. "Yeah, I wonder where he is?"

Nobody said anything for a minute. Finally Steen asked, "Steph, you were here all day. Where'd he go?"

"Well, he took me and Denilson to lunch and then split after sending us to the store for the LT."

"You left him alone in Bolivia?" Breck scowled, glaring at him through the rear view mirror.

"Don't snap at me! He's the fucking Chief –I don't tell Chief's or LT's what to do!–" Steph looked out the side window because he was a little worried. He'd kind of forgotten about him, especially after Denilson's strange face and the dented truck.

Simpson jumped in. "Chief probably has a lady in town. He's probably been down here a dozen times and doesn't want us to know about her."

"He doesn't have a secret Bolivian girlfriend. God, can you be any dumber, Simpson?" Breck turned left as the traffic slowed down.

"Everybody, calm down. Chief is fine. We are fine. And, we are here… Wait, I don't see any women." Steen looked at all the Bolivian people. "Just a bunch of families and dudes… Park this thing and let's find some beer!"

∞

They probably wouldn't have found any beer at the beach if they hadn't run into Miguel, one of the Bolivian soldiers they were training. He was with his wife, her two sisters and his brother who left as soon as he realized Miguel was going to socialize with Norté Americanos. The ladies were very quiet, but not Miguel. He showed them where people sold beer illegally from big covered buckets. He said they could buy bottles of beer from the store down the street, but this was easier and cheaper. And, as he put it, "La cerveza es la cerveza, sí?" So they stood in a group, like everyone else. The only real difference was they were louder, drank their beer a lot faster, and stood out like a sore thumb, very big, loud, cocky, sore thumbs.

"Where are all the Bolivian beauty queens?" asked Smith. "Steph, ask him where the women are?"

Steph tapped Miguel, who was nodding his head to the music and talking to his wife. "Uh, Donde están las mujeres de… la… muy bonita… uh… Cómo se dice… beauty queens?"

Miguel laughed. "Reina de belleza." And then his wife tugged on his shirt, asking him something. He whispered in her ear, and she too started laughing.

Breck pushed himself a little too close to the conversation and asked sternly, "What's he laughing at? Austin, ask him what he's laughing at."

Miguel looked confused and surprised, turned, and said to Steph,

"Uhm, the queens... they home... eat... uh, cena. No beauty queens now, aqui. Just we people."

Steph smiled, "He said you're not getting laid, Breck. Definitely not by a Bolivian beauty queen."

"What..."

Steph interrupted, "They left. He said they left, but there are other women here now. Just enjoy your beer, and follow Smith's lead." Smith was already talking to one of Miguel's wife's sisters. She had a pretty round face, smooth skin and nice teeth with a slight gap between the top front two. She kept giggling every time Smith tried to say something in Spanish while touching her hand or hair.

Steen and Simpson were trying to ask Miguel a question in their broken Spanglish, probably about the beer or los locos, maybe about food, happy to be dressed in civies and drinking beer near any women.

Steph turned to Breck, "You should try to talk to her, Breck." gesturing to the other one. "Just don't scare her."

Before Breck could do more than give him a dirty look, he and Steph both noticed an angry group of young guys yelling in Spanish. It seemed to be about them because they were pointing and looking at them and they heard "Americanos" numerous times. Fortunately, it was a small group, but it was growing.

"Something's wrong." Breck said.

Simpson took a deep drink of his beer. "Dude, you're paranoid. Relax."

"No, I think he's right." Steph said.

"Of course I'm right." Breck looked all around to see if any other groups were positioning around them. What would have seemed ridiculous a few minutes ago now seemed prudent. "Austin, ask him what's going on."

Steph and Miguel talked for a minute, and then Steph nodded and Miguel walked off. His wife grabbed his arm and pulled at the sister who was still talking to Smith.

"Hey, donde going?" Smith crooned in his softest voice. Once he realized she was really leaving, he turned and said, "Hey, what's going on."

Breck took charge. "Listen, the truck's about two or three hundred yards that way." Pointing southeast, away from the river. "If we gotta bolt, try to stay together, but break into groups if necessary. Steen and Austin. Simpson and Smith."

"What about you?" asked Steph.

"I'll stay with one of the groups. Get to the truck. Move quickly. Do only what you have to, but get to the truck." The small angry group was already noticeably larger and drawing attention to itself. More people were pointing at them. "Where the hell is that little..."

Steph interrupted, "Listen. If anything happens, and you can't get to the truck or it's gone..."

"What? I won't leave anyone." Breck growled.

"Shut up! Listen!" Steph looked everyone in. "The military engineering school is three blocks west, and one block south. It's a huge compound without any fences. Find someone in uniform and ask for help.

If you end up south of it, head down the main street, Avenida Beni Mamoré, until the truck picks you up. Worst case, go south to the airport and find the Catholic church just southwest of the south end of the airport. "

"Good idea." Breck admitted. "We'll get back to the base, get the LT and Chief, load up, and come back for you. Don't panic."

Steph knew the LT could just call the military school to determine the best course of action, but nobody wants to be stuck with an angry mob. Suddenly, Miguel called Steph toward the building to their left. He walked over, listened, and came back.

"What'd he say?" asked Breck.

"We gotta go, now." Steph said.

"What?" Steen asked.

"Somebody in a U.S. truck ran over a Bolivian kid."

"Holy…" Smith tossed his beer.

"He's dead," gesturing toward the crowd, "and they're pissed!"

Breck calmly adjusted the plan. "Stay together, no matter what. Don't run until we get around that building, and then sprint for the truck. If necessary, we'll break for the military school. Steph and Steen up front, start slowly like you're going for more beer. Smith and Simpson right behind. Go."

Steen held firm. "We're not leaving without you."

"No shit. I'll be right behind. I'll yell Alpha if I need help. Go…

calm… confident."

Steen started walking, while Steph asked a slightly drunk Bolivian if there was any beer over there, pointing toward the beach as he walked briskly toward the building. Then he asked an older guy who walked away without looking at him. He saw Simpson and Smith right behind them, actually a little too close, but he couldn't see Breck. By then he and Steen had gone around the corner and started running. He could hear the motorcycle engines of los locos screaming somewhere on the beach and hoped they would distract some of the people. He didn't need to look back because he could hear Simpson and Smith calling back to Breck, who just said "Go!"

They got to the truck so quickly and easily that it felt kind of anticlimactic. The street was dark and dusty; the only light, one large streetlamp high on a single pole at the nearest intersection, sent beams over and around the sleeping buildings. The noise from the beach seemed miles away, creating the illusion of quiet. Steph pushed Steen into the back of the truck while holding the door, gesturing the others to hurry. He looked calm, but his heart was really beating far too fast, pushing too much blood into his throat. He felt anxious. "Let's go!" he said. But nobody seemed to care they were leaving, nobody seemed to be chasing them. He could see Breck now, his face like old stone, striding for the driver's side of the truck. Steph noticed dust rising into the slanting beams of light, a fine dust that didn't float so much as rise and fall. Perhaps they had been wrong. Perhaps they overreacted, assuming the worst and ruining a good night out.

Suddenly, the back window shattered, but only partially, as the sound of broken glass tinkled into the truck bed and shards reflected bits of hard yellow light through green glass. He could see the brick, stuck for a second in the tempered glass, and then another brick hit right next to the first and went through.

"Fuck!" yelled Steen from the back seat. Part of the glass and the second brick had hit him, sending glass down the back of his shirt. He thought he might be cut, but was mostly just surprised. His instincts told him to get out, but when he tried to get back out the passenger side, he cut both his hands on the glass on the seat. For the moment, Steen was trapped in the truck.

Steph only saw them before the others because of Breck's smile and how he changed directions. A group of young, probably drunk, Bolivians came through a dark space beyond the building, maybe an alley. They were running for the truck. At least one had another brick in hand. Everyone but Steen, who was still trying to get out of the backseat, bloody hands and all, followed Breck toward the first wave. Everyone instinctively knew they had to deal with the first few guys or things could get bad, really bad. Steph completely forgot about his shoulder and felt for his box knife – not there– so he glanced in the truck bed as he went around the back – nothing– so he charge the third guy and got lucky. The Bolivian charged too, but lowered his head, as if he was going to tackle Steph to the ground. Training took over: He planted his left foot, switching his weight to his right as he twisted all his momentum by circling through his waist, driving his hips while rotating his entire upper body like a pendulum, striking his enemy's head with the side of his left fist, tightened into a hammer. This blow only glanced his assailant's head, barely stunning him, but Steph continued the rotating pendulum motion in order to strike the head/neck area with the real blow from his right fist shaped like a hammer, shifting his weight back toward his left foot and bringing all his weight and force into the second blow. The Bolivian fell to the ground like a bag of wet rocks.

Steph was amazed that it'd worked so quickly. It was his first strike in a foreign country, his first knockout ever. His eyes were wide open.

Steph instantly looked for the next threat —none— so he checked his buddies. Breck had his box knife out and had already cut two or three people. Simpson was about to kick a guy curled into a ball as Smith yelled, "Stop. Get in the truck." About six or seven guys were standing in front of Breck, but Steph could tell they wouldn't come at the knife, at least not yet. Simpson and Smith were backing toward the truck. They had to go, now. Steen was pushed back in the truck just after he'd finally gotten out. It had all happened so quickly.

Breck seemed to be growing bigger and taller right in front of Steph. "Breck! We gotta go." He backed toward the truck too, then yelled, "NOW!"

Breck walked calmly backwards as Steph ran around and jumped into the passenger seat. Smith called to Breck through the shattered back window, "Let's fucking go!"

As the crowd got closer and closer, Breck calmly pulled the keys from his pocket and got into the truck. Another brick hit the side door, just below Breck's window. The truck started right up, he backed up quickly. Steph realized Breck was still holding the bloody knife in his left hand, but he dropped it on the seat to better grip the wheel. Steph's breathing was rapid, much more frantic than he'd ever admit, but he calmly said "Don't hit anyone." If the Bolivians yelled anything, Steph didn't hear it because all his blood seemed to be pounding through his ears.

Breck sped away from the group as a smaller rock landed in the truck bed, and a final brick landed on the road, five or ten feet behind the speeding truck. Steph looked over his shoulder at the mob that seemed to be shrinking before his eyes, and then at his friends in the back. They were fine. Only then did he remember the wound on his neck, but he still didn't feel any pain. They were all surprised, but excited at the same time, filled with just the right amount of adrenaline.

"Holy shit, that was close." said Smith.

Steen replied, "I can't believe it…"

"What?" asked Steph.

Steen shook his head for a few seconds and said, "Our first action in Bolivia, and I was stuck in the damn truck!"

"Holy shit." repeated Smith.

"Only you, Steen." said Simpson. "Chief is really going to put you on a diet now… stuck in the damn truck. I'll remember that one." He laughed nervously.

"We're not out of this yet. Everybody stay sharp. Look for tails." Steph's heart was still pumping like mad, but his mind was relatively calm. He felt silly saying things like "look for tails." He looked over at Breck, who had a very different look on his face. An if only… look. "Breck, you okay?"

Breck looked at him with disdain. "Of course, I'm okay." As if it was an insult to suggest otherwise.

"I just meant…" He wanted to say something about possible injuries, normal human reactions to stress or adrenaline or even fear, but he realized that if Breck felt these emotions, he wouldn't show them. The look on his face was more disappointment. Steph was pretty sure Breck didn't want to get in the truck. He wanted something else. "Do you need directions to the base."

Breck looked at him as if he didn't know who Steph was, a distant, cold look. He stared so long that Steph almost reminded him to watch the road, so as not to hit anyone with the truck. Finally, Breck looked back at the bright headlights illuminating the dark streets and simply said, "Just watch your zone."

10 – TROUBLE ON BASE

"What?" The LT asked, not as if he hadn't heard him but as if someone had suggested something impossible.

"A riot. Or I guess I should say a mob tried to attack us." Breck said, matter of factly.

"What did you do?"

Breck tilted his head down, the way he does when he gets stubborn, "We didn't do anything! sir, but get the hell out of there."

"It's true, sir." Steph had been standing closer than the rest of the squad who didn't want to deal with the LT. It wasn't that he wanted trouble, he just instinctively tried to help solve problems, which put him in the middle of things. "According to Miguel, they were upset about a local boy who was hit by a truck, a U.S. truck... but we didn't hit anyone."

Breck scowled at Steph. He was the ranking petty officer and thought Steph should keep his mouth shut unless asked a question.

The LT surprised everyone. "Yea, we know about that." He looked over his shoulder, as if waiting for someone to come out of the control room. The door was closed. Steph wondered if it was locked. "Was anyone hurt?"

"No, sir." Breck asserted his position. "But I did cut a few guys, pretty badly."

"Fatally?" The LT asked calmly.

"No, sir. I don't think so. They ran off."

"What about the truck?"

"The back window is partially shattered, and there's a dent in the driver's door. That's it."

"Well, good job Breck. All of you. The last thing we need now is two incidents to deal with."

"What's the other incident... sir?" Steph asked. Everyone wanted to know if it was true, if somebody, an American, actually killed a kid.

"The report — not yet confirmed— is that a local boy was hit by a U.S. military truck... which left the scene." He didn't offer any other details.

Just as he finished, Chief walked out of the control room, carefully closing the door behind him. "So you boys know what that means, right?" He stood like a short ancient pillar, grounded into the middle of the jungle. Steph's first thought, *We're in deep shit.*

"Security." Breck didn't waste time worrying.

"That's right. This compound is a nightmare to secure, so we must be smart. We can't assume anything, including help from our Bolivian hosts."

The LT interrupted, "Chief, don't overdo it, keep it reasonable. We don't know the particulars yet, and I don't want any visible escalation until we do."

"With all due respect sir, we know a local kid was hit by us and our truck and an angry mob attacked us. I don't exactly know what you mean by reasonable when we're talking about security on a base like this. I know we need to get all the dirty boat drivers in here, pronto, secure this building, get eyes on that road, check on local support, and contact SOCOM, just in case."

Chief's calm demeanor never seemed to fail him. Most of the squad was a little upset the LT was thinking politically; they thought the best plan was to prepare for as much violence of force as they could muster just in case it was necessary. Instinctively, Steph's mind was racing through his memory palace map: the distances and directions of the main streets of Riberalta, the location of the police station, the churches, the airport, and the fastest route to their patrol boats. He blurted out, "What about the boats?" His mind was racing way too fast.

Chief smiled at him. "It's a good point, Austin, but not yet."

The LT reiterated, "Everyone keep calm. We need more information."

Breck was more than just a little upset. His eyes burned toward the floor just in front of the LT. "We need to set up some claymore mines, sir. Asap! And get a sniper on this roof!"

"No claymores and no snipers on the roof." The LT snapped. He walked toward the men but stared directly at Breck. "Understand me, clearly. We will set up security within this building, but that's it. Unless we see overwhelming hostile forces, we are in a clandestine, defensive security situation. The local authorities will control the locals." He paused for a minute. "Is that clear?" He yelled.

Chief answered for everyone. "Yes, sir… We got it, sir."

He looked calmly but firmly at the LT until he went back into the command room. The LT was also careful to close the door completely.

Chief turned to his men and started giving instructions. "Steen, set up the two 60's below those two front windows with some boxes at the correct height, so one man can lay down fire, but keep them on the floor next to the wall. Link up at least two or three cans of belts, and then set an extra can underneath each of those," pointing to the side windows. "Simpson, help him. You'll be the other gunner. Both of you will be on your own, so take your time, double check everything, and listen to my instructions. If I tell you to shoot over their heads, do it." He walked up close to Breck. "Get at least one sniper rifle ready underneath each of the side windows, but keep them under a blanket. Put your CAR15 on top of it... Breck, look at me." He paused until Breck looked him directly in the eyes. "As I say. You understand? Nothing else." He stepped a little closer. "Do you understand?"

"Yes, Chief." Breck hated extraneous words, but his face showed that he understood more than had been said, and that he would do exactly what Chief wanted.

"Good. We must try to deescalate the situation but be ready in case we can't." He walked toward Smith. "Smith, do you have UHF comm's with Panama?"

"Not from in here, Chief. My UHF antennae is still set up near the river, but it's a decent run over open ground from here to there."

"But if we go out there with the radio, you can talk to SOCOM, right?"

"Yea, probably."

Breck interrupted, "What do you mean, probably? You've got one damn assignment!"

"Breck! Do your job!" Chief looked at Breck with a cold stare that allowed no rebuttal.

"Yes, Chief." He trotted into the secure room where their weapons were stored.

"Don't worry about him, Smith. It probably won't be necessary, but make sure you're ready."

"I got it, Chief... I got it." He went to the secure room to get the radio, an extra battery, his morse code cheat sheet (just in case) and to check his frequencies.

Steph was the only one left in the middle of the room. Chief walked up to him and smiled.

"Chief, we've got the new Satcom radio, and I think the LT has one of those Sat phones."

Chief looked sternly at Steph, and then switched to a smile. "Yea.. We can try the Satcom radio if we need it, but it has to be a clear shot... and no clouds... How'd you know about the phone?"

Steph answered as if he should know. "The manual is in the intel documents. Also, I heard the LT saying something to Mr. Walker about Grenada."

"You know what happened in Grenada?" Chief looked at him, stone-faced.

Steph guessed Chief might have been in Grenada, so he decided to avoid the beach tragedy and describe the comm's problem. "Yes, some of it. They left their comm's in the helicopter so had to use a landline to call in

C130 gunfire support."

"Did they really? I didn't know that... I mean about forgetting the gear in the helicopter." He looked down at his hands.

"Yea...." Steph didn't know what else to say. He assumed every SEAL knew what happened in Grenada.

"How'd you know that?" Chief asked.

"I read it somewhere." Steph felt a little embarrassed that he knew more than Chief who was actually in the fight. It never dawned on him that Chief might have known more and chose not to admit it.

"Well, don't worry about it. Nothing serious is going to happen here."

Steph looked surprised. "What do you mean?"

Chief pulled a small knife from his pocket, opened it, and started cleaning underneath his fingernails. "The LT already talked to his Bolivian contact about the kid. They were already planning to station a couple of security vehicles in front of the gate. A handful of angry drunks or a small group of motorcycles won't run that."

"Well, what if they do?" Steph asked.

"They'll shoot 'em." He flicked some of the dirt onto the floor. "Not our problem if Bolivians shoot Bolivians."

"Then why..." he gestured around the room "all this?"

Chief laughed at him, and then checked himself, like a dad who remembered it was his job to teach lessons. "Practice."

"Are you kidding?"

"Well, I guess it's also better to be safe than… you know, but we don't get to do things for real often enough, especially in this war on drugs. So the more real the practice, the better." He flicked some more dirt on the floor, and put one finger over his lips, and then smiled, the way only Chief could, wrinkling all the skin above his cheeks so his eyes told more than words ever could.

Steph whispered, "Does Breck know?"

"No. But he probably suspects something. He's the real deal, Steph." Chief looked up from his fingernails, tilted his forehead down a little and raised his eyebrows. "Keep your eyes on him."

"Holy shit!" Simpson yelled from his window while picking up his M60. "Somebody's coming. Running straight at us!"

Chief ran up to the window as everyone waited for instructions. The LT opened the command room door. "Put the damn 60 down!" Chief looked carefully at the tall man trotting toward the building. "Didn't I tell you to leave it on the floor? As I say! Do as I say!"

"Yea, Chief, but… come on. Some fucking guy, dark as night, coming out of the bushes right at me!"

Chief laughed a bit and put a hand on Simpson's shoulder. "First, he's not coming out of the bushes, but through the gate. Second, he's not dark as night, more like a Nordic sunrise!"

"What?"

"It's Dr. Lukely… Do I need to add not to shoot him?" Chief went to the door to let him in.

Simpson whispered to Steph, "Who?"

"The doctor the LT called to look at my neck."

"Oh." Simpson looked a little confused, then annoyed, and then pissed, as if he'd just learned his girlfriend was having a drink with a friend from work.

Dr. Lukely was a little out of breath, but still managed to say hi to everyone after shaking Chief's hand.

"Where's your ride, dude?" Smith asked. "It's dangerous out there for us Americanos."

"Uh... they let me in, but not with my motorcycle." He nodded at Breck who'd just walked out of the secure room with his M14 in one hand and his sniper rifle with night scope in the other. "I saw your truck window. What happened?" He looked at the machine guns under the windows and Breck's sniper rifles, "Did I come at a bad time?"

A silence lingered over the room for a few seconds until Steen laughed a full belly laugh. "Did I come at a bad time... I like this guy!" Steen said. Smith and Austin were also smiling, but Simpson, Breck, and the LT just stood there. Chief was smiling, but not with the eyes.

"Why are you here?" demanded the LT.

He set his bag down. "I have some good news." Another extended silence. "Uh, should we go in... I don't know how this military stuff works, the chain of command... or, whatever..."

"If it's okay with you, LT" Chief interrupted, "the men should hear the good news." The LT nodded. "I'll get Denilson." Chief walked into the command room, leaving the door open this time. Denilson walked out first, not quite as white as before, but still obviously shaken. PO1 Renton was right behind him, as if ready to assist if necessary. Chief clapped his hands together loudly, and said "So let's have this good news."

"He's alive."

Everyone leaned toward Dr. Lukely.

"How do you know this? Are you sure?" asked the LT.

"I'm positive. I spoke to Nicolás a few minutes ago. He's in the medical facility here on the base. If you can call it that."

The tension in the room lightened. Chief smiled and shrugged as if it was just another knot that had worked itself out. The LT walked toward Dr. Lukely, unsure what to say. And Denilson sank onto a box, putting his head in his hands, trying to fight back the tears, but it didn't work.

Renton put a hand on his back, and finally said, "That's great news."

"Yea," added the LT. "Thanks, Sean. That is great... great... news." A weight seemed to dissolve from around his neck. "You talked to the kid?"

"Yea. He was a little groggy, probably has a light concussion and some bruised ribs, a broken left arm and a contusion on his right foot. But he was in good spirits and hungry. Both great signs. I've volunteered to assist the local doctor, so I can help Nicolás while keeping you in the loop." He left this last offer dangling, as if too good and too easy for anyone to reject. Steph didn't know why it seemed odd, but it did. For a second he felt ridiculous, until he saw the LT's face, and then he knew there was more to the offer and the situation. Steph knew this boy, Nicolás, and his squad were still connected, and that the Dr. and the LT were involved, whether they both understood it fully or not. He also didn't know if they were collaborating, but something was definitely going on.

If he'd had any doubt about his instincts, Chief's look confirmed them. It was rare for Chief to lose his poker face, but he also knew something was up. He looked like a Shakespearean character on an incredibly believable stage, like Brutus when he first realized Cassius was up to no good. But unlike Brutus, Chief's allegiance was clear.

"Chief," interrupted Steen, "does that mean we can stand down?"

Chief composed his face immediately. "No, Petty Officer Steen, you may not decide security protocols in order to make a peanut butter and jelly sandwich! Just because the kid seems to be okay, doesn't mean that he's completely out of the woods or that these people might not still dislike us. We are the ugly Americans, right? Especially you." He waited a moment, nobody answered. "We will stay as we are for now, but everybody can calm it down a notch and get comfortable. Especially you, Simpson. Grab an MRE and some water. Austin, pass out some MRE's, and if anyone gets one with the m-n-m's, he better share."

The LT called Dr. Lukely, Chief, Denilson, and Renton into his command room. As Steph turned to get the MRE's he saw Breck, who he'd completely forgotten about. Breck had also uncharacteristically lost his poker face, but for more than a moment. His eyes were locked, his jaw set hard, his forehead tilted down a little, and somehow, his skin seemed to be pulled more taut against the bones in his face, as if hurling down a hillside against a fierce wind, teetering on the edge of control. His breathing was almost a quiet panting, like an animal catching a scent, but Breck was different than most predators. They didn't hate their prey. Unfortunately, Steph didn't know who or what Breck had been looking at.

∞

Everyone did as Chief said. A few minutes later, the LT came out of the command room. "The Bolivian commanding officer of the base called. The police have subdued a small mob and the streets, especially around the base, are clear." The LT smirked a little, "He actually said, we have nothing to worry about." He looked around the room, nodding his head slightly, looking at everyone to make sure they didn't believe it.

Dr. Lukely came out of the command room alone and looked directly at the LT. "Chief Wendley wants to talk to you." It was odd to hear someone give orders to the LT, and then not to say sir all the time. He seemed tired, but then he smiled a little and looked at Steph. "Steph, while I'm here, I should check your neck."

Chief stepped into the doorway, licked his lips, raised his eyebrows, and nodded his head at Steph, reminding him about civilian doctors. Then he said, a little too loudly as he turned back into the room, "Take good care of him Doc, we need him."

"I will…" He looked at Chief's back, smiling. "Always do."

Steph interrupted their awkward tension. "Uh… where?"

"Let's go in this back room."

Steph liked Dr. Lukely, so he felt kind of stuck. He didn't want to undermine his Chief, but he almost felt like apologizing. But he didn't know how to say it without bordering on disloyalty, so he said nothing. It almost always seemed easier to say nothing and leave things to work themselves out. But Steph didn't like leaving things to themselves.

"Okay, take your shirt off and lean against the chair, same as last time."

"Did you really see the kid?"

Dr. Lukely was pulling items from his medical backpack. "Yes."

"How'd he look. I mean, how bad is he... I mean, really?" Steph stared at the faded and cracked tiled flooring. He flexed his hands and then relaxed them to minimize his reaction to the pain he knew was coming.

"He's fine. A broken arm, some bruised ribs, the concussion is mild, so..."

"That's it? Awesome! I mean, that's so cool that he's okay." Steph followed a crack from one corner of a tile to where it met the crumbling grout and then back around the square to where he started.

"Why do you ask... I mean, why do you care so much?" Dr. Lukely had removed the bandage and was cleaning the wound and the surrounding area. The flesh was still yellow, almost greenish in places, but much pinker around the edges than it had been earlier.

"I don't..."

"It's okay to care about a kid, Steph."

"I know. You didn't let me finish..." He focused on nothing, the way people do when they want to make a point but can't look someone in the eye. "I don't know why I care, I just do... I mean, first of all, he's just a kid, right? But also, I don't want Denilson stuck down here in a filthy jail cell or the squad shipped back to Virginia in disgrace." He paused for a minute. "I'm just really glad for everyone."

"You know, he kind of reminds me of you." Dr. Lukely was preparing two needles and a very sharp, very small scalpel. One needle would be used to conduct the same pain test he'd conducted earlier; the other to draw a blood sample. The scalpel would be used to take some very small tissue samples.

"What? How does he remind you of me?" Steph turned his head a little, couldn't finish, and then looked at the tile again. "You don't know me!" Steph's irritation was obvious.

"Hey, don't get mad. It's a compliment."

"I'm not mad! It's just..."

"What? Do you think you're better than him?"

"No!" Steph was surprised, but immediately realized that it was a fair question. The rest of his buddies didn't even try to hide their racist, Eurocentric biases.

Dr. Lukely qualified his statement to reduce the tension: "I'm sorry; let me rephrase that. Do you think you're, let's say, different than Nicolás?"

Steph paused a moment. "No. I know what you're asking. I'm not a racist." He wanted to say more, but couldn't without criticizing his teammates, his Brothers. Also, he wasn't really sure he wasn't a racist. Sometimes he felt a little better than the soldiers they trained, but, he thought to himself, *We think we're better than everyone.* Steph decided to redirect: "Please answer the original question. How does he remind you of me?"

"Well, he's really smart, he looks you in the eye, enthusiastically, when you talk to him, but most importantly, he's perceptive. He notices things most people don't, like you."

"Is your Spanish that good?"

"Yes. It's pretty good, but he speaks English quite well." He had already begun inserting the needle into the same location, waiting for Steph to flinch or yell. When he didn't, Dr. Lukely took a very small sample of the infected tissue near the needle. This time, for some reason, he didn't want Steph to know he was testing other effects of the poison or taking tissue samples. He nonchalantly dropped it into a small plastic bottle partially filled with a viscous fluid.

"What did you two talk about?"

"Mostly Michael Jordan and Chicago. He wants to live there when he's older."

"Why?"

"He loves the Chicago Bulls. I guess there might be another reason, but that's what he told me." He kept sliding the needle, which was in as deep as last time, into Steph's shoulder muscle. He was near the same depth as last time. "He wants to be an engineer, build skyscrapers in Chicago, become wealthy, and then return to modernize Riberalta."

"Impressive. All at 12 years old. That's really... Ahhhh, That fucking hurts, Doc!" Steph hissed the words, gripping the back of the chair and closing his eyes tightly as the pain rose like steam from a pressure cooker. It was different than most pain Steph had experienced because of how instantaneously it erupted deep in his muscle. That's what surprised him, the depth and immediacy of the sensation.

"Sorry." He slowly pulled the needle out, amazed at how powerfully the poison naturally neutralized the pain receptors, but also how much it had localized, on its own. "That's amazing."

"What! How stupid I can be?" Steph thought, *I should have listened to Chief.* Then said, "Dr. Lukely, please don't do that again."

"Sorry, I needed to test the extent of the damaged flesh."

"To be honest, Doc, it seems more like you're experimenting on me. Maybe Chief was right."

"How so?" He rubbed some alcohol and then an ointment over the entire area.

"He doesn't trust you... but don't take it personally. He doesn't trust any civilians, especially civilian doctors. He says you're all in it for the money."

"Would I be working for MSF in the middle of Bolivia if I was only in it for the money?"

"Maybe. It could be your front." Steph laughed. "You could be down here looking for a revolutionary medicine or poison that can be turned into a wonder drug, so you're experimenting on me right now." Steph got really excited, turning his entire body. "Is that it? Am I right?" Steph smiled, as if it were a game.

"Yeah, you got me. But now that you've discovered my secret, I'll have to kill you."

"Good luck! Wait, though, let me guess how you'd do it. You'd sick a tribe of crazy-assed killer caterpillars on me. Actually, I surrender. If you're going to do it that way, Doc, just shoot me. Those little hairy beasts are vicious." He looked at the floor again. "I mean it, just shoot me, Doc."

"Okay, if that's the way you want it." He started applying a new bandage. "Do you guys always joke this way?"

"Sure, and I'm glad to see we were actually kidding."

"Really? I'd think you wouldn't want to talk about death, considering it's always so close, or I guess I should say, so possible."

"Well, it kind of relieves the tension. We either joke or ignore the hard stuff. But there's a difference." He followed the crack around the tile again, then finished. "We never joke about killing each other. That's like the worst fucking thing you could do, a team guy killing another team guy… I can't even imagine it."

"Do you like it?"

"What?"

"Being a SEAL."

Steph hesitated after quickly guessing that Dr. Lukely might understand the complexity of the situation, his situation, but decided not to risk it. It was easier, and much simpler, to just focus on the good parts. "Yea, I like it."

"All of it?"

"No, but who likes all of anything? Do you? Do you like everything about being down here or helping kids who will probably die? I don't like the damn bugs, especially the furry bastards with vampire teeth." Steph felt a little trapped "Are you almost done, Doc? I've got work to do."

"No... I mean, no I don't like all of it. Nobody likes seeing kids die, especially not a doctor. Of course it's horrible. And yes, I'm almost done. I just need to check this, and then I'll put the new bandage on. I want to put a little extra tape on this bandage so nobody messes with it. The humidity really lifts the edges." It was strangely quiet for a moment. Steph would feel nothing, then pressure along the edges of the numb area, as if Dr. Lukely was tracing something. "Make sure nobody takes the tape off."

Steph just stared at the floor, a little angry and a little disappointed in himself.

"Okay, you can put your shirt back on." He paused for a minute as he threw away the gloves he'd been wearing and wiped his hands clean. "You know, you'd like Nicolás... if you met him. He's in the medical building just three buildings that way." Dr. Lukely pointed southeast, parallel to the jungle.

Steph had turned around as he was putting his shirt on. He and Dr. Lukely looked calmly at each other for a few seconds. Finally, Steph said, "First, that's not southwest. Second, why the hell would I want to do that?"

Before Dr. Lukely could answer, Breck, who was standing silently in the doorway, said, "Chief wants to see you."

Steph looked at Breck, unfazed by his sudden appearance. "Gotta go, Doc.

Thanks." He put his hand out to shake hands as he'd been taught as a boy.

Dr. Lukely instinctively reached out, grasped his hand, and said, "I don't know, just a thought." As Steph let go of his hand and started to leave, Dr. Lukely said, "Don't forget to leave that tape on until I come back."

"Sure thing, Doc."

Then Breck looked sternly at Steph and said, "No. Not you." And walked out.

11 - NICOLÁS

Steph knew Dr. Lukely had intentionally planted the seed, and he hated being manipulated, but it worked. He must have known that Steph would realize this and consider his motives. Steph assumed Doc wanted him to learn something about Nicolás or Bolivia or people in general. *But why not just say it? If he wants me to know something, why not just tell me? Unless, he needs me to see something... or both.* It never dawned on Steph that he might have conflicting motives, good and bad, or that he was also too damn smart for his own good.

It's much easier to get people to do things they already want to do. Dr. Lukely knew before he told everyone the good news that Steph would want to meet Nicolás, but now that he was so close and it was so easy, everything had kind of fallen into place. Steph was obviously stubborn and also a little obsessive, so once an idea caught hold of him, it clung to him like an itch desperate for a scratch. But at the same time, the itch felt slightly wrong, and the decision to sneak out of their secure barracks in the dark during a possible international situation without permission felt not only wrong, but stupid.

Steph knew if he walked the little pathway along the edge of the jungle, the one Chief had pointed out when they first got to the base, he could go most of the way unseen, but why risk pissing off Chief and the LT? He knew they'd go ballistic... *They never said we couldn't leave the building, just not to go off base. And I really do need to hit the head.* His desire to see with his own eyes that Nicolás was okay wouldn't let go of him. *He'll probably be sleeping, so I'll be in and out in no time.* He figured, *If anyone sees me, I'll just say I wanted to make sure, for the squad's sake, that the boy's okay, well taken care of.*

He told himself that he could remind Chief that you really can't trust civilians. He slipped on his camos, which would blend with the jungle, just in case. He was in a hurry, so he slipped his camo top over his Smashing Pumpkins T-shirt and grabbed his floppy hat before heading for the back door.

"Where ya going?" Chief was leaning on the door frame.

"Gotta hit the head, Chief. I've been holding it all day, kind of forgot about it, you know, with all the chaos tonight." He hadn't intended, nor did he want to lie to Chief, but it just came out. He knew that everyone would think it was a bad idea, but he was going.

"Hmmm..." Chief was cleaning the dirt out of his fingernails again. "What did the LT's doctor friend say to you?"

"Not much. Just asked about my pain. I think you might be right about civilian doctors, Chief. He keeps sticking this needle in my neck, or I guess it's my shoulder, to see how much pain I can endure." Steph felt flustered, his heart racing, his hands fidgeting.

"No, he's checking to see how deeply the poison has affected your muscles and how much pain you don't have to endure." Chief inspected his right hand, switched his knife to his dominant left hand, and started cleaning the rest of his fingernails. "I don't trust him, Steph. I don't want him examining you anymore without Simpson. Got it?"

"Sure, Chief. The LT told me I had to..."

"Don't worry about that. If he complains, send him to me. I'll tell the LT Simpson needs the learning opportunity. No need pissing off the LT and his frat buddy. But don't let him stick anything else into your neck without Simpson or me watching, got it?"

"Got it, Chief."

"It's an order."

"Got it."

"I don't know, Steph. There's something strange about how he just shows up. Ya know? I don't like it." Chief stood up straight, deftly closing and pocketing his knife. He stretched his back, smiled at Steph, and said, "Be careful, it's a jungle out there." as he snickered and scrunched up his eyes while walking out the door.

"That is so lame, Chief."

"And be careful on the toilet too. If all that…" gesturing to his own shoulder as if he had a hump, "comes from a little caterpillar that landed softly on your shoulder, imagine what might bite you in the ass out in the dark jungle?" He stopped, looked right at Steph, and said, "Hey, I wonder if that's where watch your ass came from?" He smiled again, turning to leave.

"Uh, I don't know Chief, but now I'm going to be nervous every time I go to the head down here."

"First, most South American bases, even in the rainforest, have an indoor shitter. Second, maybe it's not a bad thing to have to watch your ass more carefully once in a while." He turned his head one last time, tapping the side of his forehead as he disappeared around the corner.

It was much easier to find the medical building than Steph had expected. He'd moved briskly along the secret path, just inside the edge of the jungle, until he got to the third building, which had a large gas or water tank behind it, probably water since they didn't need natural gas for heat. *But wouldn't a water tank need to be higher?* He didn't know what it was for, but it was unique, and on a small, third-world base like this, it probably meant something medical. The building, shaped like a long, fat rectangle, looked like one of the cheap trailers his elementary school in North Carolina had stuck back behind the main building because they had too many kids for the fourth grade. It just sat on the ground like a fat, dead toad. He saw that a window near the back of the building was cracked open, but there was no reason to sneak in. Steph decided the best thing to do was walk through the front door. He had nothing to hide, wasn't doing anything wrong, just checking on a stranger's medical condition. If they said no or the kid had gone home, he'd hit the head and return to their building.

He strolled out of the jungle as if crossing the street in Chicago or New York, mindful of his surroundings but not worried, walked around to the front, stepped up two box steps, opened the unlocked door, and walked into what looked like a simple waiting room, but nobody was waiting. Nobody was there. The dark vague space was mostly empty, a few chairs, a small desk (really more of a table) no plants, no pictures, no magazines. A light emanated softly from another room down the hall, but he heard nothing and saw very little. It was eerily quiet. He walked down the dark hallway, glancing slowly into each room, looking for a young boy he assumed would be strapped to monitors, probably asleep, with an older mother or grandmother watching his breathing, making sure the fan ceiling cools the room, but not too much, and the special netting protecting him from bugs stays tucked into the bed frame.

Steph wondered, *What will I say to his mother?* The idea of seeing her, and having to explain in his imperfect Spanish why they ran over her beautiful boy, almost turned him around. But curiosity had him, so he continued down the hall. All the rooms were empty, of everything. No chairs, beds, equipment. *Where the hell is everyone? What kind of clinic is this?* His skin tingled a little. He hesitated, felt the reassuring cold metal of the box knife he kept in his right front pocket. *Why do I need a weapon? I'm just a guy visiting a kid.* It even sounded stupid in his head. He shouldn't need to be prepared with a weapon, but he was glad he had it. Then he realized, in hindsight, that he was glad he hadn't had it for the fight because, unlike Breck, he really didn't want to cut or stab anyone, but knew he would have. He tapped the knife again and continued down the hall, slowly.

As soon as he looked in the final room on the right, he knew immediately he'd found Nicolás. The boy was sitting up in bed with a book in his left hand, his right arm in a soft white cast silhouetted against his thin brown chest. He was tilting the large book toward the small lamp secured to the side of the bed. He was alone and unaware of Steph standing in the doorway. The room didn't look like a medical room; other than the bed and a small table scattered with some medical supplies, it too was mostly empty. The only light he could see was the lamp, the rest of the room filled with dark spots and shadows. Steph noticed, in the far corner, the open window he'd seen outside, covered by a light mesh screen. Maybe for fresh air. A ceiling fan whirred gently above the small metal bed. The white sheets seemed a little gray near the foot of the bed, probably an illusion caused by diminishing light. They were much whiter near Nicolás' light brown torso and long, athletic arms. He looked like any other active 12-year-old Bolivian boy, lean, healthy, and limber, except for the intense focus in his eyes. He was reading his book like nothing else existed.

Finally, Steph tapped on the door frame. Nicolás looked up with a blank face, trying to adjust his eyes to the darkness away from the lamp. Because the room's only light had been reflecting off the book's white pages, up into his face, Nicolás couldn't see anything else. He was completely helpless. Steph didn't know what to say during this awkward silence because he'd been programed for years to always show strength, never weakness, and always be cautious, prepared for anything, never vulnerable. His face probably looked stern and unapproachable, even though his thoughts were open and curious. Still, he waited, until he realized that Nicolás couldn't see him, and then he smiled.

Nicolás face transformed from focus to curiosity. Steph liked him instantly. But before Steph decided what to say —he still didn't know exactly why he was there— Nicolás smiled too. He still couldn't really see Steph, but he must have felt his smile or seen a flash of teeth because almost immediately his teeth beamed white, and only then did Steph hear the softly beautiful sounds of the insects and birds from the jungle just across the dark, open space behind the building. It was almost as if he could hear Nicolás' smile, and then he could hear the birds whistling and the insects humming, distant sounds that might be monkeys far down the river.

"Hola. Señor Lukely?"

"No." Steph wondered if the doc was supposed to be here now. "I'm Steph."

"You are American… yes?" Nicolás asked openly, the way only children do.

"Yes." Steph was still standing cautiously in the doorway, wearing his floppy hat even though there was obviously no need. Habits are hard to break.

"You are he bitten, yes?

"What?" Steph had heard the words, but they didn't register because of their awkward order and his assumption that Nicolás didn't know who he was.

"You, bitten by... oruga, uh No lo sé..." He maneuvered his fingers a little, like they were crawling across the bed sheet.

"Yes, caterpillar... I was bitten by a caterpillar." *How did he know that?*

"I sorry, uh ... for your... lots of pain, si?"

"Yes. How did you know that?" Steph walked a little farther into the room, near the end of the bed, and set his hand on the metal frame. It was cool and bumpy with layers of old and new paint.

"I also are bitten... see?" Nicolás showed a scar on his left shoulder where he'd apparently been bitten. "Doctor Lukely says it called, in English, Gigantic Silky Motha Caterpillar."

"I didn't know that."

The Doc knows the name... Steph felt his mind rearranging things, understanding a little more, trying to pull some information forward and push other information aside, like a rubik's cube combined with a slide puzzle. He was still looking toward Nicolás, but didn't see him or anything else in the room. Something definitely felt wrong.

"You... okay?" Nicolás asked.

"Yes." Steph needed time to process his thoughts, but he couldn't because this boy was so direct, with nothing to hide. It rattled Steph for a moment, so he deflected. "It's moth, not motha."

"Oh, thank you. Moth... moth... Did I say correct?"

"Yea. You said it right. What are you reading?"

Nicolás laughed a little, and said, "Sorry, so too fast... Qué dijiste?"

"Yes, I understand. Lo siento. Qué estás leyendo?"

"Ahh, no, please. You speak English. I need more to practice... So... I read of the Chicago Bulls."

"You like Michael Jordan?" Steph remembered the Doc had mentioned it, but he also knew from Panama that Spanish speaking kids learning English loved to talk about sport stars, partially because they were well known but also because they were rich. "I saw him play in Chicago once. He's pretty fucking awe... I mean, he's really awesome... really good."

Nicolás slowly set the book down on the white sheet as his mouth opened wide. "You see... Michael Jordán... play basketball? Oh, Dios mío! Qué increíble! A donde, cuando?" His excitement was emphasized by his mispronunciation of Jordan's name. Steph wondered if he should tell him that the accent is on the first vowel, but decided against it. If you love an athlete this much, who cares how you pronounce his name.

"I was stationed at Great Lakes, which is just north of Chicago, so

I went to the United Center and bought a ticket from some guy. It was fun."

"And Michael Jordán... he play good?"

"Well, he did, I think. They lost the game, but I didn't care. I couldn't see much anyway, I was way up in the nosebleed section."

"Qué es... nosableed section?"

"My seats were far, far away... from the court."

"Pero, you see Michael Jordán. Wow! I see him, and the Bulls, some day..." He looked at his book, nodding his head, as if reassuring himself. "Yes, I move to America... soon." He looked up at Steph with his wonderful smile. "I will study engineering at Chicago, and live at Chicago, and watch the Bulls and Michael Jordán. Doctor Lukely say he help me."

"Well, Chicago's a cool city, and you can learn a lot there, I mean, about engineering. The University of Chicago is a great school, with wonderful programs. It was founded in the 1850's, but it doesn't actually have an engineering program. Northwestern University does, I think it's called the McCormick School of Engineering, but it's tough to get accepted to Northwestern and it's really expensive. But, you know... you can do anything if you really want to, right? At least that's what we're told." Nicolás' looked utterly confused, so much so that he didn't know what to say. "I'm sorry. I was talking too fast... Lo siento."

Nicolás raised his eyebrows and asked him, "How you know so much? You too go to college at Chicago?"

"No, I just remember stuff."

"I go to college… in America."

"Yea, to study engineering."

"Yes. But I want… no sé cómo decirlo…"

"To say what?"

"Quiero proteger el Amazonas. The jungle is, my home place… I love much and much and more… Uhh, no sé cómo decirlo."

"Say it in Spanish."

"No is English or Spanish… No sé cómo decirlo en ningún idioma."

"Yea… I can understand that. Some things are hard to say."

"I am scared to it."

Steph looked at him oddly, "What? I don't understand."

Nicolás looked at him, then at the window, as if seeing the animals making the softening jungle sounds. "I am scared to the jungle. My father say many bad things happening. He say it will get more bad."

"In the jungle?"

"No… to the jungle."

"Yea, your dad sounds like a smart man."

Nicolás' face lit up. "Yes, very good father. Very good man. For him, I must go to college at Chicago. Learn el Amazonas engineering."

Steph didn't know if that even existed, but then said, "I'll probably go to college someday, but, who knows."

"Yes, you go. I know you go. You know so much."

"Well, right now I know so much because I read a lot, it all just settles into my palace, and then I just remember it." He shrugged like he'd just finished making a sandwich or taught someone how to open venetian blinds.

"What is palass?"

Steph paused. He hated talking about his memory palace because most people either didn't understand or thought it was weird, but Nicolás seemed genuinely curious. "Well, it's just a memory trick, a way to remember many things."

Nicolás looked expectantly at Steph. "You... teach me?"

"Sure, but it's boring." Steph felt confused and embarrassed, but didn't know why.

"To learn engineering, I must remember...You teach me. I no boring."

"Sure. It's simple to understand, just takes practice. The more you practice, the easier it gets." Steph walked over to the other side of the bed as he pulled off his floppy hat and jammed it into his pocket. "So, you take a room or house, someplace you can easily remember, and you create loci."

"What is lo-key?"

"I'm sorry. It's a Latin word for... uhm... spots, specific spots. Then you tag, or connect details to the same spots along specific paths you created through a room or multiple rooms... That's it."

"That's it?" asked Nicolás' in disbelief.

"That's it."

"I no understand."

"Okay. So, in this room, the door is a loci, we'll call it a spot, the open window is a spot, the bed a spot, the table a spot. If you want to remember Michael Jordan's stats from his first year in the NBA, uhh..."

"1984, from University de North Caro-lin-a to Chicago Bulls."

"Wow, yea, so you envision the... envision means to see in your mind or imagine," Steph tapped his head. "his shooting percentage during his first year."

"What is per-son-tij?"

"Uhh, do you know porcentaje?

"Sí. 51.5 Field Go In porcentaje." Nicolás smiled after he said it.

"Wow, you know that? Maybe you don't need a memory palace."

"For Jordan, easy. Engineering, no easy."

"Well, you just add data... uh, info, or information to the spots,"

Nicolás interrupted, "The lo-key."

"Yea, after doing it for a few years, your mind starts just putting things into the appropriate spots. It's kind of a pain in the ass because then all these images just pop into your head, often connecting with other images or loci, spots, taking over your brain, and then you realize connections that may or may not be important. So you're trying to get laid –I mean, meet a new friend– and your mind keeps trying to connect crazy images and facts when all you want is to have fun."

Nicolás had lost Steph's train of thought toward the end, but he understood that this would help his memory and mind. "Teach me more, another?" Nicolás set the book aside.

"Alright. So, let's use the Doc."

"What is doc?"

"Doctor Lukely, call him Doc, he'll get a kick out of it.

"What is kick out of..."

"Nevermind. Just call him Doc, okay?

"Okay."

"So, imagine the last three times you saw him, and something interesting or important he said each time." Steph felt a little bad digging into Dr. Lukely's business, but the itch had to be scratched.

"Okay. First time, he was at my house after I wake up, after truck, talking at mi padre, I no remember good because... ohh, so much pain. Second time, later when he shoot me, for caterpillar, and he bring me this book and check the... mi herida... no lo sé..."

"Your wound." Steph added.

"Yes, my woond, and he tell me about Chicago and how he maybe help me... go there."

"What about the other times?"

"Only two times I see him, before here."

Steph raised his eyebrows. "Wait, really?"

"Yes. He say he go to my house, talk my parents more, to talk more, if maybe I can go Chicago this... now mes, este mes." Nicolás was obviously getting tired. "Doctor Lukely very good man." He looked at and then touched the book lightly, as if imagining something very valuable.

"He's going to take you to Chicago este mes, this month?"

"Yes, he say... this mownth."

Steph blinked and shook his head a little, something was definitely wrong. "When?"

"This mownth."

Steph realized he'd completely missed something Nicolás had said. "Wait! You were bit?"

"Yes."

"By a caterpillar? Like me?"

"Yes."

"No way... When were you bit?"

"Today, I think, but not sure. Maybe... ayer." Nicolás looked for something on his table.

"Bullshit!" Steph responded without thinking. He didn't mean to challenge Nicolás, but the boy had to be wrong.

Nicolás looked at him, puzzled. "What is this? No lo sé." Nicolás was genuinely curious about the phrase because he didn't realize Steph didn't believe him. He hadn't seen Steph's face, and he was genuinely naive, genuinely innocent.

"Nicolás, me infectaron hace tres días… three days ago, and look at my neck. You could not have been infected or bit, stung, whatever, by the same type of caterpillar this morning or yesterday."

Nicolás smiled, "Sí, yes… is… increíble, pero … is true. Doctor Lukely here, soon after…" He made a gesture like a needle poking into his shoulder. "The pain, all over, stop very fast… Uh… no más hinchazón. Good man, nuestro amigo, Doctor Lukely." He smiled again. His smile was light and clean.

"Well, yes, that is amazing… increíble!" Nicolás assumed he meant the healing, but Steph really meant that the two of them had both been bitten within three days. And then another thought came to him. "You said, maybe. Do you know this word? It means tal vez."

"Sí. Entiendo. I understand."

"How can you not know when you were bit? Didn't it hurt?"

"I were… como se dice… inconsciente?"

"Unconscious."

"Sí. Un-con-shus. After the accident."

"So you just woke up with all this…" Steph was trying to process what seemed impossible. This boy had been hit by an American truck, then attacked on the same day by a deadly poisonous caterpillar while unconscious. It didn't make any sense. And then, to end up in a military hospital bed, alone. All in less than twenty-four hours. Steph needed time to think, but he had another question that had to be asked now. "You said he gave you a shot. Where?"

"Si. Yes. Here." He pointed at the base of his neck.

"Where were you bit?"

"Si. Same. Here." He pointed at the same spot.

"Can I see?"

"Si, por supuesto." Nicolás leaned forward and twisted his neck a little. Steph leaned closer and saw a small bandage. He lifted the edges carefully, afraid it might hurt Nicolás, but he didn't flinch. Two small red spots sat next to each other. Steph imagined that must be what his wound looked like under the swelling and bandages. But if he gave Nicolás a shot, where is the third hole? Maybe he misunderstood Simpson, but he thought he'd said there were two holes or punctures.

If Doc gave him a shot, where's the other hole?

"Mister Steph... Okay?" Nicolás was trying to look over his shoulder, probably wanting to lean back, but Steph was so lost in thought he'd forgotten about him.

"Yea, sorry." Steph pressed the adhesive back onto the skin.

"Okay? It... look okay?"

"Yea, it looks great. That shot must have really done the trick."

"Si. Very good. And you? He shoot you?" Again he made the gesture of giving a shot, but this time toward Steph's neck.

"No. No shoot me?"

"I no understand. Por qué no para usted?"

"I don't know, Nicolás, but it's a very good question that I will be asking Dr. Lukely. Why he no shoot me?"

∞

Steph felt a little bad rushing out, but something was very wrong. He could feel it across his skin and along his spine, a strange tingling. He needed to get back to his squad, so he told Nicolás he'd come back tomorrow if he could and hinted that maybe they'd watch a Bulls game together in Chicago. As he walked out the door, Nicolás waved a small, left-right good bye gesture at Steph, the way kids say goodbye, and went back to his reading. The last thing he noticed was the little pool of light on his lean, brown arms and a slender hand opening the book's cover.

On his way back to their barracks, he walked down the semi-hidden jungle path rather slowly, not as a precaution, but because his mind was sorting, or at least trying to sort through, a tangle of disorganized details. His greatest talent, as much as he hated to admit it, was not toughness, leadership, or courage, but insight and deduction. Common sense, basic logic, was strongly suggesting specific conclusions, but they were either extraordinary or extremely unethical. It seemed imperative that he organize his mind before allowing them to suggest an idea that might be too big for him to handle, or worse, contrary to the squad's best interests.

He knew he should have already cultivated this talent more, before it was needed in the real world, the way Breck practiced marksmanship at the range, Simpson took EMT classes back home, and Smith practiced his morse code, just in case it really mattered. Even in this moment, when he needed all his mental focus, his shame distracted him, embarrassed him. Finally, he made a decision that would dramatically affect the rest of his life:

No matter what, starting tonight, I'll do my duty. It seems odd to consider thinking, remembering, and understanding situations as my duty, but, as Chief says, we all have our part to play for the platoon, for the Team, for our country. So, I guess I should add… for the truth. I'll solve problems, even mysteries, for the Team and for the truth.

He could see most of the small Bolivian base from the path, with maybe fifteen buildings, a weak gated entrance, and a few tower lights facing the road and town. On his right, or more accurately, behind his right shoulder, millions and millions of acres of jungle seemed to protect him, a dark vegetable wall. For some strange reason he felt safer with the jungle behind him. He stopped again, wondering about the statistical likelihood that both of them had been bitten within a few days. Steph loved numbers, probabilities, statistics, percentages, anything that clarified the world, or at least made it appear clearer. They seemed like fixed points in a chaotic universe, a language everyone could use to discuss the unseen and, maybe, sometimes, even the unknown. *10%? No, way too high. Think of all the people in and around this one town, maybe fifty or sixty thousand. If five or six thousand were infected, I'd have read about it or the doc would've said something. 3%? 2%? Maybe. I could probably find out how many people are bit, divide that by the number of…*

That's when he heard it, an unmistakable snap, somewhere behind him, probably on the same hidden path he was walking, considering the approximate direction of the sound. He froze, listening as intensely as possible. If it came from the jungle, it could be a large rodent, a tapir… or a puma? Unlikely. *No. It's not an it, but a he, and he's on this path. Maybe not. 50% chance he's on this path. 20% chance I imagined it —no, 15%— What else? Think. Fallen branch? No, the sound was too crisp. Now… nothing.*

He wanted to be thorough, but he intuitively knew someone wasn't just on the path, but following him. *Stay calm, don't let him know you know. Walk slowly.* He took a few steps, and paused. Nothing. His pulse rose. He instinctively checked for his box knife, then remembered he hadn't put his floppy hat back on. It made him feel safer, so he slowly placed it on his head. If he knew the full extent of what was really going on, he might have realized the most important thing was to figure out who else was on the trail, not the likelihood that he was correct or how far back the person was. But then he remembered that he'd lied to Chief, snuck to an unauthorized section of a Bolivian military base, and was now alone and potentially in danger on the edge of a very dark jungle.

Walk. Listen carefully between footfalls. Pause.

After a couple minutes of slow, silent walking, he realized a few things: *He's not stalking me, only following me. He's either very good, or not moving. I am not in control. I must get back to the barracks, now.*

He walked calmly, but briskly, along the path, stopping every 30-40 seconds for 5-10 seconds to ensure the situation hadn't changed. He heard nothing but his heartbeat and the silence of the jungle, as if the animals knew to be quiet. He could see the barracks, so he walked quickly from the edge of the jungle to their well-lit back door and glanced back at the path. If someone was in the bush as he believed, especially if camouflaged, he'd never see him. And then he remembered something else Chief had said, "If someone has the right training, right weapon, right opportunity, and is comfortable in the tension, there's not enough luck in the world to stop the inevitable." It gave him the shivers and motivated him to get off the well-lit porch and into the relatively safe barracks. He turned the handle. Locked! He looked back at the jungle, more nervous this time. Nothing. He didn't want to run around the building, past the windows to one of the other three entrances, in plain view of anyone who might be watching. His mind churned, but he did nothing.

Knock on the door. Better to be written up than shot down. But I really don't want Breck to know. Alright, just knock.

Just as he was about to knock, announcing to everyone he'd been gone and couldn't get back in, the door quietly opened. He slipped in, and the door immediately closed behind him.

12 – THE FIGHT

"Dude, where the hell were you? And don't tell me you went to the head, because I did and you weren't there." Steen's face radiated a complicated mix of concern and anger. He was wearing his most comfortable camo pants, a green Navy issued T-shirt, and his Walkman headphones around his neck. "Well, where were you?"

Steph looked at Steen for a long minute and decided to tell him the truth. "I went to see Nicolás."

"Who the hell is Nicolás?" Steen's eyes bunched and focused a little.

"The kid... who Denilson hit."

"Why?" He looked at Steph as if he were either a confused child or an irresponsible idiot, but then seemed to remember who he was talking to and rolled his eyes. "Dude, they said he was okay."

"No, they said he wasn't dead." Steph walked past Steen, sat on a cruise box, and started taking off his boots.

"What's the difference, and more importantly, why do you care enough to go AWOL?"

"I wasn't AWOL. I went for a walk on base."

"Steph, are you stupid? You went for a walk on a BOLIVIAN base just after we were attacked by a mob..."

"No." Steph didn't know what else to say.

"No, what?"

"No. I'm not stupid."

"Or, wait, I get it. You think... I'm stupid."

"Shut up. I don't think you're stupid and we weren't in any real danger. It was just a fight. They weren't the killer types." He started working on the second boot.

"How the hell do you know? You're the least qualified of all of us to know the killer type, and mobs get ugly, especially drunk ones."

"Okay. You're probably right." Steph turned his head toward the door, thinking about the open window.

"And although you have read a few Bolivian books, that doesn't mean you understand these people. They were pissed? I know, I felt the brick and the glass!" Steen tended to get overexcited.

"Alright. Chill out." Steph pulled out his box knife, clipped it into his right boot, and tossed both boots by the wall. It was a trick Chief had taught him, so he'd never forget to put his knife back in his pocket.

"The LT is stressed. We were almost smoked by a mob, and you're playing nurse man with a kid you don't even know, who might sue the hell out of the Navy, by the way."

"Man, just relax." He looked down at his worn, greenish brown socks. "I said you're probably right."

"Probably?" Steen looked out the window.

"Okay, you're right. But I wanted to make sure he was okay... and,

I don't know. I wanted to meet him." Steen turned toward him, with a dumbfounded look. "I know! It doesn't make sense, but I just felt like I needed to meet the kid."

"Why?"

"I don't know." Steph rubbed his forehead a little, and then cupped his hands around his eyes. "Well, actually, I don't know if this is... important. I don't know exactly how to say it, but I figured out that ..."

"What? You figured out what?" The harsh confrontational question came from the doorway. Steph knew before he looked that it was Breck, and he had some mad bug up his ass. "You found... what, while you were... where?" Breck's eyes mockingly questioned Steph. "Does the LT or Chief know you were wandering the base? Do they know you compromised our mission and our safety playing with some little river rat you don't even know?" Breck walked past Steph toward the back door, ignoring Steen.

"Why do you have to call him that?" Steph stopped rubbing his eyes. He felt like too many disorganized parts were crashing around inside his head, and he needed a little quiet to let them settle into place.

"Call who, what? That kid?" Breck walked over to Steph, leaning over him, and said, "You are in deep shit, Petty Officer Austin. Don't you realize that? You should be less concerned about all this politically correct crap and more about yourself and this squad."

Steph could feel something loosening in the back of his head. He already disliked Breck, but he suddenly hated him. The rubbing had created little red and white spots in front of his eyes. He stood up, right into Breck's face, as if unaware of his words or that he was wearing slippery green socks or that he didn't have his knife or that he was yelling at Breck.

151

"Why do you have to call him a rat, and be all racist and… and…?"

"What?" Breck was smiling at him, mocking him.

"an asshole! A psycho asshole! What did he ever do to you? He's just a nice kid who didn't say one fucking thing about us running him over with a truck!"

Simpson came into the room, having heard the yelling. "What's going on?"

Breck ignored him, his eyes burning and his words flying like sparks. "What? Are you fuckin' kidding me. You're going to choose a little jungle-monkey river rat over team guys. I should…" Steph's loosening had turned into a loud crack. He suddenly charged up into Breck, grabbing him by the shirt with one hand and the throat and chin with the other. They went first into the wall and then onto some of the metal cruise boxes. Breck was caught off guard for a second, but it didn't take long for him to get his balance, pivot as they were falling, and land in a slightly better position. He was wearing boots; Steph's socks had already started sliding down his feet. Neither of them threw a punch, it wasn't that type of fight. Steph just wanted to silence Breck. He wanted to stop him from talking. But Breck, once started, always wanted the same thing, to destroy.

By the time they hit the hard-tiled floor, Breck was on top. If Steph hadn't been so emotional, he would have known that his position was bad, and if he wasn't careful, it would quickly become worse. All he could think about was that he didn't want Breck on top of him, so he pushed on Breck's right leg with his foot while trying to spin to free himself. It was a mistake. Breck moved his leg, took advantage of Steph's twisting, and released one arm in order to get Steph's back. He instantly locked him in a choke hold.

"Let him go Breck!" Steen yelled, stepping toward them.

"Stay back." Simpson said as he grabbed Steen's arm. "He started it and has to learn his lesson."

Steph tried desperately to get a hand inside Breck's forearm, to create just enough space for a little air. He turned his body and pushed up on his knees and then twisted his body enough to slam Breck against the cruise boxes. It must have hurt, but not enough. In the end, it did nothing but put him in a position to better see Breck's incredibly taut forearms and clenching fists as well as his own legs. Steph tried to pull on Breck's fist, and then tried to elbow him in the ribs. Nothing. He felt his strength going, and then his eyesight got blurry. He could hear someone talking, as if from far away, and he could see Breck's legs and the tiled floor. He tried to head butt any part of Breck, hoping to get lucky, but it did no good. He was done. The last thing he saw before the world went grey and splotchy and then black was the beads of moisture and flecks of vegetation on Breck's boots.

∞

Unconsciousness is like a light switch. Drifting away seems like regular life being slowly dimmed, but once you're out, you're gone. Steph didn't remember any thoughts or sounds or pain, just the flecks of vegetation on Breck's black boots and the look and smell of his camos. Becoming conscious again was a strange and wonderful surprise for Steph, even if it was filled with coughing, gagging, and the realization that he'd been completely powerless in Breck's arms. He felt jolted awake, but in slow motion. He looked up from his camo pants and saw the room, but recognized or acknowledged the sounds and colors slowly. He turned his head a little, and realized that he was sitting up against the wall and that Chief was sitting next to him with a canteen of water in his hand. Breck was nowhere in sight.

"You okay?" Chief asked, with a caring but condescending look. "You want a little water?"

Steph shook his head and blinked his eyes a few times. He tried to swallow his own spit, but changed his mind. He looked at his right hand and his fingers, which he kept flexing and rubbing together, and realized that even though his mind was clearing up, his body wasn't reacting as it usually did.

"You'll feel better in a few minutes." Chief set the water canteen down next to him.

Steph tried to ask him a question, but no words came out, just little puffs of aerated sound.

"What?"

Step looked at him, focusing intently to say just one word, "Breck?"

"Why, you want another try?" He laughed. "I wouldn't advise it."

Steph shook his head, took a sip of water, and spoke slowly and quietly. "I don't want... just want to know where he is." Steph rubbed the back of his neck.

"Well, he's on watch in the front for a while. When you're up to it, I want you to hit the rack. It's been a long day for you." He was cleaning his nails with his little knife again. "Damn, a long-assed week."

"Chief, I... uh" Steph looked at the canteen for a long moment, still groggy and unsure of himself. He wanted to tell him that something was wrong, not with Breck, but with their situation. But he couldn't think straight. It was hard to speak, much less articulate a rational argument. "... uhm, I need to tell you something."

"Don't worry about it tonight..." Chief switched to his other hand, not able to find any more dirt under his right hand fingertips. "Yeah, I can still remember the first time I was choked out. I was drunk as hell, in a motel room just outside Fort Benning, in Georgia. We were there for jump school. You remember how boring it is. Well, I was shit-faced, acting the fool, starting to break shit, and a tough-assed second class, PO Canty, decided I needed a nap. He walked up behind me and turned the lights off. I later cruised with him. Great guy, half-Korean, his mother was from the South, married a grunt, of course. And that was just the first time I was choked out." He picked up the canteen, took a sip, and handed it to Steph who stretched his jaw a little and took another sip. "Don't worry about it. We'll sit down with Breck tomorrow. Gotta work this shit out before it becomes... well, you know!"

"Yeah, Chief, but that's not what I'm talking about." He looked at him through slightly glazed eyes.

"Well, don't worry about it, whatever it is." Chief stood up and walked toward the door. "We'll talk about it tomorrow. Get some shuteye." Chief offered him a hand.

Steph nodded his head, took his hand, and stood up. Although a little wobbly, he was good to go, so he walked into the other room, laid on his cot, and covered his face with a T-shirt. He would have done whatever Chief said anyway, but he was tired, his head was starting to pulse, and he felt embarrassed. He hadn't lasted even a few minutes with Breck, who handled him like a child. More than anyone else, he just wanted this day to end and for tomorrow to be different, a chance to do better. But he didn't think that was going to happen. He knew everything was going to be different when he woke up, and not in a good way.

13 – GRAB YOUR GUN

"Get up! Grab your gun."

Steph wasn't sure who'd yelled at him, his mind felt furry, like the inside of your mouth after an all-night bender.

"Austin!" Chief was right in his face, lightly smacking him and squeezing his jaw. "Wake up, now. We have a situation out front. A new one. They're back." Chief knew the after-effects of being choked out, so he pulled Steph's legs off the cot, set his boots next to him, and held out his CAR15, safety on, barrel down. Steph slipped on his pants and boots, pulled his knife from the edge of his boot and put it into his pocket, took the CAR15, and followed Chief to the front room. His eyes were open wider now.

Everyone was stationed as they had been before, but they seemed even more tense. Steph could hear distant yelling from somewhere near the base entrance.

Smith looked at Steph and said, "About fucking time."

Steph ignored him, "Where do you want me, Chief?"

Breck answered, "Watch the east side of the building, and the back, but be prepared to support Smith at the 60." Steph glanced at Chief, who nodded his head.

Steph took his position and looked out into the darkness. No movement, no threats, no noise. Nothing but darkness. He turned toward the squad. "What's up now?"

"They're pissed about the kid." Smith answered.

"Why?"

"He's dead and they want a big chunk out of our asses."

"Yea," added Simpson. "And Uncle Sam's checkbook."

"But he's not dead. Why do they still think he's dead?" Steph assumed he must have misheard something. Or, more likely, it was just another mistake.

"Well, they say he's dead and they're screaming, freakin' mad. You know, I can't understand why they don't..."

Breck barked at him. "Simpson, shut up and watch your zone."

"What's your problem? Have you gone over too?" gesturing at Steph.

"Shut up! Every stupid-assed sound that comes out of your mouth distracts all of us. So shut up before I shut you up."

"Piss off, Breck!" Simpson leaned his M16 against the wall. Breck smiled at him for a second until Chief intervened.

"Simpson, go to your station. All of you, calm down, focus on your zone, and do your job. They won't get on the base, so this is all just-in-case." When he was done, he glared at Breck, who stopped smiling, nodded, licked the teeth along the top of his mouth, and went back to his position.

Steph waved Chief over. "Chief, I need to talk to the LT, right now."

"You can't. He's in with Denilson, Renton, and the Doc."

"Why's Dr. Lukely here?"

"I don't know."

"I need to tell them Nicolás isn't dead."

"How can you be so sure?"

Steph looked directly at Chief until he looked up, "I was there, earlier, in his room. I talked to him just... What time is it?"

"About eleven."

"...just, over an hour and a half ago."

Chief looked at him, smiled, and pulled out his knife to work on his fingernails. "And why were you there, without authorization?"

"I don't know. I just wanted to make sure he was okay, I felt responsible."

"Why? You didn't hit him."

"Yea, but... we're all in this together, right?" Chief raised just his brows while still looking at his nails, tilted his head a little, and waited. "Okay... Dr. Lukely told me about him, and I was curious. He said Dr. Lukely had been helping him since the accident."

Chief's expression changed, but he didn't look up. "Lukely knew him this morning?"

"Yea... Dr. Lukely examined him after the accident."

"Why?"

"Nicolás said the Doc showed up right after the accident, talking to his parents about helping him out. Then he came back and treated him for an insect bite like mine."

"What?" Chief, face hard as bone, looked up. "How, like yours?"

"Same kind of bite, same place, but the kid was getting better right away."

"How did he know about the bite?" Chief said.

"Who?"

"Dr. Lukely."

"I don't know."

"What else did the kid say?"

"Well... that the Doc offered to help him get into school, or something like that. He said he might be going to Chicago with him. It sounded fishy to me, but..."

"What did the kid say to you about the shot?"

"What?" Steph looked at Chief, who had looked back down at his fingernails. "What shot?" Steph's skin started tingling.

"You said he treated Nicolás."

"Yea, but..." Steph's mind was rearranging frantically. "I didn't say anything about a shot, Chief,"

Steph was about to press him, ask how he knew about the shot, when the LT opened the command room door and yelled, "Chief, send in Austin. Now!"

Chief closed his knife and looked Steph right in the eye. "Listen, don't get cute. Tell the LT the truth and I'll cover your ass if necessary."

"But, Chief..."

"No buts." He stood up, "Hey, I made a funny, get it. Asses and buts... Get it?" Chief looked directly into Steph's eyes and laughed, but not his full belly laugh. "Now get in there. I'll cover your zone." He took Steph's weapon and pushed him toward the command room.

Steph, his mind frantically trying to sort this new information, arrange it in its proper place and time, tapped on the door as he walked in. Denilson, sitting in a frail wooden chair in front of the desk, looked exhausted. His LPO, Renton, was leaning against a wall near the corner, as if leaning away from Denilson would minimize his own problems. The LT was sitting behind the desk, watching Steph enter, reading him, while Dr. Lukely poured himself a cup of coffee in one of those tiny styrofoam cups, awkwardly keeping his back to Steph.

"Have a seat, Austin." The LT watched his face the entire time he was in the room. "Petty Officers Renton and Denilson, will you please see if Chief Wendley needs help with anything?"

"Yes, sir." Renton seemed grateful to be leaving the room; he pulled at Denilson's sleeve as he went by. Denilson rose like a zombie, following him out the door without looking at anyone.

"Petty Officer Austin, do you have something you want to tell me?"

As Steph considered what he thought the LT wanted to hear, he wondered if the LT had heard him talking to Chief or if he was talking about something else. He decided to play it safe, finishing what he'd already started. "Yes, sir. The boy, Nicolás, isn't dead. This…" waving his arm toward the front room, "must be some kind of mistake."

"And how would you know that?"

Steph did not want to admit he'd snuck out, but he didn't seem to have any choice. "I talked to him a couple hours ago."

"What time?"

"Uhh, around 9:30, I mean 2130. I think." *Why isn't he asking me why I jeopardized the squad and its mission by disobeying standing orders, exploring a foreign base at night, and talking to a kid Denilson had almost killed while the entire town hates Americans even more than they did before?*

The LT leaned a little closer to Steph and asked, "Are you sure of that time?"

"Not exactly, sir. It's a guess, but it's close."

"Well, try to be sure." The LT was acting way too sympathetic, too considerate.

"Well, sir, it was pretty dark when I left, so it had to be past 2100 hours, but I didn't check my watch."

The LT interrupted, "You should get into the habit of checking your watch, Austin."

"Uhh, yes sir, but why does it matter so much?" Steph looked at Dr. Lukely, who was walking toward the desk.

"Steph," Dr. Lukely said kindly, "Nicolás died an hour ago."

Everything went very quiet. Steph thought he heard a strange whirring, as if someone had turned on a distant fan, but he quickly realized that the sound was in his head, like when the wind seems to create background music during a storm. He glanced from the LT to Dr. Lukely and back to the LT. When neither of them said anything, he looked toward the right corner of the desk for what seemed like a long time. Nothing happened. His mind seemed frozen, except for the strange whirring sound. He didn't consider anything or understand anything, he didn't feel any emotions or formulate any ideas. It was an oddly pleasant experience to think nothing, but it didn't last long.

I barely knew the kid. I didn't hit him or kill him. Actually, if he died after... then we didn't kill him, so that's good. He was fine when I left. But how... The room was still silent, as if everyone was waiting for Steph to speak, but he barely noticed them.

Maybe it was the bite? Like mine... But I feel fine, even after all this... And he seemed free of pain. What is going on... I barely knew the kid, so why should I care? He didn't know why he should, but he did.

Suddenly he realized, *Oh, damn. I was the last one to see him alive, unless...*

The LT finally broke the silence. "We already know you went there last night, Austin. And if we know, then other people might know... other people might have seen you. So, first, what the hell were you doing there? And second, did anybody see you?"

163

Steph looked up slowly. He'd understood both questions, but didn't feel he should answer them, not yet. He didn't know why, but he needed time to think. So he just waited. It was obvious to anyone watching his face that he was thinking, but they probably didn't know he was actually processing, analyzing, organizing, comparing, remembering, evaluating, judging, imagining, planning, and questioning everything at the same time. *Do they think I killed him? Probably not. I'd have absolutely no reason, and the LT knows I'm not like that. But that doesn't mean other people might not suspect me.*

He'd almost forgotten they were in the room. He could see Nicolás, innocently lying on the white bed with his Chicago Bulls book on his lap and his dreams reflected in his big, brown eyes. It would be a mistake to say Steph was angry. If there's one emotion that balances anger, determination, and a driving, indescribable need, he was filled with it. He was also filled with one purpose, one question: *Who?*

After almost thirty seconds, the LT asked, "Austin, did you hear me?" The LT was trying to remain calm. It seemed obvious someone had told him to proceed carefully, but he was struggling. First, he had to deal with an idiotic 3rd class SBU driver who ran down a kid with a U.S. issue truck and didn't tell anyone until the town was ready to skin them all alive. And then one of his SEALs wandered around a foreign military base in order to talk to the same kid... who ends up dead. He wanted to scream to every current and future idiot in the building that this was his op and he would gladly court-martial anyone who violated even the smallest regulations, interfering with his plans in any way. He seemed about to explode when Dr. Lukely cleared his throat, gave the LT a sharp look, turned, and said, "Steph. What did you and Nicolás talk about?"

Steph was still processing. He appeared a little helpless when he looked up, like a soldier or athlete trying to recover from a concussion, but he was really working the problem without letting anyone know. Steph was starting to realize the power of silence, patience, and controlled tension. *He wants to know what Nicolás told me, not what happened. He's nervous.*

Steph watched Dr. Lukely's face carefully as he answered, trying not to show too much or cause a confrontation. "Not much. College, the Chicago Bulls, reading, the Giant Silkworm Moth, memory…"

The LT stood up slowly, leaning on his desk for support, his face reddening, his eyes blazing a fiery blue Steph had already seen. "You disobeyed my orders, snuck around this base at night WHILE we were locked down, and jeopardized our mission to talk to some kid you didn't even know about memory and MOTHS!" His neck muscles flexed.

"Yes, sir, but that's not why I went there. I went to check on him."

"To check on him? You went to check on him? Who are you his nanny?"

"Yes, sir. I mean, no, sir, I'm not his nanny. I just felt like… I had to make sure he was okay."

The LT squinted, as if he felt the beginning of a serious headache, and sat back down. "So, you're saying you went there to protect him?"

"I don't think so, sir." Steph was looking at the corner of the desk again. "If that's right, then I did a really bad job. It was more curiosity for the squad and…" He paused. Something seemed ready to fall into place. Steph seemed on the edge of understanding how a few things connected or related.

"And… what? Are you kidding me? You were… curious?" The LT's face was darkening again.

Dr. Lukely interrupted. "Andy, it sounds like Steph meant well…"

"Sean, this is the Navy, not the Peace Corps. Good intentions don't mean anything if they start with a violation of direct orders."

"Yes, but perhaps they should. And at this point we are focused on the wrong question." He turned back to Steph. "You haven't answered the more important question yet, Steph…

The LT interrupted, "Yea. Did anyone see you?"

"Well, somebody obviously saw me or we wouldn't be having this conversation."

The LT barked at him, "Don't be a smartass, Austin! You're already in a world of shit. Answer the question. Do you think anyone else saw you? Answer the question. Now!"

"Other than who, sir?" Steph wasn't sure why he was being difficult, but it felt necessary. He had to stall. *Something's not right. Why did he say "anybody else"? Why is the Doc in here? Why did the LT interrupt him… because they have different priorities. They are asking different questions.*

"Petty Officer Austin, are you aware that your actions could merit a court-martial?" The LT looked like the first heavy clouds of a storm about to break.

"Yes, sir, but I don't think my actions deserve a court-martial."

"Perhaps not, but since I decide who to report for court-martial, not you, I advise you to answer the question as I asked it, just in case."

"Sir, to be honest. I thought I heard someone on the path behind me when I was returning to the barracks, but I decided not to investigate. It seems likely that the person knew where I had been. But, sir, that is only meaningful in relation to my question." He looked straight at the LT, who stone-faced him.

Then it was Dr. Lukely's turn to be surprised. "What path?"

Just as Steph was contemplating if and how to answer, Breck burst into the room without knocking. "There's a Bolivian at the front door asking to talk to you."

The LT stood up. His frustration was boiling up, he needed to vent some of it and Breck was an easy target. "Petty Officer Breckendae, I am a Lieutenant in the U.S. Navy, outranking you by a couple thousand promotions. I can bust your ass any time I want, so you better add the appropriate SIR in the appropriate place when you talk to me. Do you understand?"

"Yes, sir, but I was talking to him." pointing to Dr. Lukely. "A little Bolivian with wire-rimmed glasses wants to talk to Dr. Lukely, sir."

They all watched as Dr. Lukely left the room. Steph noticed that Dr. Lukely was the only one who didn't seem surprised. He looked at the LT, shrugged and walked out, as if he didn't know what to say.

The LT sat back in his chair. "Petty Officer Breckendae?"

Breck, already on his way out, eager to get back to his station, leaned back into the room. "Yes, sir?"

"Sorry about that."

"No problem, sir. I agree one-hundred percent. Without order and discipline, the shit'll hit the fan every time, and then we're all screwed." He waited a minute. "Am I excused, sir? I need to get back to my post."

"Yes, of course. Keep up the good work."

He hesitated. "Sir, can we have Austin back? Every set of eyes, you know."

"In a few minutes."

Breck closed the door. The LT was looking at a sheet of paper on his desk, but didn't seem to be reading. Steph assumed he was gathering himself, covering his need to get control behind the illusion of responsibility. Even the smartest, sharpest people need to disconnect for a moment or two. The brain is a complicated organ, and the mind is a funny thing. Steph and the LT sat quietly in uncomfortable chairs for what felt like a long time.

Steph was also resting, in a way. He was partially lost in a new type of thinking he hadn't known he was capable of, and wasn't sure he could handle because he didn't feel like he could control it. His mind, as if by some independent power, was rearranging, replacing, prioritizing, and sometimes creating images: objects, details, colors, sounds, quotes, facial expressions, gestures, probabilities, statistics, possibilities, events, and facts flashed and rejected each other, fighting for attention, working themselves into place, like sand and rocks and foam and small animals on a beach. Slowly, visual hypotheticals started forming, most of which Steph didn't like.

Hypotheticals, or what if's, are essential in mission planning: What if our comm's go out? What if the squad is separated? What if someone breaks a leg? What if… But these hypotheticals weren't planning contingencies, partially because they didn't support the squad's interests, and partially because they evolved organically and visually from Steph's palace, and thus weren't initiated and then guided by rational logic. Some of the images flashed and disappeared or evolved into something else, never to be seen again. If they were going to end up identifying suspects, motives, means, or blame, it wasn't happening yet. At this point, they were like a chaotic visual soup that one day might become an accusation.

Not that it mattered, but Steph didn't like this part of his mind. Secretly, he enjoyed cultivating his palace, knowing details other people couldn't remember or understand, and intentionally creating an elaborate network of thought, a mental ecosystem. He knew most people couldn't do it, so he felt special in his palace. But every gift has a cost. Sometimes, no matter what he tried, he couldn't stop it. Steph had learned too much and gone too far to deny that Nicolás had been murdered, that he was involved, that he didn't know who or why, and that he wouldn't be able to stop thinking about it until he found the truth.

Dr. Lukely came back into the room. Chief followed right behind him, asking nervously, "Who was that guy?" Steph had never seen Chief nervous.

Simpson was trailing behind Chief, as if he too was now a part of the command team. "Yea, who was that guy?" Nobody seemed to notice him.

Dr. Lukely sat down in a chair, looking really tired all of a sudden.

"Hey, I asked you a question. Who the hell is that guy, whispering in your ear while a small mob wants a chunk of our asses? Spit it out, Doc!"

The LT looked at him, "What's he talking about, Sean?"

Chief yelled, "Well?"

"He's here..."

The LT stood up, suddenly nervous. "Who's here?"

"Quirános.

14 - QUIRÁNOS

"Who the hell is Quirános? Sounds like a fuckin' sandwich?" Simpson stood in the entrance, biting his nails and sweating mildly even though he wasn't doing anything but worrying.

The LT looked at Chief, then off into space, as if trying to figure out their next move without knowing their opponent's last move, or even who they were playing.

Chief turned toward Simpson. "Simpson, don't you have something to do? A position to watch?"

"What? A guy can't ask a question?"

"No, dumbass! And you should know that by now. What do you think this is, the United-States-of-I-Give-a-Shit about your opinion? Go back to your station." Chief was a little tired and stressed, but he still knew how to talk to his guys. Wrap a command in sarcasm, and it becomes a joke. Serious, maybe, but still less like an officer's order.

"Just asking a question, Chief." While leaving, he looked sternly over his shoulder at Dr. Lukely, then went back to his station.

The LT nodded at Dr. Lukely. "Tell us."

"Put simply," He paused and looked at the SEALs, "Marcel Quirános is trouble. He's a politician, but not your typical South American politician. He's tough and connected, but also virtuous, or at least he seems virtuous. He's a writer and a university professor, which means he's good with words and knows a lot of influential people, has lots of connections. He's considered a firebrand, always looking for a fight, which has gotten him into a lot of trouble —created a lot of enemies— but he has a lot of supporters in congress. And the Bolivian people love him. He's been in jail, a lot. To be honest, I'm surprised he's still alive."

"Why?" asked the LT.

"Lately he's been writing editorials and lawsuits instead of academic articles."

"So."

Sean looked at the LT. "Andy, if you're going to succeed down here, you need to understand the history and politics of the region. The courts, at the moment, still have some autonomous power." He paused for a minute, then surprisingly said, "You should ask Steph, I mean Petty Officer Austin."

"Why would I do that?" He looked as if he'd been insulted.

Chief interrupted, "I think he means because Austin is our intel rep, sir."

Dr. Lukely said, "Well, that's part of it, but really it's because I think he has a unique mind and knows more than you think… Just ask him. What can it hurt?"

The LT stood, walked a few feet, turned, shrugged, leaned against the wall, and started spinning a pen on the edge of his hand. He'd flip it with his middle finger as it sat in the cradle near his thumb, sending it spinning one full rotation only to land back in the cradle of his hand, as if ready to write in midair. It was a habit he'd started during lectures in college. "Is that all you know about this Quirános, Sean?"

"Mostly."

Chief looked at Dr. Lukely differently now. He'd known for a while he was, at minimum, holding something back. But now he was a potential threat to the squad, how much and what kind was yet to be determined. He watched him the way an older smarter cat might watch its prey before instincts start making the decisions.

Finally, the LT said, "What the hell. Austin, tell us what you know about Quirános, what's his first name again?"

Chief answered, "Marcelos."

"Yea, okay. Tell us what you know about Marcelos Quirános?"

Steph had been listening to the conversation, but indifferently. For a while, it seemed like they'd forgotten about him after everyone else walked into the office. He'd been thinking about Nicolás and pain and innocence, about the jungle, predators and prey, about running and searching. Although his eyes saw what everyone was doing, they'd glazed over when his thought soup started forming into clearer ideas, when he started imagining Nicolás running through Los Amazonas. Nothing seemed out of focus, but Steph didn't really focus on any of the particulars. Nicolás' short hair didn't really stream behind him, it wasn't long enough, it bounced a bit, softening the silhouette of his head above his naturally pumping arms and expanding chest. Steph could hear all the jungle sounds he'd noticed during the insertion and smell the rich, humid earth he'd held in his hands. He could almost feel the branches and leaves as he imagined them easily giving way for the boy, inviting him further into the never-ending green. No matter how hard he tried though, he couldn't imagine Nicolás' feet, couldn't see modern running shoes or sandals or light boots or bare skin. From deep within the maze of his memory, three or four ghost-like figures appeared on the trail in front of and behind Nicolás. Steph knew instantly they were not actual people. They looked too old to be real, like the great Tarahumara of Mexico, possibly the best long distance runners in the world, or like ancient Bolivian warriors on a hunt. But why here? Some of them wore white cloaks with hoods, partially hiding the shapes of their faces while others showed unfocused but beaming smiles. They seemed to be encouraging Nicolás, but maybe they were just laughing pleasantly, not at him, but enjoying his youthfulness. Maybe, like some of the indigenous people of North America, they needed to help the dead along on their journey somewhere else. Or maybe they just wanted to run in the jungle, to feel a new place, to connect to new people. Or maybe...

"Austin!" Chief barked, a little annoyed.

Steph blinked, looked at the LT and Dr. Lukely, both of whom were staring at him, and then looked at his Chief. "Yea, Chief?"

"Did you hear the LT?"

"No... Sorry, I was..." He didn't know what to say, but he knew he'd never tell them about his strange visions.

"He asked you a question."

"Sorry, sir. Can you repeat it? I guess I'm a little tired." Steph looked down at the floor, not because he was tired, but disappointed the vision was gone.

"Can you tell us anything about this Quirános?" The LT asked again.

Steph nodded his head up and down. "Yes, sir." He closed his eyes for a few seconds, and then opened them a little as he entered his memory palace. First, he walked very quickly, almost in flashes of movement, down stairs and past doorways until he visualized the library. It was a relatively small room but certainly the largest mental space in his palace because he stored his read memories in the most obvious places: books. He mentally walked to the shelf opposite the door and stopped. The books starting sliding quickly by until the Q's appeared and then they stopped moving. One book glowed a little. He mentally reached out, pulled it from the shelf, and started leafing through pages (his real fingers actually moving a little in his lap) until he saw the word Quixote at the top of a page with a dilapidated horse actively carrying a wonderfully ironic knight, who looked more like a skeleton than a warrior, across an arid, hot road as a funny-looking fat guy smiling on a donkey ate a hunk of meat. Realizing he'd gone too far, he flipped back over more pages until he came to a page labeled Quirános. He saw a hard-faced, dignified man typing on an old fashioned, floating, black typewriter with one hand as he banged the other on a podium with a big, black hunk of rock. The man looked Steph straight in the eyes while standing on stone steps with hungry people looking up at him from the sides. A few of the people looked angry, one of them held a pistol at his side, smiling. Only then did Steph answer the LT's question.

"He's a socialist in congress who helped start the Bolivian Socialist Party. For a while he was the minister of mining, which is a big deal in Bolivia because of all the mineral resources, which many people believe will be even more important in the next century. Before that he was a journalist and freelance writer. I don't know much about his commercial writing, but he complains about corruption –a lot– especially political corruption. He's considered an isolationist but doesn't necessarily think Bolivia should align with other socialist nations, at least not yet. He's an idealist, so he can't help seeing the flaws in other South American socialist movements. He definitely hates the United States' intervention in South America, especially in Bolivia. He once called the U.S. "an evil shadow unworthy of the sun." He never does anything in public these days without an important social or political benefit because of assassination threats. He's been targeted at least three times, that I know of. He's probably sincerely idealistic, probably believes political power is the only thing that can help the everyday people of Bolivia, and is definitely brave... maybe fearless."

When Steph looked up, everybody was staring at him, but nobody said a word. They weren't shocked that a Bolivian politician would dislike the U.S. so much, but amazed Steph knew so much about this surprise adversary on the spot. He looked back at them, assuming they wanted more information, so he looked more carefully at the page and saw the number 31 playing with three little kids on a coach, two girls and one boy, and then an image of Pablo Neruda crawling out of a poem. "He was born in Cochabamba in 1931... He has two sisters and a brother... I don't know much about them. When he was young he wanted to be a poet, like Pablo Neruda, but realized he didn't have the talent..."

The LT interrupted, "How do you know that?"

"He admitted it, that he had no talent, I mean... and then switched to journalism. But honestly, I don't know for sure, sir. I mean, I've never read any of his poetry."

"No... how do you know all this information about this particular guy who shows up in the middle of nowhere?"

"It must have been in one of the

briefing books at SOCOM, sir. Maybe some of it was in the Bolivia book I read at that bookstore in town." Steph looked at Chief, a little confused. His eyes raised a bit, as if asking, *What?*

Chief reassured him. "That's great, Austin. I mean, more than great; it's kind of freaky, but very helpful."

The LT interrupted, "Austin, tell me the truth, did you know we'd be asking about this guy?"

"What?" Steph felt the same tingle in his spine, as if being watched by someone not in the room. "What do you mean?"

"That's my point. How the hell… I mean, that's some specific information you just told us. Nobody remembers information like that unless they've prepared."

"No, Sir…" He looked at a dirt spot on the wall, and then back at the LT. "I didn't know you'd ask me about Marcelos Quirános." Steph suddenly felt embarrassed. He straightened his spine a bit and stared at the dirt spot again. "But I did assume it my responsibility to know about Bolivian politicians, geography, history, you know. I can tell you about other Bolivian politicians if you like. Enrique Komani hates the United States more than Quirános. He comes from a rich family, oil money…"

"That's okay, Austin." Chief interrupted.

"He went to college at Harvard, and then worked in New York for a financial company, probably to figure out how to grow his family's oil money. I can't find the name at the moment, but if you give me a minute I'll remember it."

"That's enough, Austin." Chief ordered.

Steph stopped talking, never taking his eyes off the wall.

Dr. Lukely stepped toward him. "Steph, I asked them to ask you because I think you have a mental gift, and I want them to know. I'm sorry. Nobody's testing you, it was me... I shouldn't have... pushed."

"You don't have to apologize to me, Dr. Lukely." He looked from the wall to the LT. "Anything else, sir?" He badly wanted to go back to his position and grab his gun. *Just let me stare out the window, looking for someone to shoot, like Simpson and Breck.*

"Yes, Austin. I need you to stay here, listen to the situation, and share anything you know that might help us understand why this Quirános is here."

"Yes, sir." Steph nodded and switched his gaze from the wall to the floor.

Dr. Lukely answered the question. "You don't have to be an expert to know why he's here. I can tell you. He smells blood. Even a little blood is enough. Steph's right. He's an isolationist who doesn't like any American intervention: military, financial, medical, humanitarian, nothing."

Once again, Steph couldn't suppress the feeling that something important was absent from the conversation. The question of why Quirános was here was obvious. *But why everything else? Why was the LT more angry and confused about what Steph knew than what Steph had done? Why did Chief seem so angry at Dr. Lukely? Why hadn't anyone mentioned Denilson or his dangerous situation? He could go to a Bolivian jail! Why was Dr. Lukely here at all, answering questions and partially running the show?*

And then, what seemed to him the biggest question of all just popped out of his mouth. "Why aren't we talking about what happened to Nicolás?"

The room went quiet. Steph would soon learn that when and how you ask a question is often more important than what you specifically ask. If he'd waited, even just until he could carefully watch their expressions, who they glanced at, and how long they took to answer, he could have learned a lot. The LT, angry and defensive, stared straight at him, clearly showing he was embarrassed he didn't know the answer. Dr. Lukely, unsure of what to say or whether to say anything, but clearly knowing something, avoided Steph's honest gaze by looking at the LT as if this sticky mess was his responsibility. And Chief pulled out his knife and started cleaning his already clean fingernails. Even if Steph had implemented this helpful tactic, he would have learned very little from Chief, but that in itself meant a lot.

Finally the LT answered, "Because we know what happened, Austin." He looked at Steph like a man who didn't know how to talk to a kid about a hard truth without oversimplifying it.

"Well, what happened to him, sir?" Steph pushed.

"He died." The LT looked at him through harder eyes.

"But that doesn't make sense."

"Why not... Petty Officer 3rd Class Austin?"

"Because he was fine just a few hours ago, after being examined by a doctor this afternoon." Steph gestured toward Dr. Lukely.

The LT sighed, paused, and then simply said, "Chief..." and walked over to the coffee maker.

"Austin, come on." Chief walked toward the back room, assuming Steph would follow him. Steph kept looking at the back of Lieutenant Hensen's head, knowing he probably wouldn't say anything else. Finally, he followed Chief out of the room. They walked all the way to the back of the building, out of earshot, and sat on a cruise box, near where Breck had almost killed him.

Chief had grabbed two cans of soda, looked at the moisture on the side of one can and said, "Take it."

Steph took the can and set it next to him on the cruise box.

Chief opened his can, gulped a bit, played with the silver lever that opened the can, and looked at the ground, nodding his head a little. "You liked the kid. Didn't you?"

Steph looked down at his boots. "I don't know."

"You seem... affected by his death."

"Yea..." Steph didn't know what to say. And even if he did, he wouldn't know how to say it. He probably was upset, but that wasn't why he asked the question. Deeper in his mind, he knew something wasn't right. But he also realized this was an opportunity to cover his curiosity. *If they think I'm just sad...*

"People die, Austin. Sometimes they're kids." He took another gulp of his soda. "Did I ever tell you about Grenada?"

Steph looked up from his boots. "No."

"Yea, I was green, like you are now, hadn't seen much action yet, but I was there, scared out of my wits, just trying to stay alive, do what I was told... I remember the first dead kid I saw. I think it was a girl, but I'm not sure. She was mostly covered in rubble, not blood, but lots of dust. The image is mostly blurry, but I can clearly see her hand. That's why I think it was a girl. We were hauling ass to a new evac site after we'd lost comms. I was scared. It was early morning, I think, and out of the corner of my eye I saw her hand, as if reaching out from under the pile, asking for help." He twisted the silver lever and traced random letters in the moisture on the side of the can. "I ran right by."

Steph waited for a second, hoping Chief would keep talking. It was unusual, to see a chink in his armor. But Steph's compassionate side couldn't wait any longer, "You were doing your... job. I mean, you didn't kill her. She was obviously dead. You had to keep going."

"Yea. That's what we have to do, Austin, keep on going while living inside the fight, but that doesn't mean it's easy." He looked up abruptly, staring directly into Steph's eyes like a hypnotist. "We keep on going. That's what we do... keep on going while doing what's best for the Team. Do you understand, Austin?"

"Yes, Chief."

"Good. Now get back to your station. I'll call you if the LT has more questions."

"But he said he wanted me to listen and..."

"Don't worry about that. And Austin, no matter what anyone says, watch your back. I have this terrible feeling the LT is... too nervous, too... Well, let's just say he seems really tense, and I just can't trust really tense people who won't calm down. It's important to maintain the tension on our enemies, live in it, embrace it, but not be too affected by it. Like in a choke hold, you must maintain complete pressure, the way Breck did, no hesitation, no weakness, while not being affected by the consequences. Once you're in it, you have to be all in, no hesitation."

"Got it, Chief." Steph wasn't sure if he could do it, but he believed it.

"And remember, you appear to be the last person to see Nicolás alive. At least the last American."

"So."

"So? What do you mean, so?" Chief looked surprised, and a little angry.

"I didn't do anything. I mean, I went there, but I didn't do anything but talk to him… Why would I…"

Before Steph could finish his thought, Chief moved a little closer and spoke a little lower. "Something's off about all this, Austin. And you sense it, don't you? I don't know what it is, but I think it's above our pay grade. And we know what shit does, right?"

"Yea… it rolls downhill." Chief loved cliches, so Steph threw one back at him. "But doesn't the buck also stop somewhere, Chief?"

"That's what I'm worried about. The LT has plans, big American plans, back home, and he doesn't want the buck, or the shit, anywhere near him."

"Well I don't want it anywhere near me, either." Steph said instinctively, not really thinking about what it meant or how it sounded.

"Then stay out of it, and watch your back. I know you're smart, but don't be too smart. Also, the LT's loyalties seem out of whack."

"What do you mean?" Steph knew what he meant, but hoped for more information. Sometimes, the best questions are the ones you already know the obvious answers to, if they get people talking.

"His frat buddy. Dr. Lukely shouldn't even be here… So why is he? Either he and the LT are into something, or the LT is covering for him when he should be focused on Team priorities, or the LT isn't as smart as I think. The LT, and… well, all of you, should always remember the most important rules."

"Yes, Chief."

"Say them."

Steph sighed, partially because he felt like a kid being tested but also because he was uncomfortable with Chief's most important rules. But this was his Chief, so he listed them: "Watch your ass first, protect your Brothers second, and then follow orders, no matter what —unless they're stupid, and then ask Chief–."

"And?…" Chief asked.

"And… when in doubt about anything, ask Chief."

"That's right. Now get to your post. I'll keep you posted." He laughed the full belly, heartwarming laugh Steph loved. "I made a funny. Did ya get it? Post…?"

"I got it, Chief, and it's called a pun."

"Whatever it's called, I got it, even in Bolivia." He patted Steph on the shoulder and went back through the main hall into the LT's control room. Steph picked up his soda can, stared at it in the palm of his hand, trying to rearrange the mess swirling in his head. It was unopened, a few drops of moisture still sliding down its side. He looked at the other soda can, the one Chief had left open on the floor. The tab was turned to the right, forming an L. Traces of letters hinted at Chief's thoughts. The sides of the can were slightly indented. He put his back in the cooler and tossed Chief's can in the trash.

He wanted to be a good SEAL and do as his Chief said. Something definitely wasn't right about the LT and Dr. Lukely, but also about Chief. He wasn't sharing everything he knew. Steph wondered, *Where did he go earlier?* Steph couldn't believe all this had happened in one day, which still wasn't over. He knew he should be tired, but curiosity fueled his body as well as his mind. He felt a strong urge to solve this mystery, even fix it, for the Team and his Chief, if possible. His curiosity was deeply stubborn. He hated unsolved problems, but also didn't want to cause trouble. Steph truly wanted to be a reliable Team guy, and he probably felt about Nicolás the same emotions Chief felt about the little girl in Grenada. The difference... for some reason he couldn't just run by. He believed and trusted his Chief, but he still felt a deep need to solve the problem. Like an itch that had to be scratched or an urge that had to be satisfied, he had to arrange the broken pieces, solve the problem, and know the truth.

∞

As Steph walked back to his post, he realized the guys were talking about the situation, too, but their discussion was less political and more practical.

"I think it was the LT," Smith said quietly, but with conviction.

"What? That's the dumbest thing I've ever heard!" Simpson laughed. "Why? Wait… I mean, forget it! I mean, it's so dumb I don't know how to explain its dumbness… or your dumbassness."

"Well, he didn't want him to i.d. the SBU guy, what's his name…"

"His name is Denilson, and that's even stupider than not talking! Just stop talking!"

Smith was not as aggressive as Simpson, but he'd had enough. "Don't tell me what to do, or not do, you skinny-assed prick!"

"How would the little shitter dying help the LT? Now we're in a huge mess. All we had to do was just give the family a cow or a couple goats and fix the bike, maybe leave them some cash. Now, we all might have to stay here." He gestured with his arm and then looked out the window. "God… I don't want to stay in this fucking hole any longer than we have to."

"Yea, it doesn't make sense." Steen was leaning against the wall, picking the best parts out of his MRE entree. "It wasn't the LT. Maybe it actually was the accident, you know, he seemed okay, but really wasn't." He didn't really care either way and immediately regretted joining the debate. Steen looked at Steph, hoping he might say something to take the attention off him. Everybody knew he'd gone to see the kid.

Steph looked at him, stone-faced. "It wasn't the accident."

"How can you be sure?"

"I saw him." They just stared at him, as if expecting more. "I assume you know I went to his room, so... " He paused for a few seconds, trying to determine what to share. "I mean, he was fine. He had a broken arm and maybe a sprained ankle or something. But he was sharp, coherent..."

"Are you a doctor?" Breck asked, still staring out the window.

"No."

"Then stop talking shit. You don't know anything about concussions or internal injuries." Breck turned his head, glared at him for a second, and then looked back out the window. "Besides, it doesn't matter. The kid's dead. They'll blame us. The truth is irrelevant."

Steph wanted to argue with Breck, to prove Nicolás' death was important, that knowing the truth was, and always is, important, but he was tired of Breck.

Simpson changed the topic. "Well, I don't really care about any of it, but I'll tell you one thing for sure, I don't want to listen to this damned Quizános socialista, communist mother fucker talking shit about America or us. Somebody should just waste his ass before he can get trouble going for us."

"I'm fine with that." said Breck quietly, but unlike Simpson's empty complaining, he meant it.

"You can't just assassinate a Bolivian politician because you don't like him." Steph said without looking at them.

Simpson replied, "Why not?"

"First, it's illegal. Second, it's politically stupid. Third, it would complicate our leaving, and finally, it's immoral. He doesn't deserve death because we don't like his politics."

Breck turned from the window, glared at Steph, and leaned his rifle against the wall. "Who's side are you on?"

Steph looked at him, surprised by the question, "What?"

"I mean it, really? Whose side are you on?"

"This isn't about sides. Of course I'm on our side, but spontaneously killing a politician in his own country because we don't like him is stupid!"

"It's stupid to protect the LT and this squad?"

"Just talking about assassinating Quirános while we're in this mess is stupid, especially when we don't know…"

"What? Don't know what?" Breck was intentionally pushing Steph's buttons again.

"Don't know what really happened. Don't know who's listening outside the door or even in this room." Steph gestured to the lights and walls, tapping his ear before continuing. "Don't know what's going on. And yea, don't know how Nicolás died."

Breck ignored Steph's suggestion of possible surveillance. "We know what happened. Denilson hit a kid with a U.S. truck, and the kid died. And now we need to keep our heads and get the hell out of here. So stop talking shit. Just stop talking, all of you, and do your job."

"That's not what happened." As soon as he said it, Steph wished he hadn't.

"What?" Just when it seemed like the tension couldn't get worse, Breck and Steph were facing off again.

Steph didn't want to say it again, but he couldn't back down from Breck, especially after being choked out earlier. "That's not what happened. He didn't die from the accident."

"Man, you just don't get it, do you?" Breck walked toward him slowly until Steph lifted the stock of his CAR15 up toward his shoulder, still pointing the barrel down. Breck stopped, but his face transformed into the mask Steph had seen during the riot in town.

"Dudes," Steen was up and walking toward them. "Chill out!"

"You're not going to touch me again, Breck. I don't care... what the fuck happens... Don't touch me!"

Steph felt like an alien in his own body, all frozen blood and forgetfulness and rage. He couldn't really hear anything but a strange thrumming in his ears until Chief asked calmly, "What's going on out here, guys?"

What's going on? I was ready to shoot this psycho... Almost ready to shoot. It's amazing how easy it would have been to kill him. He's good, but he wouldn't have expected it here. He wouldn't have expected it from me.... But he's my brother... Right?

And then he heard Breck say, "Nothing, Chief. We're just talking about the situation."

"Well don't." Chief walked to a spot between them. "It's above your pay grade, and even if it wasn't, you probably wouldn't understand it."

"What's there to understand, Chief?" asked Simpson. "We have the might and that makes us right. Let's blow this place."

"Well, that's not your call, now is it, Seaman Simpson? That has a nice ring to it, doesn't it?" Chief looked up at the ceiling and then at all the other guys.

"Uhh, Chief, I'm a 3rd class…"

"Not for long if you keep saying stupid shit and forgetting your place. That goes for all of you." He walked to the approximate center of the group and repeated himself. "That goes for all of you. Remember my rules, and everything will be fine." He looked right at Simpson. "What are they, Seaman Simpson?"

"Watch your ass, protect your buddy, and follow orders unless they're stupid and then do whatever you say."

"Very good, Petty Officer Simpson. And now, all of you, calm down, watch your zones, settle in for the night, and stay alert. Except you, Austin. The LT wants you again."

They walked back and Chief told Steph to sit in a small blue chair just outside the door to the control room. "I'll be right back." And he went back to the front room.

As he sat there, Steph realized the LT and Dr. Lukely were arguing again, but about something that happened a long time ago, not this situation, maybe what they were discussing earlier. He heard the LT whisper something about transferring from Duke to John's Hopkins University, and then Dr. Lukely confidently reassuring the LT. It was much easier to hear Dr. Lukely, perhaps because he was more confident, or perhaps he felt even more entitled than the LT. Maybe he's just closer to the door. "Andy, you worry too much. I'm a big boy. I can take care of myself." Then Steph heard the LT whispering, but only a few of the details: testing... medecine... death.

Suddenly, the door opened, and the LT looked angrily at Steph. "What are you doing, Petty Officer Austin?"

"Just waiting, sir."

"Waiting for what?"

"You, sir. Chief said you wanted to see me."

The LT looked annoyed for a second, then yelled, "Chief!"

Chief walked up, "Sir?"

"What's Petty Officer Austin doing here?"

"I thought you wanted to see him?"

"No." The LT looked suspiciously at Chief

"Sorry," Chief looked defiantly at his LT, and then added "sir."

Steph just sat at the bottom of the long, awkward silence, until the LT finally said, "Both of you, go back to your stations. And Chief, tell them to stop making things worse."

15 - LOYALTY

Steph went back to his position and looked out the window. Nobody asked him any questions. For the first time in years, he felt almost alone while being with his buddies, his Teammates. Ever since he was hazed, on his third day at SEAL Team Four, he'd felt like an integral part of something. He grew up a poor kid, raised by a single mother who moved him and his sister from Michigan to California and back, then from Michigan to North Carolina and back, so he had never felt grounded. Other than his maternal grandparents, he had almost no family. So the SEAL Brotherhood, one of the most intensely loyal fraternities in the world, the blood and death promise to always protect, support, and choose Team guys over everything else, even siblings, wives, and children, had touched something deep in Steph. Something connected to home and security, to a permanence he'd never felt. But Steph knew very well that one wrong step, one disloyal move, could, and usually did, cut any SEAL from the Brotherhood. And that was the step his mind seemed to be suggesting he take.

Steph's tragic flaw was simple, stubbornness. It got him through BUDS and STT, but he couldn't control it. He knew other Team guys who lost their way and were kicked out of the Teams because they couldn't control their temper or an addiction, but he couldn't control his curiosity. No matter how hard he tried, he couldn't stop thinking about something once it grabbed him. And this idea had grabbed tightly. *Why can't I just let it go, walk on by like Chief said?* More than anything, he wanted quiet to figure out a solution. Perhaps if he could find some mental space, he could control his need to know. *Maybe I can hide my thoughts in another part of my palace. Could I create a black hole for ideas? A place to erase thoughts?* But he knew it wouldn't work today, partially because he'd never find any quiet.

Simpson and Steen had been discussing who to blame for quite a while, but Steph had just realized they were no longer talking about Quirános. "Somebody has to take the fall… better him than me."

"Yea, Simpson, always better someone else than you." Steen replied.

"Well, duhh! Do you want it to be you or Austin or Breck?" Simpson pulled out his pocket knife, flipped it open, tapped the sharp blade on the tile floor a few times, closed it, and slipped it back into its pouch on his belt.

"Thanks for including the rest of us in your exit strategy." Steen pulled a candy bar out of his pocket. He bit off a chunk and kept talking through a mouthful of caramel and nuts. "But why him?"

Simpson shrugged his shoulders. "He's a wanker."

"Maybe, but he's still an American."

"Yea, but not one of us."

"What if he didn't do it?"

"Well, then he can ask his parents to get him an expensive lawyer and get him off. He can fly home in their jet or whatever. The truth is, I don't really care because I don't trust him."

"Is it because he won't let you treat Austin? That's a dumbass reason. Didn't you take civics classes in high school?"

"What?"

The First Fall

"You know, innocent until proven guilty?"

"Guess I was absent that day."

Steen turned his head and leaned up against the wall. "You probably were. Well in America you're innocent until proven guilty. It's a Constitutional right."

"We're not in America. I doubt these people even have rights."

Steph realized they were talking about Dr. Lukely, suggesting he might have killed Nicolás, or at least suggesting he should be blamed for it. He turned and looked at them, about to ask why they suspected him, when a series of images slowly floated into his mind, partially materializing right in front of his face: A giant silkworm moth, Nicolás' trusting face, Dr. Lukely strangely wearing a suit and talking to a lot of people as if on stage, children being injected with medicine, Dr. Lukely giving Nicolás a shot, another giant silkworm moth.

"I guess we could blame that sandwich guy."

"Why, genius? How would we blame him?"

"I don't know. He's trying to frame us."

"But he wasn't even here, and that doesn't explain how."

"How do you know?"

"What do you mean?"

"How do you know he wasn't here before Denilson hit the kid, and this guy saw an opportunity, and he grabbed it. You know, Blame the Americans! That's what everybody else does. I mean, shit, we're helping

193

people all over the world and all they want to do is blame us for shit."

"Yea, that's true. I don't know for sure. Maybe it was him… But then again, maybe it was you."

"Nah, I wouldn't waste my time, unless Chief or LT asked me to. Then…"

Steen looked right at Simpson, checking the look on his face. He was looking out the window again. "Would you really?"

"Yea. An order is an order. I mean, that's what we do."

"Do you think the LT would order us to do something like that?"

"Sure. His primary responsibility is to America's interests, and the Teams, and us."

"But kill a kid to… what? Just to cover up an accident? No…"

"Sure. Maybe the kid saw something or would testify or something? LT's gotta do what he's gotta do. And like Chief says, we gotta do what's best for the Team. If I'm okay and you're all okay, I'm supposed to follow orders… or ask him. The real question is… Wouldn't you?"

Steen hesitated. He knew everyone in the room was listening to their conversation, and he knew what they wanted him to say, but he couldn't say it. "I don't know. It doesn't seem… I don't know… I mean, how does somebody decide something like that? What decides something like that?

Chief, who'd been listening to most of their conversation, answered for him. "Loyalty! And if you dumbasses can't remember that word, then just follow my rules and everything will work out." Steph noticed a harsher tone underneath the words, a seriousness that was supposed to make them uncomfortable.

"Chief, but what if..."

"No buts, Simpson. No what if's when it comes to orders. Just do what you're told. The UCMJ will send you to prison for not following orders, and send me or the LT to prison for giving you an illegal order. So, shut up —everyone— and stop making the situation worse. I need quiet to think."

Steph didn't think Chief really cared about them making the situation worse. He only stopped their discussion when they started talking about something he didn't want them to explore.

After just a few minutes, Simpson said, "Uhh, Chief?"

"Damn it, Simpson. Can't you shut that pie hole of yours? Not even for a minute? What is wrong with you, son?"

"Uhh, a bunch of cars and trucks are heading right toward us."

Breck came over to Simpson's position to look out the window, "What kind of trucks? How many?"

"I don't fucking know, three or four."

"Look out." Breck pushed Simpson to the side, squinting as he looked at the approaching cars. "They look more like cops. I see lights on the top of at least one vehicle."

"Steph," Chief looked over his shoulder, "get the LT."

The Bolivians walking up to the door included a couple military personnel, but most of the men wore local police uniforms. Three of them wore suits, which looked strange because it was so late. Marcelo Quirános led the group toward the door with a purpose-driven step that could be understood better by the calm but determined look on his face than his pace or gait. He was a handsome man with European features, a well groomed beard with a streak of gray on the left side of his mouth. He had strong brown eyes and stood taller than most Bolivians, accentuated by his nicely tailored suit. His hands were empty.

One of the suits was Quirános' assistant, a shifty looking politician with a decent suit and a forgettable face, neither handsome nor ugly. He was probably related to someone powerful. The mayor of Riberalta finished the trio. His suit was wrinkled and clearly of lower quality, but he walked just as angrily and defiantly as the others. His features were a little rounder, his fat a little more obvious, but he too looked European. More than anything else, he looked tired and angry, as if he'd just been dragged out of bed.

The LT walked through the room with Dr. Lukely behind him. "Everybody stay put. Keep your weapons out of sight from the windows. Most importantly, don't do anything." Chief started to follow him out the door. "Chief Wendley, stay inside and make sure nothing happens." Dr. Lukely followed the LT and closed the door behind them.

"Damn! Stone cold!" Simpson said while shaking his head from side to side.

"Shut up, Simpson." Chief was obviously upset, but tried not to show it. "Everybody get back to your stations. Keep your weapons down, but be ready. Breck…"

"Yes, Chief."

"Keep a close eye on what's going on out there."

"Got it, Chief."

"I want to know who does most of the talking, if they exchange documents, everything."

"Chief."

"What?"

"They're leaving, and the LT and Dr. Lukely are coming back,"

"Already?" Chief seemed surprised

The LT and Doc walked in, closed the door, and stood in the middle of the room.

"That was quick. Well?" Chief asked.

"They weren't in the mood to talk..." Dr. Lukely replied. "But they'll be back sometime tomorrow morning."

"What for?"

"To take Denilson, and anyone who resists, to jail."

16 – KILLERS

It was amazing how the tension slackened after Quirános and his entourage left. They gave the LT until noon to hand Denilson over to the police and promised that he would be well taken care of and nobody else harassed. The Mayor told them not to leave the base, Quirános adding that it was for their own safety.

Chief decided to post sentries at the front and back entrances, just in case, but told everyone else to get some sleep. He could see how tired most of them were after coming straight from the field and into this mess. "Get to sleep, now. Tomorrow could be intense, so we need to be sharp."

Chief assigned Breck to watch the front because he could rely on his inner fuel to keep him alert on duty, and told Steph to watch the back since he'd gotten more sleep than anyone lately. Chief probably also wanted to make sure they stayed away from each other. He knew Breck would never leave his post.

After everyone else settled in, Steen walked into the back room and sat on the floor with his back to the corner, feet flared out wide with a peanut butter sandwich roll in one hand a soda in the other. "So. How's it going?" He took another big bite of his sandwich and let his stupid grin spread across his face.

"Fine." answered Steph, not in the mood to be calmed or reassured.

"You know what they say about people who say they're fine, don't you?"

"No. Aren't you supposed to be asleep?"

198

"In a minute. I sleep better with a full stomach."

"Okay... So, what do they say?"

"Oh yeah, that people who say they're fine are really freaked out, insecure, neurotic, and emotional."

"That's stupid. Where'd you learn that?"

"I don't know, probably a movie, but it's sometimes true. Don't you think?"

"Yea, sure, if you believe in the law of large numbers."

Steen looked up from his sandwich. "What do you mean?"

"Almost everything is sometimes true if you wait long enough. The statistical odds of success go up a little bit after every non-experience. It's just a matter of patience. Most people simply die long before they can experience a lot of improbabilities. So, like I said... patience."

"Man, you are one weird dude."

"Yea..."

"How's your throat?"

"It hurts a little, but not bad. To tell you the truth, I'm kind of glad to know what it feels like. I mean, I didn't want to be choked out, especially by Breck, but as long as I woke up... Now I know."

"Know what?"

"Being dead and all... It's like turning off a light. But still, no thanks."

"Good advice." Steen rolled his eyes as he pushed the last hunk of sandwich into his mouth.

"By the way, why'd he let go? I mean, it wouldn't surprise me one bit if he hadn't."

Steen paused for a sip of his soda. "Chief made him. Pulled out that little knife he's always cleaning his nails with after Breck didn't listen the first time."

"Really?"

"Yea, it seemed like Breck was in a trance."

"He was going to kill me?" Steph sat up, realizing that he hadn't really thought Breck would kill a Team guy, even if he hated him.

"I don't know. I was about to grab him, I think even Simpson was ready to help, but Chief came in and told him to stop. It wasn't like Breck was disobeying him, more like he couldn't hear anything. So Chief clicked open his knife in front of Breck and gave him that stare he gives when he's really serious, like he's about to flip the switch. And then Breck let go. Man, you dropped like a sandbag." Steen finished his soda. "He's one dangerous dude... kind of a psycho. So, watch out."

"Yea..." Steph was concerned about Breck in the back of his mind, but he was really focusing on the situation.

When Chief entered, Steen didn't need a hint or order to walk out. "See you in the morning."

"Goodnight." Steph waited for Steen to leave before asking, "Chief, what's the deal with Breck?"

Chief sat down next to him. "What do you mean?"

"Well, is Breck losing the bubble? I mean, is he psycho?"

"Maybe a little, by civilian standards, but every squad needs one." Chief's reply surprised Steph, and it showed on his face. He looked directly at Steph, "But that's my problem. Besides, you weren't in any real danger. He's a killer, for sure, but not for you, or anyone else in the squad. Definitely not while I'm here."

Steph nodded his head for a minute. "Well, he seems dangerous… It felt like a long time to be out, but then again… how would I know?"

"Nah, don't worry about it. Most people wake up after being choked out, even after what seems like a long time. It's not a definite kill move unless it's intentionally held long enough, and for some people it can require a few minutes or even more. It's just that you're totally incapacitated. He had the right lock, and he kept the pressure tight, but he wasn't trying to kill you, just scare you."

Steph shook his head. "That's nice to know."

"Petty Officer Austin, you're smart, but you need to learn to control yourself, especially your emotions and your expressions." He tapped Steph's forehead, "I can read you like a map. And if I can read you this easily, they can read you. Remember, Admit nothing, deny everything, and make counter-accusations, even with your face; otherwise, you'll never be great at what you're good at." He looked toward the window, "I know… You don't like some of the realities of our job. I've done it for a long time, and I know what you think you're doing here. Finding yourself or your strength or some other personal self-realization bullshit…" He looked directly into Steph's eyes again. "They aren't like you; they're more… Well, just don't underestimate them. Remember the puma I saw? Some animals will literally finish their business while you're still alive, leave you half-eaten, and then saunter off, belly dragging on the ground, while you're still bleeding out. Trust me. I know what I'm talking about... You're not a puma, Steph. And no matter what you do, you can't turn yourself into something you're not." Chief looked down into his hands, rubbing them together. "Damn, I wish I still smoked. I'd kill for a cigarette right now." He stood up and stretched. Steph watched him, feeling a little like Isaac from the Bible. "Don't waste time being what you're not, Austin. Become great at what you really are, what you're already good at. That'll answer your question."

Steph was looking at the floor. "Chief... what if I don't want to be like that? What if I'd rather be something else, more like them?"

Chief had a faraway look in his eyes, one Steph had never seen before. "Well, then I guess you're screwed. A man divided will eventually fall. As hard as it may seem, you've got to be what you are, and then... I guess you have to change your life to fit your truth."

Steph already knew this, he just didn't want to admit it.

"Well, I need some sleep. Turn the lights out so you're not silhouetted and you have better night vision. But don't fall asleep! If Breck catches you sleeping on watch he might finish what he started. And Austin,"

Steph looked up, "Yes, Chief."

"Watch your back... As a matter of fact, until we get out of this mess, watch your front too."

Steph didn't know what to say. "Okay... Thanks, Chief."

"Actually, stand up for a second. Time for a quick lesson."

Chief showed Steph the best way to escape a rear choke hold. "Remember, its best to stop it before the lock. Come at me from behind." Steph walked behind him and went for the choke. "Strike with the back of the head, for a little shock and some space, then quickly strike or clutch the groin." Chief moved so quickly, Steph wouldn't have seen the moves. "Then leverage the arm and twist and pull, after stopping the attacker, become the attacker! Slip into your own rear choke hold if possible." Chief showed Steph by putting him into the position. "Lock the arms, using leverage and, if possible, the target's weight against him, stay close to the body and constrict from all sides." Chief locked Steph in, showing him how a little more pressure actually closes off airflow. "It takes twenty to forty seconds to render unconsciousness, which seems like a long time when you're choking someone. Be patient. And if you want him dead, best to finish him with your knife afterward."

"Thanks, Chief." Steph was tired, and didn't really want a hand-to-hand lesson in the middle of the night. But Chief wasn't done.

"If you can't slip behind to go for your own rear choke hold, pull your knife, stab and twist, then finish the job another way. But you must be decisive. Once it's started, you must end it as soon as possible, for your safety, and the Team or squad's safety."

"Thanks again, Chief." During his lesson, Steph thought about the importance of physical touch between men, how much trust it builds. He knew he felt a strong paternal connection to his Chief, but he also knew how difficult it was to talk about. If there was a way, he set it aside for later.

As if realizing Steph wanted to say more, but couldn't, Chief simply smiled and said, "You're welcome. Now stay alert." And he walked out.

Steph got up and flipped the light switch off, then looked out the only window in the back of their building. At first, he saw nothing but darkness, but his eyes slowly adjusted until he could see the contours of the jungle, and then the difference between the dark of the base and the dark of the jungle. Nothing happened. And it seemed obvious that nothing would happen until at least tomorrow. Quirános would honor his word, and they could rest until at least daylight. There wasn't really anything else they could do.

Steph sat down on his cot, leaning against the wall. He knew he wouldn't fall asleep, especially with so much on his mind, so he closed his eyes and went back to the beginning of the blackout, considering again how similar it felt to his idea of death. He didn't fear death, at least not consciously, but it unsettled him to think of Breck deciding that for him, of Breck controlling him. No matter what Chief said, Steph believed Breck would kill him, but he did agree that Breck would do it like the puma. It might seem personal to other people, but once he started, emotions would have little to do with it.

If something happens now, how will people know it was him? Killers can get away with a lot down here, especially if it's done right. His thoughts drifted toward Nicolás' death. *Somebody murdered Nicolás. It wasn't an accident, but nobody seems to know who or how. Or, at least, nobody seems to care. Can it just be me?*

Then, whispering aloud, as if it could only be true if said aloud. "Yes, somebody murdered Nicolás." The next thought sprang from the first like a chain reaction. "And if somebody murdered him, somebody must know why..."

Steph realized, in that moment, that his life had changed, not switched directions, but been redirected. He believed he could be a warrior, a soldier, and even a killer if absolutely necessary, but he couldn't let people murder a kid and get away with it. No matter what Chief or anybody else said, he had to do something.

Steph was now actively cultivating his palace for more than memory. It was a place to create, a thought arena where his special talents could work freely. He actively pulled and culled ideas and images, floating up from dark places, from imaginary spaces, forming images that spoke to him and each other and gestured toward new connections and possibilities. Although he felt vulnerable working his palace around other people, Steph loved the mental freedom. It never failed to invigorate him, to connect seemingly disconnected ideas. But most importantly, he trusted himself –his true self– while working his palace. And there, in the dark room free from distractions and observers, he could let loose.

The first image to rise was a quote he couldn't attribute at first. The words slowly became focused, as if someone adjusted the distance until each letter was clear.

A matter of… rational contemplation.

The words dissolved quickly, like a candle running out of wick, and he saw a large, eery head appear from a faint bookshelf with a giant P on its forehead.

Of course... Poe.

Steph relaxed even deeper into his palace.

Denilson started everything, but somebody else is behind him, guiding him through the streets of Riberalta. He certainly struck Nicolás, but it was almost certainly an accident. Dr. Lukely...

Steph could see the Doc carrying an unconscious boy into the jungle.

What's he doing with...

He couldn't see clearly into the jungle, just enough to know Dr. Lukely was doing something to Nicolás.

The medicine. But how did he get bit?

No moths appeared, no bugs of any kind.

Maybe he didn't... Maybe Dr. Lukely intentionally infected Nicolás to test the drug.

It made complete sense, but once again, someone else was behind them, a shadowy figure that seemed to either control, or at least know, what everyone else was doing. Quick flashes of faces and moments looped through his field of view: Quirános and the suits, the mob of angry men downtown, everyone in his squad, some more clearly than others, but one, who he couldn't see, seemed more present than the rest.

One person seems to be controlling or at least aware of everything... But who?

Suddenly, Steph realized he was asking the wrong question, considering what he knew. With so many people involved, he couldn't be sure of who, but maybe he could decipher why.

Why would anyone watch Dr. Lukely experiment on a kid and not do anything?

He could see Dr. Lukely looking at or for someone who was looking at him, or at least watching him. The vision slowly became clearer once one image started flashing again and again, becoming more and more obvious, more powerful, until Steph said what seemed undeniable.

"The LT... The LT's to blame."

Unfortunately, Steph said it aloud and then opened his eyes abruptly. He knew he'd made another mistake as he heard the door quietly closing.

17 – WITHOUT BORDERS

Steph didn't know what to do. He was certain the LT was to blame, but he didn't know exactly why or how. As the OIC, he's technically responsible for everything, but Steph knew it was more than logistical responsibility.

The LT is guilty of something. But murder? He has done something terrible, or has let something terrible happen. Steph rubbed his eyes. *I wonder who was listening at the door? It doesn't matter. The shit's gotta come to light for any of us to get clean. I shouldn't have said it aloud. Have to be more careful.*

As he was trying to figure out who would most likely be spying on him, the door suddenly opened, letting a soft beam of light from the LT's office angle across the floor. A figure stood in the doorway. "Petty Officer Austin, the LT wants to see you." It wasn't Simpson, Breck, or Steen. He finally realized who it was.

Steph asked, "Ensign Walker?"

"Yea?"

Steph paused for a moment, realizing he could have misjudged time. When lost in his thoughts, time seemed different. Someone else could have been at the door before.

"What, Austin?"

Steph looked up at Mr. Walker. "Uhhm, how long have you been standing there, sir?"

"What do you mean?"

"Uhhm…" *I guess it doesn't really matter. He either heard me or didn't. If he did and doesn't say anything, ask me what I meant, he's hiding something. If he didn't hear me, then I'm acting suspicious. I gotta let it go.*

"Austin!" Ensign Walker seemed annoyed, not an emotion conducive with spying. "What do you mean?"

"Nothing sir. I'm just tired."

"Well, get going."

"Yes, sir." Steph stood up and walked out of the darkened room, wondering if his time had come, if he'd really screwed it up. Part of Steph felt like a kid called to the office, but another part felt like he was watching himself walk across the room, in charge of his ideas and actions. This person seemed in charge. When he got to the control room, he could hear the LT yelling and Chief trying to talk him down. Steph partially heard phrases like court-martial and formal referral. He decided not to sit down.

When Chief finally came out of the room, shaking his head and tightening his lips across his face to show just a bit of his gritted teeth, he waved his hand slightly for Steph to follow him. He didn't need to tell him to stay quiet.

"But Chief, Mr. Walker told me the LT wants to talk to me."

Chief waved his arm to follow.

They walked to the front of the barracks. "Breck, wake up Simpson and tell him to take watch in the back."

"Yes, Chief." Breck took his M-14 and left, not even looking at Steph.

"Trust me, Austin, you don't want to go in there right now. I told the LT I'd talk to you." Chief looked out the window, pulling the cheap blinds up a bit, then to the side, so he could look both ways. "You know... I don't really know what to say. Sometimes..." He looked out the window again. "Sometimes you're as dumb as a bag of rocks. No, not rocks, a tied up bag of puppies or kittens or something." He rubbed his forehead and eyes.

Steph felt bad for Chief, he looked so tired. But Steph also felt a strange indifference. He wanted to say something... *I don't know. I can't stop the truth, about Nicolás, about the LT, any more than I can stop anything else down here. I know he wants me to just leave it, just let it go, but I can't. It just won't be released. Something else has taken control. I just have to play my part... Why can't I tell Chief this. I'm going to just tell him the truth.*

He didn't get a chance: "Damn... I'm tired. You know, everyone thinks I want to do this forever, that I can do this forever, but it's not true. Did anyone tell you? I'm probably going to retire from deployments after this cruise? They'll put me in Ops, and I'll get even fatter and slower, but I'll get to spend more time with my kids. Who knows, maybe in a year or two I'll leave the Navy, really focus on my family and give the civilian world a shot." He reached into his pocket. Have you ever seen my boys, Austin?" Steph shook his head. Chief took out a photo and looked at it for a long moment, and then handed Steph the photo of his two boys.

They looked just like him but shorter and thinner. Steph smiled at the thought of a father and sons camping trip or a morning of quiet fishing. "They look healthy."

"Yea, they like to eat like me." He took the photo from Steph's hand, looked at it, and slipped it back into his pocket. "Yea... I'll take care

210

of them soon. But first, I have to get everyone out of this mess. It's my job, Steph —not the LT's, not yours, not the Bolivian government's— It's my job to fix this and bring everyone home safe, if possible."

"And what if it can't be fixed?" Steph didn't mean to antagonize. The comment just came out on its own, unfiltered.

"Well," Chief looked out the window, tapped the glass a couple times, as if testing its strength, and said, "I'll fix what I can and bring the rest home broken." He walked up to Steph, a little too close for comfort, and slowly leaned even closer. Their eyes locked for a strange moment. "It's my job. I couldn't stop myself if I wanted to, which I don't." He turned to leave the room. "Simpson's going to watch the back. Go to sleep." And he walked out.

Steph had felt out of control before, but now his rational mind seemed disconnected. He knew what he had to do, but was unsure about Chief. He walked to the back room, changed into his dark cargo pants, a dark hoodie, put on his boots, clipped his knife in his pocket, and slipped out the door before Simpson showed up for his watch. He didn't think anyone had heard or seen him leave, but at the same time he didn't really care. He knew it was naive to think he didn't hear or see something.

∞

As he quickly but calmly walked the open space from the barracks to the jungle, he felt free and determined. The thrill of pulling his hood over his head and slipping into the groove of the clandestine path energized him. He hadn't put his watch back on, but it must have been around one or two a.m. The clouds blocked out the starlight, so it was pitch black everywhere but around the few streetlights on the other side of the base, a few hundred yards from the edge of the jungle.

He knew exactly where he was going. He ran smoothly past the medical building where Nicolás was killed, slipped a bit deeper into the jungle to get around the edge of the base, and headed toward Adolphos.

Yes, the LT's to blame, but he didn't do it.

The small house was right next to the bookstore. It only took about ten minutes to get there, but he had to figure out which house.

Is it east of west of the store? Steph didn't second guess himself at all. He knew he was right.

It didn't require special skills. All the houses were dark except the one just west of the bookstore. And after a few minutes, Steph saw Dr. Lukely walk by a window. He snuck up to the house, looked for an open window. None, all were closed and locked.

Strange for Riberalta, where it's so humid.

So he checked the back door. Locked, but the door was built poorly, so he pulled out his knife and quietly slipped it between the door and the frame, loosened the latch bolt, and went inside. The hallway was mostly dark, but residual light from one of the rooms to the right made it easy to avoid the boxes in the hallway. They were mostly closed, but a few showed chemistry equipment poking out the top or leaning sideways against some newspaper, as if packed in a hurry. Steph listened patiently, heard someone, probably just one person, rustling papers around the corner. He was confident Dr. Lukely was alone in the house. He listened for a few minutes to calm his breath and make sure of the situation. Then he calmly tapped his knife and slowly walked around the corner.

Dr. Lukely was quickly sorting and filing some of his papers into an accordian file, placing others in a burn bag beside a big, old table covered with more papers, a few empty cans, and some scientific equipment. Steph was confident he hadn't been heard because he didn't look up from his task or change his frantic demeanor. This was the first time Steph had seen Dr. Lukely flustered, nervous. The room was randomly filled with more chemistry equipment, including burners, flasks, strips of chemical paper, hand-filled charts leaning against the wall, and other scientific equipment Steph couldn't identify. A laptop computer —high tech for the late 1980's— sat on a small table near a big blocky phone with a modem and other expensive electronic equipment. Steph was impressed with Dr. Lukely's secret pharmaceutical lab.

Steph didn't really know what to do now that he was in the room. He was shocked at how easy it was to enter a well-lit room, stand a few feet behind a person, his life in your hands, and not be seen or heard. The tension was building, which might work to his advantage, but at this point it was only making him nervous, causing him to doubt himself. Something had to happen, so he lifted his arm and scratched his neck.

Either the slight noise or the movement, which might have reflected some light on the windows, caused Dr. Lukely to raise his eyes from his work. He still didn't actually see Steph, but he suddenly realized that a dark, undeniably human figure with a dark foreboding hood covering much of his face seemed to appear out of nowhere. All his mind registered was a hand slowly lowering, as if reaching for a weapon, a knife, a gun, or something worse.

"Holy shit!" Dr. Lukely yelled as he stumbled away from the shape, bumping into the table and falling toward the window. He quickly turned his body and raised his arms in defense, not knowing what else to do since the only way out of the room was blocked. He regained his balance, breathing heavily, and waited. He still hadn't realized it was Steph. Fear and adrenaline can have a powerful effect on our observational skills. He just stood there, terrified.

Steph hadn't intended to frighten him. He hadn't even thought about the hoodie or his dark clothes, but instinctively dressed to hide himself for the trip to Dr. Lukely's house. He waited a moment, surprised Dr. Lukely still didn't know it was him. Then finally said, "It's just me." Steph slid the hood down the back of his head and looked at the doctor's terrified face. He almost said it again to try to calm him down, but remembered what Chief had taught him about tension and that Dr. Lukely was almost certainly responsible for Nicolás' death.

"Damn, you scared the hell out of me." He picked up a chair he'd knocked over, leaning on it with one hand. "What the hell are you doing here? Why..." He breathed deeply for a minute, then sat down on the chair. "Why did you do that?"

"Nicolás was killed." Steph stared at him, watching closely for any slip that might give him away.

"Yea, probably an aneurysm from the accident... Maybe,"

"No. Not from the accident. He was either murdered or killed. Not by the accident." They both stared at each other for a moment. "And I think the LT's to blame."

Dr. Lukeley's expression changed. "Wow, that took guts. Can't you get in big trouble just for saying that?"

"Yea."

"Well, let me save you a lot of trouble. Andy didn't kill Nicolás."

"I didn't say he killed him."

Dr. Lukely looked confused. "But you just said…"

"How do you know?"

"What?"

"How do you know the LT isn't to blame?" Steph was prodding, changing the focus, trying to lead him into a mistake.

"I just do. I know a lot more than you think, which I can't tell you right now. But I promise you, I will. And I know Andy didn't do it." He took another deep breath, which seemed more like a mental reboot. Steph just stared at him, believing what he said about the LT, but still trusting him less the more he watched him. "I think somebody is trying to frame him, or you guys, any American."

"Didn't you hear me?"

"Yea, I'm listening."

"I know the LT didn't kill him. I said he's to blame."

"I don't understand what you…"

"And he certainly didn't die because of the truck accident."

"Well.. No, he didn't. It's much more than that."

"What do you mean?"

"It's political."

"You mean…"

"Yes. Quirános. I don't know whether or not he killed Nicolás, but he's definitely trying to pin it on Andy, who definitely did not do it. Andy's a soldier, so I assume he'll kill people if he has to, but he's not a murderer, especially not a child murderer."

"How can you be sure?"

"Because he'd risk almost anything to avoid that. He already did, once."

"What do you mean?"

Dr. Lukely rubbed his eyes with both hands, then ran them through his hair. "We were in a fraternity together, a long time ago, and we drank a lot. During our senior year, I was the president of our house…" He looked down at the floor, as if remembering someplace else. "One night the plebes were rushing, and we were making them drink… and it got out of hand. One of them, a small, brainy guy from Florida, was struggling to keep up, and then he passed out. We all thought he'd just fallen asleep, but he was actually slipping into a coma. We were all drunk, but… I know, that's no excuse… Well, somebody realized he wasn't just sleeping, just passed out, we panicked. Andy knew exactly what to do. He called 911, went with the plebe to the hospital, and took responsibility. He always does that, takes responsibility, does the right thing." Dr. Lukely kept looking at the floor long after he was done.

"What happened to the plebe?"

"He died."

"What else happened?"

"Nothing. We were put on probation or something. Andy spent less time at the house, but I just kept on. Just like before… I just kept on… It changed Andy."

"That doesn't prove the LT isn't involved."

"I didn't say he wasn't involved. —We're all involved. — I said he didn't kill Nicolás."

"Well, if it wasn't him, then it was you." Steph was surprised at how calmly he accused Dr. Lukely of killing Nicolás.

Dr. Lukely looked at Steph a long time before responding. Steph knew that innocent people show genuine emotions when wrongfully accused, while guilty people work to control their responses. Dr. Lukely was working hard. "You think I'm capable of killing a kid? I tried to help him. I still want to help him, or at least his family."

"I think people are capable of many things, astounding things." then paused and decided to ask him point blank. "Doc, did you murder Nicolás, or was it an accident?" He stepped closer to him.

"No."

"Did you cause his death… intentionally, accidentally, negligently, for the sake of science? I know you treated him. He told me you were giving him shots."

"No, I didn't kill him… Yes, I treated him, so I guess there's a chance he reacted badly to one of the treatments, but…"

"What the fuck does that mean? Reacted badly!" Steph yelled. Then, quietly warned him, "Doc… don't bullshit me."

"I'm not. I really think this is political."

"Really?"

"Yes. Steph, I need to ask you a favor."

"What?" Steph couldn't believe what he was hearing.

Dr. Lukely stood and faced him. "I did not kill Nicolás, and I don't believe Andy is responsible or should be held responsible. The only way for us to know what really happened is to figure out how and why Marcelos Quirános is involved."

"You know, Doc, you're in over your head."

"Yes, I am, but that doesn't mean I'm guilty of Nicolás' death. I mean, I could have done better, but we all could have done better… We all should have done better."

He seemed to know exactly what to say. Steph suddenly doubted himself. He suddenly felt guilty. *What if the LT doesn't know anything about this and Quirános blames him, arrests him, and it's really Lukely and he gets out of the country? What good is this newfound ability if I can't protect my Brothers?* Steph stared at Doc more intensely. *I have to know, for the LT and the squad's sake. And he fucking knows that I must know.*

Dr. Lukely was good at manipulating people, and he knew better than to show anything on his face. "You have to trust me, Steph, just for tonight. I mean, where am I going to go?" He paused for a few seconds, looking Steph in the eyes the entire time. "I know I screwed up, but I didn't murder Nicolás. I didn't do that. But no matter what, they will blame the Americans, regardless of the truth. And that means they'll blame Andy, and put him in a Bolivian jail cell. He'll never leave without Denilson. We have to know, for everyone's sake. We must know the full truth."

"How the hell am I supposed to figure out what he knows or is going to do?"

"For years, Quirános has kept a notebook he uses to organize his life, his travels, issues, everything. It's a kind of journal, a kind of work diary, because he has a terrible memory. We need to see if anything in it, or in his other papers, hints at his real motives. Something in there will indicate he's preparing to arrest Andy. You grab it, and we can use it to convince him to just let us out of the country."

Steph's first reaction was to refuse. *Why should I risk my ass for this. It makes sense, but so does the other explanation.* He just stared at Dr. Lukely.

"And Steph, if you see anything else we might be able to use, grab that too."

Steph glared at Dr. Lukely, hating him and all his privilege and audacity. He wanted to be more like Breck, for just a minute.

Dr. Lukely, seeing Steph's hatred, simply said, "Steph, I didn't do it. I can understand why you doubt me, there's no good reason for you to believe me, but if we don't find out what happened, they'll blame all of us, all the Americans, and that means Andy, and all your friends… He doesn't deserve to take the fall." He paused, letting the suggestion sink in.

Steph was tired. He hadn't really slept much the last few days. BUDS and STT had trained him for sleep deprivation, so it wasn't a question of doing what needed to be done, but thinking clearly was a different matter. The brain must have rest to function properly. One part of him, the thinking part, wanted to refuse, drag Dr. Lukely back to the base, and let Chief and the LT get the truth out of him. Let them take charge. But the LT was Doc's friend, his close friend, and Dr. Lukely was good at manipulating people. He might persuade the LT to let him go. Another part of Steph wanted to give him to the boys for a few minutes, tell them the truth, and let them work him over. But there was also the curious, rebellious part of Steph, and it too wanted to know the full truth. He wanted to find a clue or detail other people didn't know. He knew he was becoming obsessed with Nicolás' fate, but he was too tired to clearly consider the consequences.

"Where is he? What does the journal look like? Does he travel with security?"

"I don't know, uhh… I don't know." Dr. Lukely was looking around his room as if some missing papers might answer Steph's questions, an imaginary intel brief or operations folder, but really he was just stalling.

"Do you know anything, where he's staying?"

"No, I mean, yea. I know that. He's staying at the Hotel Colonial. It's over on Placido Mendez… Uhh,"

"I know where it is, northeast of the airport, by the river."

"Yea, by the river."

Steph saw the motorcycle keys on the table. He also saw a box of latex medical gloves. "I'm taking your bike. Stay here."

"Sure. It's full of gas. Do you need any money?" His nerves were fraying.

After picking up the keys and putting a pair of latex gloves in his pocket, Steph walked right up to Dr. Lukely, their eyes just a few inches apart. "Is there anything else you should tell me?"

His face was paler than before, anxious. "Uhh, I don't... I can't..."

Steph stared at him for a long minute, angry, suspicious, intense. "You didn't answer me."

"No... There's nothing else I should tell you."

Steph could see Dr. Lukely's face trembling just a bit, so he paused, realizing the power of controlled anxiety. Finally, he said "Doc, I agree the LT shouldn't take the blame, but that doesn't mean he's not partially responsible. Quirános might be planning to use this politically, to keep us down here, and you know I have to figure that out. But we both know you killed Nicolás. The only question is whether or not it was an accident."

"But I..."

"Shut up!" Steph pulled his knife and clicked it open next to his leg. Dr. Lukely couldn't see it, but he knew it was there. "If Quirános is plotting, we're screwed, but at least we'll know." Steph leaned in even closer, "But if you run, you're dead. I don't care if it was accidental or intentional, or if you meant well, trying to save kids from kissing bugs, or trying to make up for the mistakes of your youth. You started experimenting on him, intentionally infected him with this shit so you could cure him, and now he's dead. And now we're all fucked!"

"I didn't… " Dr. Lukely was sweating, blinking way too much, and having trouble controlling his facial expressions, almost smiling, then looking sad.

The moment seemed about to explode, but Steph forced himself to stay in it a little longer. He waited for quiet again, and then said, "Doc, I liked you."

Dr. Lukely interrupted him, "I like you, too. Steph."

Steph stared at him until it he realized he wasn't supposed to talk. "I'll be back in a little while, and we'll go to the LT. You'll tell him everything, truthfully. He can decide what to do with you."

"Yes, I will. The truth, I swear."

"And Doc, if you're gone… we'll find you. And it won't be me or Andy who decides what to do with you."

Sweating more than he should have been, "Yea, of course… Of course. I mean, I'm not going anywhere. I'll be right here. Where would I go?"

Steph stared at him for another long minute, then turned and walked out.

18 – THE FIRST TIME

Steph put on the helmet, which would draw a little attention since so few Bolivians wore motorcycle helmets, but a lot less attention than his blonde hair. His hood would never stay up on a motorcycle ride. He knew exactly how to get to the hotel while avoiding the police station. It was very late, so he wasn't worried about civilians. His main concerns were more complicated:

Doc's lying, but that doesn't mean he's the one. Quirános would benefit politically if an American intentionally or accidentally killed a Bolivian, even more so if it's a Navy lieutenant. The hard question is whether he has anything to do with Nicolás' death, and what does he plan to do with us, or to us? What if he's sleeping in his hotel room? I'm not a Ninja, I don't know how to sneak through someone's dreams. If I do get into his room, what do I expect to find? Proof that he's framing us? What if Nicolás did die because of the accident, and I'm entirely wrong? Then we actually are to blame, and the LT and Denilson are responsible. Doesn't matter, none of us are going to a Bolivian jail. No way!

Steph realized that although he wanted to know the truth and find justice, he would never leave a Brother in a Bolivian jail, even if he was guilty. He realized in that moment that his quest for the truth did have limits, clear limits, but he still wanted to know. He also remembered his duty. *From one perspective, as the intel rep, this stupid AWOL excursion is technically my job.*

El Hotel Colonial was beautiful, even in the early morning darkness. The lush flowers spilled over sculptures, drainpipes, doorways and rooftops, which might offer cover. He drove slowly past the entrance and then around the block, searching for ingress and egress routes, a place to hide the bike, alternatives if he lost this transportation. He parked across a side street at Riber Plaza, a nice park filled with shadows. He removed his helmet, pulled on his hoodie, and slipped across the street, behind the supermarket, entering the hotel from the alley. It was easy to climb over the high wall and hop down into the courtyard, where most of the doors faced inward, like an old motel in a tourist town in New Mexico or Arizona. His first problem became obvious, he had no idea which room Marcelos was in or how to find out. So he sat in a quiet spot in the shadows, pulled on the thin, latex gloves, and waited, for inspiration, help from the universe, or just dumb luck.

I should just go back? I'm probably in a lot of trouble; they must know I'm gone by now. But then again, maybe they think I'm just asleep, or they're not thinking about me at all. The LT might not notice, but Breck has probably tried to kill me a couple times, pissed I'm not available for his craziness, and Chief... The idea of Chief realizing he was AWOL stabbed a little. Steph realized his second problem, *I don't know how to break and enter stealthily, pick a lock, cover my tracks... I'm not a damn spook. What the hell am I doing here?*

Then he really started doubting himself, especially his decision to do Dr. Lukely's bidding. *Why did I trust him? Well, I don't. Then why am I here? How do people like him and the LT get people like us to do their dirty work? Money. Yea, and maybe that privileged look. Maybe if I looked like a Greek Olympian with a trust fund I could get Steen to do my laundry. Fuck this, I'm going back.*

Just as Steph was about to leave, a door across the courtyard opened and a man and a woman walked out. He stopped, locked the door behind him, pulled on it a couple times to ensure it was locked, causing a loose rattling sound, and walked toward the courtyard entrance. Once they moved into a slightly lit area, Steph could see that Quirános was leaving with a local prostitute. She was not elegant, a bit thick in the middle, wearing clothes so tight they almost looked threadbare from behind. They didn't talk to or touch each other. They simply left.

Steph didn't hesitate. He'd asked for help, for a sign or a bit of luck, and he got it. He slipped through the shadows, to the door, listening carefully while quickly peeking in the small gap in the curtains. A weak light near the back of the room allowed him to see that nobody was in the visible part of the room. He didn't need to pick the lock, he just took advantage of the loose doorway and the old locking mechanism by wedging his knife into the door lever and pushing his foot consistently and quietly on the jam while pulling the handle toward himself. With a little extra force from his knife, he was able to force the door open without turning the lock at all, just scraping the old wooden door jamb and lock a bit.

Once in the room he put away his knife away, unlocked the handle from the inside, closed the door silently, and relocked it. The room was eerily lit from a fluorescent light left in the bathroom. The bed wasn't made. One heavy bottomed scotch glass sat on the table next to a notepad and an ashtray with cigar ashes and a butt rubbed into the corner. In addition to the bed, a hammock hung near some windows surrounded by hanging and potted plants. An armoire closet split the room on one wall, with one door hanging open revealing one nicely tailored suit and a couple white shirts on hangers. Steph could hear the fountain in the courtyard, water trickling through layers of rock.

His heart was pounding, even though he didn't feel any danger. If Quirános had security, they weren't with him tonight, at least not in or near this room. But Steph still waited, listening. He heard nothing but the fountain, an occasional motorcycle from the street, and the hum of the fluorescent light. It was amazing how much he could see after sitting in the dark shadows for so long. Then he saw the desk. Somewhat hidden by the armoire cabinet, it was covered in loose pages of a La Paz newspaper and one notebook. Steph walked over, leaned down to see if he could decipher anything from the articles, and then picked up the notebook, remembering which direction it faced and that it had been closed so he could replace it correctly.

Of course it was written in Spanish, which would take more time, but the real problem was Quirános' handwriting. The ornate, tiny script was very difficult to read, especially in the dark. Steph needed more light, but he hadn't brought a flashlight and didn't want to go into the bathroom, afraid he might be trapped. Steph decided to read the last pages first, tilting the book toward the feeble fluorescent light.

As best Steph could tell, the diary was mostly about Marcelos Quirános struggle with himself. The entries described his consistent self-doubt, his failure to stop the crime or corruption he knew was stifling Bolivia. He wrote about his failure to control his urges, his drinking, his temper, the prostitutes. Steph found no mention of Americans or Nicolás. It appeared to be just a diary.

As he read, Steph instinctively settled into the space between the desk and the armoire with the open door offering more cover. Even if someone looked in the window, he didn't think they could see him. The more he read, the more he believed Quirános was a good man trying to protect his ideals and country, no matter how much pressure he had to put on himself. Steph didn't agree with his politics, but he respected him since he too was plagued by self-doubt.

He was just about to return the book and slip out when he heard the key in the lock and the rattling sound of the door. Steph froze, unsure what to do. He heard the door open, and then close with a push and a careful turn of the lock, as if someone didn't want to wake a roommate. He heard the keys fall on the table, a sigh, and then a soft, "Qué he hecho?" Steph's mind stopped thinking, just listened and processed. The urge to flee grew like a fever in his temples, but at the same time, Steph felt a calm in his legs and hands. Quirános dropped something else on the table, then picked something up, probably the scotch glass. But he set it back down, as if deciding it was too early in the morning for a drink.

Suddenly, Steph realized he could see Quirános in a small, ornate mirror outside the bathroom, above a little dressing table. The room was still dark, so he couldn't see clearly, but it was enough. He could see him taking off a light jacket, flipping off his shoes, and unbuckling his belt.

If he gets in bed, I have a chance… Quirános dropped his pants to the floor and sat on the edge of the bed, rubbing his face and head. Lie down… Then Steph's started second-guessing himself again. *What the hell am I doing here? I should never have trusted him. It's so obvious now, he's covering his tracks. He sent me here to buy time, or to walk me into a trap. Oh shit…*

Steph saw in the mirror, and heard from the soft release of the bed springs, that Quirános was leaning toward the lamp. As he flipped the switch, the room filled with light, illuminating the plants, the desk, and the mirror, which partially illuminated the dark American hiding behind the armoire door. Steph tilted his head, and thus his hoodie, so he could see everything but still hide his face and hair as much as possible.

Quirános walked around the bed, toward the bathroom, and stopped just in front of the desk. Steph's heart was pounding, at first he felt like a hunted animal, until he realized that he was not the prey, but the predator. Quirános just stood there, as if he'd forgotten what he was doing, as if he was sleepwalking. Steph knew what he had to do, but still hoped for a miracle, hoped that Quirános would simply go back to his bed and lie down, or even better, go in the bathroom and turn on the water.

If he goes through that door, I'm gone. No matter what. I'll be as quiet as I can, but if he goes, I'm going.

Quirános picked up one of the sections of newspaper from the desk. He stood just past the edge of the open armoire door. All he had to do to see Steph was turn his head, to look over his right shoulder or look down at his feet. He looked at the newspaper in his hand as Steph tried not to breath. Steph had been looking at Quirános' hands and papers, afraid that if he looked at his face he'd draw his attention, but he couldn't resist any longer. Steph slowly raised his eyes until he could see the side and back of Marcelos' head, still facing down, and that's when Steph saw them both together. A man in boxer shorts and a slightly stretched white T-shirt reading the newspaper next to an assassin in dark clothes and a hood. The mirror was like a portal into a different room, a different room and different people. A different Steph. It wasn't him. It couldn't be.

How have I become this?

Subtly, as if someone had whispered his name, Quirános looked up. The two men's eyes met for a moment in the mirror. One set of eyes looked cold and indifferent, but were really sad and hesitant. The other set transformed from relaxed and clear to terrified. Steph didn't hesitate. In less than a second he'd nudged the armoire door out of the way and stepped behind Marcelos, locking his arms around the soft neck, driving the right forearm upward under the chin into the larynx while locking the right hand behind his own left forearm as the left hand grasped the back of Quirános'

228

head, pressing forward with all possible strength. Marcelos dropped the paper and reached back to try to release the powerful arms, but he was no soldier and it was already too late. He didn't know what to do, so he tried to call for help, but screams need oxygen, and there was none. He flailed at the papers, but they couldn't help. He flailed a little more, tried to twist his body, and then his legs turned rubbery and he slowly sank toward the hard tiled floor. When the two men settled on the ground, one because he could no longer stand and the other to keep constant pressure on the throat, Quirános put his hands palm down onto the cool tile. His face turned a deeper, darker color, but he still held his weight up. Steph kept the pressure, just as his Chief had taught him. Even after the body went limp, and Quirános' forehead rested on the cool tile, Steph kept the pressure.

Steph's mind usually worked and worked, thinking, sorting, comparing, analyzing. But during his accidental assassination, it went blank. He didn't look at Quirános' head, but did glance down into the tangle of clothes between his chest and Marcelos' back. The black and white fabric didn't blur at all; they were clearly different. Steph was all black and dark and awesome, while Marcelos Quirános, the courageous Bolivian patriot who fought for what he thought was right, was light brown and white and dying. Steph could hear the throaty gasping noises and the attempts at words. Maybe they were pleas of help or curses, but they were broken, weak, and in Spanish. But it didn't really matter because Steph wasn't listening. For the first time in his life, he'd really flipped the switch. His mind, also for the first time in a long time, was blank, like a new sheet of dark paper.

Marcelos went out relatively easily, as almost everyone does. The human body simply must have oxygen. No amount of toughness can change that. Steph waited a little longer, then let go, softly and quietly settling Quirános onto the floor. Then he walked to the door, listened for anyone outside, carefully unlocked the handle, opened the door a bit, locked it again, slipped out, and quietly closed the door. He immediately walked toward the shadows, the alley, the park, and the motorcycle. He didn't look back, but checked his flanks instinctively. The bike started easily, and he drove away, straight for Dr. Lukely's room.

19 – THE DOOR TO THE TRUTH

As soon as the wind started blowing through his helmet, Steph's mind rebooted. *I've killed an innocent man.* He didn't notice any exhilaration in his pulse or breathing, actually the opposite. He was physically calmer than he'd expect. The streets were mostly empty, except for the occasional stray dog or a drunk slumped against a wall. Steph wasn't sure what he'd say to Dr. Lukely, but he was certain the Doc had lied to him.

Why? It doesn't make sense for the Doc to want Quirános dead… unless… Steph wondered if Dr. Lukely was connected to Quirános in some nefarious way or, more likely, that he had no connection to him, and that he'd sent Steph there because he had to be sent somewhere. *Fuck, it's not politics, it's just money… Drug money! Jesus… He's working for a drug company, not MSF. He's not a doctor without a border, he's a scientist without a conscience.*

Steph's anger was rising up and out of control. He hadn't needed his palace to clearly see that Dr. Lukely had intentionally infected Nicolás in order to test his drug, but he hadn't realized that it was about money. *Maybe he just gave him too much? Why didn't he give it to me? Maybe it's partially about his sister, but it's probably more about money.*

Steph was almost at Dr. Lukely's small house. Then he wondered again, *How much does the LT know? What am I going to do to Doc when I see him?* He wasn't sure, but it wouldn't be good. Steph pulled the motorcycle right up to the front door, turned it off and leaned it on its kickstand. He walked in the door carelessly since he didn't need to be stealthy. First, the motorcycle announced his return, and second, he didn't care if Dr. Lukely was ready for him. He wanted him to be ready. He wanted the fight. Everything would be so much easier if they could fight, man to man.

"Doc! Get the fuck out here!"

He strode into the room angrily, aggressively, like a boxer in the center ring, until an undeniable feeling stopped him dead in his tracks. His arms tingled as a slight but highly pitched ringing sounded softly in his ears. Something was very wrong. First, the house was deathly silent but the lights and equipment and boxes and notes were just as when he left. Not a hint of escape. Second, a faint odor of struggle floated through the rooms, like the taste of metal in your mouth after you hit your head. Steph looked quickly over his shoulder toward the door he'd entered and left open. He pulled his box knife from his pocket and quietly clicked it open, then turned the blade to hide it behind his forearm, grasping the handle way too tightly. He stood a few feet into the hall for a long minute, sixty grueling seconds, listening, waiting, hoping he was wrong, hoping nothing had happened and nobody other than Dr. Lukely was there.

For a second he thought to play dumb to regain some advantage, call out again as if nothing was wrong, but it was too late. Chief would have told him to always get control of his emotions before, not after. He felt he had two choices: run for the bike and get to the base asap, ignoring stealth and caution, or quietly and carefully move farther into the house. He stepped forward, enough to see into the main room where he'd confronted Dr. Lukely earlier. It looked the same, perhaps a few papers were different, Steph could see a backwoods backpack leaning against the table, two cans of soda with just a bit of moisture on the side, one opened, one not, some papers on the floor, as if knocked over accidentally and then ignored. The lights felt blinding and invasive, revealing, almost frightening. He wanted badly to turn them off, but it would take his eyes too long to adjust to the darkness. He peeked into the back hall, where he'd entered earlier, and noticed two open doors. He turned his knife to face the blade out, extending it about a foot in front of him. He slowly pushed the first door partially open. It was a dark bedroom with an unmade bed and little more.

The other room.

Steph stepped toward the other room, which he knew was the place because of the smell. A pungent odor that wasn't there before, a rich, earthy human smell, like a little kid who'd been sweating for a couple days without a shower and hadn't changed his underwear, got stronger with every step. The door was closed but not locked. Steph felt surprisingly calm as he opened the door to the lifeless room. He knew before he saw anything in the dark bathroom.

It was him. It was definitely him. He killed Nicolás, but did he do it on purpose? Did he do it intentionally or accidentally? Did he intentionally try to blame it on us? Does it really matter?

Steph flipped on the lightswitch. He wasn't surprised to see Dr. Lukely hanging from his belt fastened around the shower pipe. He'd urinated after he died, staining the front of his pants. His arms hung loosely at his sides. His face was a splotchy blue, which Steph assumed meant he'd only been dead for a little while.

Why'd he wait? If he killed himself after I left, wouldn't he be less blue by now?

The note was on the counter. Just a simple "I'm sorry" written in neat cursive script. Steph remembered instantly. *Dr. Lukely didn't write in script, only print.*

Steph reached into his pocket, pulled out his gloves, and put them back on, just in case. Then he looked up at the throat, it was badly bruised, a wall of bruises, but some of the darkest spots were high above the rope. *Doesn't look right, but I'm not a doctor.*

Then Steph decided to lift his fingertips. As he feared, there was something under a couple of his nails, something white, like wax... *Or skin. Could it have been Quirános' men? Does he travel with his own "men"?*

He looked down at the rug, it was perfectly squared in the center of the floor. Everything was too convenient, too neat. *Man, you were a little too careful. And the light.*

Steph wondered why a suicidal Dr. Lukely would have turned the light off to kill himself in the dark. *The killer instinctively turned the light off on his way out.*

Steph suddenly realized his situation, standing in a murdered man's bathroom at four in the morning, AWOL, dressed in all black clothes with latex gloves covering his hands, just a few minutes after he'd murdered a Bolivian anti-American socialist. He also realized he was very tired. He didn't know exactly what he should do, but knew he had to get back to the barracks. *How did I not see this?*

He walked out of the bathroom and past the table, setting the keys down and walking out the front door carelessly. Instead of walking towards the jungle, toward safety, he walked along the edge of the street, like a lonely kid pulled toward unfortunate acquaintances.

Could it have been Quirános? He wondered again. No, that makes no sense. I already know that. Think... Think! His feet moved heavily, but automatically, scuffling the rocks along the edge of the road. *Could it be the LT? Parts of it, maybe, but not Dr. Lukely. He'd do a lot for the Teams and his career, but not this. It had to be him. It had to be Breck.*

He should have been more careful getting back to the base. He should have used his memory map to find the quickest way back to the safety of the jungle, to fewer lights and fewer Bolivians, to the secret path, but he didn't really care anymore. He wondered again about Quíranos.

My first kill. It didn't feel anything like what I thought it'd feel like. No fury, no battle, no fear; just cold adrenaline and death. But… it's not that… It's… he was… just reading the paper, in his underwear… Not what I thought it would be like.

Steph suddenly realized he'd have to tell Chief and the LT what he'd done. *Yea, I'm screwed! They'll be pissed… Yea, I'm probably going to prison.*

All his remaining energy slowly seeped out of him. He'd betrayed his Brothers, allowed an innocent kid to be killed, murdered an innocent man, possibly allowed an American doctor to be murdered, and ruined his career and future because he wanted to solve the puzzle himself. Because he needed to do it alone. He pulled his hoodie back up over his head, noticing he was still wearing the clear plastic gloves he'd forgotten to remove. Steph looked extremely suspicious, but he was too tired and depressed to care. The sky was just beginning to show the first hints of dawn when he saw a big, new truck pulled over by the side of the road. A tall, fat man, dressed in nice clothes, was arguing with two smaller, thin men who looked more indiginous than European and seemed out of place on the outskirts of Riberalta, even on the edge of the jungle. They were bartering or arguing about something in the truck bed. Steph walked right up to them, indifferent to his safety or the political situation. The men were so focused on their argument they didn't notice him. The big man, with all the confidence of wealth, status, and power, finally tossed a small bundle of money at the men and yelled something in Guaraní. As he turned away from them, they all looked directly at Steph, who was standing on the edge of the group staring at the limp, pathetic carcass.

She was obviously dead, but still seemed alive, as if just pretending to be dead until the stupid men went back to town, back to their loud music, yelling, and motorcycles. The sleek spotted coat seemed electric, like it still pulsed with coiled energy. Steph reached out to stroke the tense, smooth coat. As soon as he touched the tan fur he pulled his hand back, shocked. It seemed inappropriate to caress and fondle her, but he couldn't resist. He removed the glove and slid his hand to her head, traced the contours of her eye sockets with one finger. The glassy eyeballs looking at nothing, seeing nothing. Then he slid his finger into her mouth, sliding it over her incredibly hard, white teeth, pushing the jaws apart a bit more, rubbing the edge of his finger over her rough tongue. A pungent earthy, living smell floated from her mouth, almost like decomposing grass or fungus. Steph lifted her powerful paw, his own hand engulfed by the massive but light miracle of soft pads and razor sharp claws. Although they were retracted, he could imagine the terrible force they once wielded. Still holding the puma's paw, he looked at the fat man, his eyes burning a new hatred he'd never known. Steph didn't think at all, he simply slid his box knife from his pocket, hiding it along the side of his leg. The only sounds they heard was the tall, fat man's heavy breathing and the click of razor sharp metal locking into place.

"I no kill." He didn't move, didn't step backward or give an inch. "They say... hit by auto bus." The fat man seemed angry and worried at the same time. He could see the silver gleam of the blade as Steph dropped the paw and turned completely toward him, but his eyes were wide and aggressive. "They find... on road. I pay."

The smaller men didn't seem to know what was happening. They said something in Guaraní. Steph held the fat man's gaze for a minute, then looked back at the puma. All his hatred left him, like air from an untied balloon, until de didn't feel anything at all. The anger gone as fast as it arose. His mind blank, he closed his knife, looked at the indigenous men about to lose their puma to a greedy, rich man. They all knew a puma skin was very valuable, and illegal, especially as the cats were hard to track, rare, and protected by the Bolivian government. Steph felt bad for the smaller men, so he tossed his box knife to the closest one, looked one last time at the dead puma, resisted the urge to touch her one more time, and walked toward the jungle.

∞

Despair carries a weight that pulls from within, not like gravity, but more like dehydration, as if the pull comes from all directions at the same time. Steph didn't care about any of it anymore. He walked along the edge of the jungle, occasionally drifting into the bush and then back out to the grasses along its edge. He didn't think about the path or the squad, but subconsciously walked toward them. His decision to head back toward the jungle was not for security, but privacy and solace. He wanted rest, a calm space, a quiet alert mind. He didn't need to think his way back to the bush or the path, he just walked.

The wall of green that had been so exhilarating just a few days before, now calmed him like a deep breathe. As it absorbed him, his anxiety lightened, his legs strengthened, but most importantly, his mind settled. He adjusted the hoodie so it tilted enough to cover most of his fair face and all his blonde hair but allowed him to see a little better. He pulled off the other plastic glove, shoving it into his pocket. He stopped walking, kneeled down, grabbed a handful of soil from the jungle floor, lifted it toward his face and deeply inhaled the rich smell of life and death. Then he rubbed the soil all over his hands, letting most of it fall to the ground. He walked the secret trail back toward the barracks.

I wish I had some camo... I could lose myself in Los Amazonas for a while. It's a difficult, violent, intense reality, but it's honest. It's fair and honest... At what point did we become so dishonest... to the realities of life, to our better interests, our better nature? But then again, all the animals and even plants are trying to devour each other, trying to sneak up on each other, trying to kill each other... What's the difference? They'll calmly stare while they eat each other... Why do I feel so low? Why do we second-guess ourselves... Because we're human. Because, right or wrong, we're moral and ethical creatures, not pumas or killers, but sons and daughters.

Steph hadn't realized how close he was to the barracks, so he was surprised when he found himself walking past the medical building. Part of him wanted to go in, to check if Nicolás was in there. *Maybe it was a mistake. Maybe he's not really dead.*

But Steph knew... there was no point hoping any longer. He continued walking to the same spot as last time, looking at the barracks, imagining the conversation he'd have with Chief and the LT in a few minutes. He remembered Marcelos Quirános, heard the gurgling sound of his collapsing throat, felt the pressure of his own hard forearm against the soft throat and the sensation of dropping limp, dead weight to the floor. He could almost see him lying there, awkwardly, like the puma, devoid of that inherent gracefulness not all of us enjoy.

He leaned sideways into one of the young adolescent trees, still big by suburban standards, but small by Amazonian standards. After a few moments, he heard a few birds and was able to really quiet himself, especially his mind. Slowly, his palace arose on its own. He didn't know why, but still closed his eyes and saw the squad, Steen and Breck, Simpson and Smith, Chief. Steph was happy to see them, but knew they'd have to quietly distance themselves from him. He saw the LT, his face contorting into a rage about to explode, then realizing there was no point, resigning himself to the inevitable. He saw Dr. Lukely, still hanging from the pipe in the bathroom shower.

Should I have cut him down? That would have left a trace… But, I already left a trace… Doesn't matter, I'll tell everyone the truth. Whatever…

After a long moment of swirling images, his mind shifted, not to a different space, but a different way of thinking that includes but goes beyond memory, that includes but almost surpasses, or at least circumnavigates reason, not to answer questions, but to solve mysteries. Up to this point, Steph had mostly been arranging details and images, charting motives and actions, deducing and rationalizing, reasoning, weighing and thinking. Now, without any effort, his mind did the opposite. Details, images, ideas, and motives fell away, dissipated. His palace became clearer, less confusing. Steph didn't really notice the fading away of Steen or Simpson, the softening of the LT and Dr. Lukely, as much as he saw the one image slowly coming into clear focus, as if of its own accord, as if it finally wanted to be seen.

Lights… If I open my eyes, I'll see the lights of our barracks, and I can just walk out of this jungle and into the squad. Maybe the boys will be glad… Maybe they'll be proud… Yea, maybe they'll believe I did it for us…

But he stayed where he was, alone, on the edge of the jungle, and didn't open his eyes. He stood in the same spot, as if waiting for a sign, waiting for a final moment. The sounds of morning were rising. He heard another bird call out. A harsh screech. Then the jungle went almost silent again. He felt the air tightening.

He didn't open his eyes because at the same time he was hoping
for light or a sign from somewhere else, the violent face was still coming
into focus. He thought he knew the truth, but still wanted to actually see it,
to be sure. Something was different. The birds suddenly cawed and cawed
from what seemed like right overhead as the face of another murderer
looked right at him. He was wrong, so very wrong.

As he realized his fatal mistake, Steph heard what sounded like a
shifting of weight, a quick step and a soft creak that gave the murderer
away. But it was too late. He finally realized his mistake, realized the truth,
and realized everything that mattered. With his last breath, Steph said aloud,
"Mother of God!"

The choke hold was different this time, tighter, a different kind of
instant, like a boa constrictor tightening every muscle in the world. Steph's
hands instinctively reached back toward his attacker, wasting critical time.
He remembered what Chief had taught him, but, once again, too late. He
arched his back, trying to strike with his head, but the iron grip was
relentless and the murderer kept his head carefully off to the side, just
enough. The attempt to strike with his butt, to create space to turn and
maneuver, didn't work. Steph reached for the box knife that wasn't there,
remembering how he'd stupidly given it away. He punched and grabbed,
twisted and fought, knowing it was futile but still wanting his nemesis to
respect his willingness to fight to the end. The lack of oxygen was already
weakening his muscles, reducing his abilities and willpower. Once again,
Steph felt like a kid lost in a violent, ruthless adult world. As his legs started
to give out, his attacker didn't settle to the ground, but leaned back,
allowing Steph's weight to help finish the job. The last thing Steph saw was

the lights of the barracks and the overarching branches of the jungle hiding his death. He blinked his eyes, saw white spots and then dark spots. Steph's arms fell to his sides, and his last thought was that he was right the first time: Death is like flipping a switch.

20 – THE REST IS SILENCE

Regaining consciousness comes in two seemingly contradictory waves. First, the light simply switches on. You come alive again in a flash, a silent lightening, a foggy awareness. But mind and thoughts are different than consciousness. They roll in behind the crack, like a slow rolling thunder. This is what most people remember, the gradual clarity of thought. Steph came alive again in the barracks, disoriented, his throat wasted, his head pulsing, the right side of his face cold while the left side felt hot, almost burning.

Why am I sideways? Why can't I see anything?

He tried to turn, to get up, but couldn't. His shoulders ached from a relentless pulling strain. He realized his arms were tied at the elbows and wrists with some type of soft, wide bands.

Oh, yea... He remembered what happened on the edge of the jungle. Then he thought about the bands, *Yea, less likely to leave a mark.*

He struggled to blink, then squinted and tried again, roughly managing a few blinks before realizing he was blindfolded and tied to a chair laying on its side on the floor. He couldn't speak or scream, even if his throat wasn't partially crushed. The gag in his mouth seemed to fill every centimeter of space, keeping him from moving his tongue and making it difficult to breath. His throat hurt, inside and out, a lot, on the sides as well as the front, which was different than last time.

Perhaps this is what Quirános felt?

He could hear him, behind, sorting or arranging items, probably

242

something small. He heard a zipper, and then glass clanking lightly.

Sounds like Dr. Lukely, before he inspected my neck. Could it be... A needle abruptly entered Steph's neck in almost exactly the same spot the caterpillar had bit him. The swelling was almost entirely gone, but he probably still had a mark.

A target for another murder. Smart... it might look like a delayed reaction, which could help explain why I've been acting so strangely, going AWOL, attacking Bolivian diplomats, walking the streets of Riberalta. Oh man... he's going to blame me for everything.

The burning started almost immediately, the same pain shooting around the shoulder, down the arm, and into the scalp. He moaned incomprehensible, animal sounds reverberating into the gag for a minute, wishing he could grit and grind his teeth, trying to twist, to move, to relocate the pain. Finally he decided to just press his cheek into the cold tile floor and suffer.

I'll take this pain. I brought it on myself.

Steph heard boots walk around his head, stopping in front of his face. He knew he was squatting down, probably looking at him, maybe checking the soft straps or the effects of the poison. The pain was more intense this time, but since Steph was familiar with it, he actually suffered a little less. Unfortunately, he knew what was coming. This time, he knew he'd probably lose consciousness, probably drift in and out of delirium, especially if this poison was a large dose of the same venom.

Maybe it's just an overdose of whatever Dr. Lukely was working on? Maybe...

Then Steph heard him. "I warned you, and saved you, and then warned you again, over and fucking over!" Chief tapped Steph's head. "But you're just too damn smart for your own good. Aren't you, Austin?"

Part of Steph had known it was his Chief when he saw the dead puma. He still didn't know why, and still didn't want to believe it. Even when his deadly face finally materialized in Steph's palace, he hoped he was wrong. Secretly, lying on the cold floor in agony, he still hoped it was Breck. At least that seemed to make sense. But deep down, he'd known for a while. As much as he had wanted the blindfold off and the gag out, now he wanted them to stay where they were, to block the truth, to hide him from his shame. But Steph also didn't want to die, so he knew he had to do something.

Chief pushed lightly on Steph's neck, as if testing for circulation or blood flow, the way doctors check circulation during a heat stroke examination by pressing on your fingernails and waiting for the color to change. "I warned you…" Chief continued, leaning in a little closer, "too smart in this business is worse than stupid."

Steph knew he had to do something, to stall, to plead, to incite, so he mumbled something through the gag.

Chief looked at him for a minute, then leaned even closer. "What'd you say?"

Steph mumbled again.

Chief waited another minute, then started pulling out part of the gag. "Don't try to scream. Your throat is badly damaged, so you won't make much noise anyway. And then I'll have to quiet you again. Understand?"

Steph, still lying on his side, blind and mute, nodded.

"A good choke hold really bruises and weakens the larynx." Chief pulled out some of the gag. "Sorry about the sides of your throat. I know it's not very elegant, but I couldn't leave the front bruised and not the sides and back. Appearance matters sometimes."

Steph nodded again, sure that Chief hoped people would think it was the poison.

Chief pulled out the last of the gag. "Now, what did you say?"

Steph licked his lips, created some saliva in his dried out mouth, and whispered, "Not smart or stupid, just curious…"

"Well…"

Then Steph added, "Couldn't just walk by."

Chief nodded his head. "Yea, I can accept that. We are what we are." He looked, almost tenderly, at Steph's face, mostly covered by the blindfold. "I can't really blame you for being curious, Austin. You're a pain in the ass, but you're honest and tenacious."

Steph felt like a heart-broken son, but still tried to turn his head toward the door.

"Don't. It won't work." Steph could hear Chief tapping the floor with his little pocket knife. "I hate to do this. I mean, I like you, always have, but you screwed up." Chief continued in a sing-song rhythm, "You broke the most important rules, and a puma's a puma, right?" Steph could hear the slight sarcastic smile in Chief's voice, which sent a chill down his spine and goosebumps along his arms. "Well… better get on with it."

Chief stood and walked behind Steph again, arranging something. Steph felt a clammy sweating start around his neck and head, then more burning inside his shoulder area, more intense than in the jungle. At first he wasn't sure if it was fear or the poison. He felt Chief checking the restraints, then heard him whispering from behind.

"Steph, I really am sorry about this, but we can't have an in-platoon "detective" asking the wrong kinds of questions when we get you back to the states… Did you know? We're leaving today, before the situation gets any worse. The political situation, I mean."

Steph realized he only had a few minutes at most, that Chief was about to finish the job. He tried to yell, but his throat failed him. He couldn't believe nobody had walked into the room, but then again, Chief probably took care of that.

"If you're hoping somebody will find us, forget it. They're all quietly transporting our gear to the airport. And the LT's so busy with the last minute logistics for our departure, he won't hear a thing. He doesn't even know you were gone. So, for the most part, it's just us."

Steph whispered, "How will you…"

"How will I explain your death? Do you really want me to tell you?"

Steph nodded his head.

"Of course you do. You're curious. Well, when we leave, you'll be in the throes of a relapse, from the attack. No Dr. Lukely to help you or realize what's really going on, only simple Petty Officer Simpson, a corpsman who'll do whatever I say, to confirm the poison. I'll suggest

246

relapse if he doesn't, maybe add that the Doc probably tried something experimental on you. He won't contradict me, especially considering how badly he wants to get out of here. I'll suggest the possibility of staying, to find a Bolivian doctor, simultaneously pointing out the many problems facing all of us here. We'll decide to take the chance with flight, especially considering how well you recovered last time. Hopefully, you'll die soon after we get into the air, but either way, considering the situation, nobody is going to divert us to a foreign hospital. We'll fly to Panama. You won't make it."

Steph whispered, "Small doses…"

"Yea. It's too bad, Petty Officer Austin, you could have been a good one. But…" Chief leaned in close, "we have to do what's best for the Team. So, no hope. None."

He started to walk off, but Steph's slightly louder statement stopped him. It hurt like hell to say anything that loudly, but Steph still held out a little hope. "You killed Dr. Lukely."

Chief paused, "Yea… That was unfortunate, and, ironically, what sealed your fate." He came back, squatting in front of Steph this time, most of his weight on his right foot. "I'm sure you realized he started all this mess with his experimental drugs, medicines to cure the world. God! I wish I would have known the LT was calling in a civilian. Remember, I told you, nothing good comes from trusting civilians. By the way, how'd you know it was me? I assume you're not guessing."

"The soda can and the handwriting."

"Shit. I turned my soda tab didn't I? I'm usually so careful."

Steph's mind was racing for ideas. "And the writing."

"What was wrong with my note?"

"Doc only wrote in print."

"Well, can't be perfect."

All the missing parts had fallen into place, but Steph needed to keep Chief talking. "He killed Nicolás."

"Yea, but in fairness to him, I think it was an accident. Not that it makes any difference to me. He risked that kid's life, and, come to think of it, your life and our futures, for that damn voodoo caterpillar medicine."

Steph spoke without thinking. "It could have saved a lot of kids' lives."

Chief leaned in a little closer and whispered, "How'd that work out?" Then he got up and walked to the far side of the room.   Steph tried to deduce what Chief was doing, but focusing was becoming more difficult. The burning and pain were getting worse.   Chief came back quietly and squatted behind Steph again. "Just so you know, I didn't plan any of this, and it'll be over soon. As soon as I give you the rest of this venom, you'll slowly slip into a delirium and then, hopefully, a coma. So, you should make your peace with the world now."

Steph was suddenly very angry. His pain seemed to transform into fury, but he still couldn't break the straps or the chair or Chief's resolve. Even if he wasn't in so much pain, he couldn't free himself or create a miracle. All he could do was die stoically, but his anger got the better of him. "Well, fuck you then! Asshole! Just do it. Be a man, end it now."

"Sorry, it's a really strong dose, so it must be spread out or it'll read differently... if they do an autopsy. Chief paused for a moment, as if he was second-guessing himself. "You know, If you had just stayed in the barracks tonight, none of this would've happened. You've really screwed the squad, our platoon, the Team, the LT, and even Dr. Lukely." The volume and intensity of his voice rose a little. "If you had just stayed in the barracks, Petty Officer Austin, we could have left all this on Dr. Lukely, where it belonged. I didn't want to kill him, but what was I supposed to do? Let him get away with it?" Chief leaned even closer to Steph's ear. "Why couldn't you just follow orders? And don't tell me curiosity." He leaned even closer. "Why!? I think I have a right to know. Tell me why."

Steph wanted to stall, but also wanted to answer. He wanted to live, but also wanted to tell Chief to end the pain. *Nobody's coming. Even if they do, would they stop Chief? Would Simpson or Smith stop him? Could they stop him? He's kind of right... I got myself into this mess... Steen would stop him... I know he would...*

"Austin, I asked you a question. I want an answer."

Steph couldn't believe he was being lectured by his own murderer, but every minute he stalled was another minute of hope, or at least life. "I don't know, Chief. I guess I'm just stubborn."

"Bullshit! Breck is stubborn. The LT is stubborn. I'm stubborn. You're different."

"I guess... I'm just compulsive."

Chief paused for a minute. "What do you mean, compulsive?"

"I mean, sometimes I just can't stop thinking about a problem until it's resolved."

"Well, once again, even though you've screwed us, I like you, and wish I could give you some morphine or something, but the autopsy has to be clean." Steph could hear and sense him leaning toward him.

"Chief, wait. You know, if you like me at all," Steph whispered, "you could not kill me. I won't tell anyone. I can give you something on me."

"Too late for that, Austin."

"No, Chief, wait. I killed Marcelos Quirános tonight. I mean, I didn't want to or mean to, it was an accident..." Steph paused, remembering the sound of Quirános' guttural pleas for help.

"Austin, stop. It won't work."

Steph realized immediately that Chief didn't believe him. "No, it's true. Check it out. Or, you'll hear about it... on the news."

"Relax, Austin. It'll be easier. It's too late. It's done."

"But you're Chief, you can do anything down here. I won't tell anyone you killed Dr. Lukely. I mean, he murdered a kid. Right?"

"Austin... just stop."

Steph knew he should keep pleading, but for some reason he couldn't beg anymore, and it wasn't the poison. He was lost in a swirling current of emotions. Chief was like a father figure to him, and he did want justice for Nicolás. He himself had killed an innocent man, and he was so tired. His mind was so tired. *Is it crazy to kill me over this, or is he right? Do I deserve this? Is all of this my fault?*

Chief interrupted his thoughts. "Sorry, Austin, but the timing has got to be right, and they'll be back soon." Chief focused intensely as he tapped the needle. "Sometimes, bad shit just has to be done."

"Chief, what's going on?" The LT's voice was strong and stern. He filled the doorway, tall and confident. They hadn't heard him push open the door. Chief didn't answer, but quickly stood up, and turned toward the LT. Steph knew Chief was still next to him and that he was still holding the needle with the rest of the poison. The tension was incredible. Chief still hadn't answered the LT. Steph thought about asking for help, but decided to wait.

The LT stepped just inside the doorway and repeated his question, "Chief Wendley, what the hell's going on?"

Chief went on the offensive. "Well, for starters, your frat buddy, civilian doctor killed the kid, Nicolás, as part of a medical experiment and then tried to pin the blame on us."

"Petty Officer Austin, is this true?"

Steph couldn't believe the LT was asking him to participate in the discussion while partially poisoned and tied to a chair on the floor, but his LT had asked him a direct question, so he answered honestly. "Yes, sir."

Then nobody said anything for a long time. Steph worried Chief would suddenly stab the needle into his neck. The burning was spreading to other parts of his body, especially his lower shoulders and even around his spine. The feeling was definitely different this time, less heat but deeper and scarier pain.

Finally, the LT asked, "What does that have to do with Petty Officer Austin being blindfolded and tied to a chair on the floor?"

Chief paused. "Well... sometimes... someone has to do the dirty work."

"What dirty work are you talking about, that has to be done?" Chief didn't reply.

During the tense pauses, Steph wanted to scream for them to untie him, give him some pain killers, do almost anything but this ridiculous standoff, but he knew he had to keep quiet and hope the LT would do the right thing.

Steph could hear the LT step forward, as if just realizing something important. "Chief, where is Sean?"

Chief didn't answer at first, as if he was waiting for everyone else to realize their mistakes. Then he finally asked, "Who's Sean?"

"Dr. Lukely. Where is Dr. Lukely, Chief?" The LT took another step toward them. He couldn't wait any longer. "Austin, where is he?"

Steph was barely part of the conversation now, the pain starting to block out their words and his own thoughts, but he heard his name and the question, and answered as best he could in the circumstances. "Dead."

The LT pulled his Glock 17 Compact from the holster on the back of his right hip and yelled "Step away from Petty Officer Austin, Chief! NOW!"

"I appreciate your emotions, sir, but get a hold of yourself. Sometimes we have to do difficult things. It's about time you learned this lesson."

"You want to teach me a lesson? Are you out of your mind?"

"No, sir. I'm doing what's best for the squad, for the Team, and America, which I shouldn't have to do alone since it's your fucking job."

"My job? How is killing Americans in Riberalta, Bolivia good for the Team, for America? How is that my job?"

"We can't have more bad publicity down here. People are going to connect him to you, and then we'll be responsible for not only the kid's death, but for Americans performing drug experiments on children during a war on drugs."

"They're not connected."

"So what? How naive can you be? People don't care about what it is, just the way it looks."

Steph had stopped listening to them. He could hear their words, but they meant nothing. He knew the LT wouldn't shoot Chief, talking about politics and the history of the Teams, the reputation of SEAL Team four in Bolivia and South America. He knew Chief was explaining how, if they didn't cover it up, all the blame would be laid on the LT. But it wasn't until he heard Chief say, "Your career, sir. Think about your future." that Steph started to worry the LT might still let Chief kill him. "Nooo, no, no." He moaned.

The LT hadn't heard Steph, all his energy and anger were focused on Chief. "So you're suggesting we sacrifice one SEAL for the SEAL Teams?"

"No, sir. Not just for the SEAL Teams, but also for the Brotherhood, which is certainly bigger than any one person." Chief turned the small syringe, with the last dosage of poison, toward Steph's neck. It was the last step that would make his death look like an unfortunate, fateful accident.

"Don't do it, Chief." The LT shook his 9mm pistol, as if making sure Chief could see it. "I'll shoot."

Chief Wendley replied calmly, "No you won't, sir. We all know you won't shoot me. Think about your career. You know I'm right. You want me to take care of the dirty work... Besides, you're a good officer and a good American, but you're too much like him." gesturing at Steph with the needle, "You're not a killer. You're a good American, but you're not a killer." As he started to bring the needle down to Steph's neck, the entire room exploded with noise and light.

The sulphurous smell of gunpowder filled the small room. The echoing sounds reverberated back and forth across the room for a few seconds, as if more shots were being fired. Since he was on the floor, Steph could hear a little better than the LT, but Steph's ears were ringing way beyond the norm. He didn't need to be able to see to know that his Chief was gone and that he was still alive. No needle, no mentor, no matter what.

Then he heard the LT yelling far too loudly. "Awww! Shit! My ear!"

Steph knew he only had a little consciousness left. Physically exhausted, poisoned, emotionally spent, depressed at the unnecessary loss of so much life, guilt-stricken, but still alive, Steph sank into the cold, hard floor. He was drifting, not into his palace or rational thought, but a soft, painful, state of semi-consciousness, which he assumed would lead to unconsciousness.

Maybe I'm dying anyway. Maybe Chief gave me enough poison or I didn't feel the second shot… Either way, I'm sorry for everything. It's my fault, and I'm sorry.

The last thing he heard was the LT giving orders, telling someone to do something immediately. Then he felt someone untying his arms and heard the LT asking him questions, maybe about Dr. Lukely, but the words were lost in a mist of smoke, noise, guilt, regret, and pain. He felt the blindfold being removed, but he kept his eyes shut tightly.

He heard the LT ask, "Are you okay? Austin, can you speak?"

And then he heard Steen's voice yelling for Simpson.

And the rest was silence.

21 – THE END OF EVERYTHING

Steph sat stiffly in the plastic chair outside the Commodore's office. He'd been waiting for this day for weeks. His recovery at Naval Hospital Portsmouth had gone relatively well, partially because he was mostly unconscious. By the time they'd medevac'd him to Panama and then Virginia, he'd slipped into a deep delirium, almost a coma. Nobody'd ever told him whether he was actually in a full coma or not, but he assumed he wasn't because he could remember his dreams and bits of memories that seemed real. Weird walks in the jungle surrounded by pumas and kids playing in the water mixed with images of Marcelos Quirános slouching toward a hardwood floor. Great, expansive birds that were far too big and brave to be real and then the sleek, spotted coat and ceramic white teeth of the very real puma deflated in the back of a civilian pickup truck.

He reached back to his neck and slowly traced the border of the crescent scar where his Chief had shot him with poison. A soft, fleshy purple bump, just starting to harden around the edges, rose in the middle. He liked feeling its edges, knowing it was there but couldn't kill him, at least not now. He pulled the stiffened collar of his freshly starched camo's up a bit, trying to hide the reminder that his mentor, the father-figure he'd trusted more than anyone, had decided to kill him.

He was surprised when Mr. Walker, soon to be Lieutenant Junior Grade Walker, told him he didn't need to wear his dress whites when he showed up at SEAL Team Four's headquarters. He assumed a court-martial required dress uniforms, and there was no doubt in his mind that he was going to a military prison. It was just a question of when and for how long. He almost asked an attendant at the hospital to help him find a copy of the

UCMJ so he could learn more about his fate, his future behind bars. But he decided to leave the future to the future for once. He'd learned a lifetime of lessons in Riberalta, especially that it's sometimes better to leave well enough alone, not that he was sure he'd be able to. So he just sat in his bed reading until the doctor told him he could start rehabilitation, until he was able to function on his own, until Mr. Walker told him when to show up for his hearing. He was also surprised he hadn't been arrested or handcuffed to the bed or at least warned about not going AWOL.

He set his hand back in his lap, nervous, but glad to get this day over with. While lying in his hospital bunk, Steph had thought the details of Riberalta through many times, analyzing everything carefully. Although he'd made many mistakes, and broken Navy protocol as well as violated documented and undocumented Team protocols, he couldn't find a different path, another set of options that would have saved Nicolás, Dr. Lukely, and Chief, and kept him from murdering a Bolivian politician and going to prison.

Not murdering... assassinating. I wonder if they'll use that term in the trial.

He wasn't proud of the results of his actions, but he believed he tried to do his duty.

The XO's assistant, a brawny, muscular lieutenant waiting for a platoon, walked up and said, "Come on Petty Officer Austin, he's ready for you."

Steph didn't really know how to proceed, other than to do what he was told. He assumed he was in legal, professional, and maybe even physical danger. Chief Wendley was an old-timer, well respected and liked at the team. Steph was an odd, newbie who'd caused a SEAL death and embarrassed SEAL Team Four during an international operation. He wondered if he'd have a lawyer in the room, still a little surprised that nobody had contacted him.

I must be a total idiot, not even asking about a JAG lawyer; will this be like an arraignment? I should have done something to prepare, but, to be honest, I don't really care. I've screwed up so much, I really deserve whatever I get. A court-martial is the appropriate end of everything I've worked so hard to achieve.

The lieutenant took him past the CO's office to the XO's door, knocked twice, opened the door, and gestured Steph to enter. The Executive Officer, second in command at SEAL Team Four, sat behind a big desk covered with neatly organized piles of papers, like an asymmetrical chess board covered with monochromatic pieces nobody else could understand. Behind him hung about a dozen photos of SEALs and politicians shaking hands, inspecting training sites, or just socializing. The remainder of the room was sparsely decorated. There were no windows. Steph expected to see a panel of officers, like in the movies, but he realized immediately how naive he'd been.

This is not my court-martial, just my ass chewing, or maybe full-on ass kicking.

The XO got up from his seat, walked around the desk, and gestured toward two chairs at the side of the room. As he was sitting down, the XO said, "Son, I have been in charge of this unfortunate investigation as the CO has been… well, busy with more important things. Lieutenant Hensen told me everything. I'm confident I understand what happened down there."

Steph, still surprised that he was alone in the room with SEAL

Team Four's executive officer, paused as he was sitting down, suspended in midair.

What does that mean? Everything, as is it seemed to the LT, or everything? Did the LT know more than I thought? How could anyone else know everything. I'm still not sure I know everything.

The XO looked up at Steph, still half-standing with two hands on the chair. "Go ahead, son, sit down."

Steph sat and wisely decided to keep his mouth shut in order to let the XO reveal his cards, a lesson he'd learned from his Chief the hard way. But he had to say something, to not appear rude. "Thank you, sir."

The XO leaned toward Steph, as if he had to be quiet in that big spacious room, as if people might be listening. "Yes, it was a bad situation."

"Yes, sir." Steph badly wanted to apologize and explain his actions, rationalize his decisions, but he stayed quiet.

"Well, as you can probably guess, we need to contain the damage while being true to our ideals. Would you agree?"

"Yes, sir." Steph replied, not exactly sure what he was talking about.

"There's no doubt that Chief Wendley had... medical issues, mental health issues." He paused, as if waiting for Steph to play his part in the conversation.

"Yes, sir."

"I'm really sorry about what happened to you, but we have to think about other factors, bigger factors." Steph didn't know what to say, so he just nodded his head up and down while trying desperately to maintain eye contact. The XO continued, "Not just SEAL Team issues, but his family… we need to consider his family… Wouldn't you agree?"

In all his time in the hospital, Steph hadn't thought about Chief's wife and kids, who he used to talk about all the time. He let his head fall toward the floor a bit, looking at his finely polished boots, even more ashamed than he'd been before. "Of course, sir." He raised his head. "Whatever can be done for them. Whatever is best for them." He wanted to maintain eye contact, but couldn't, so he looked at the wall over his right shoulder.

The XO smiled, "Good, son. Good. I'm glad you agree. His family won't survive without his death gratuity and housing benefits, and then there's the life insurance. That's why we've decided to report his death as an accidental weapon discharge."

Steph's entire body tightened up. He kept looking at the wall, pressing his lips firmly together, furrowing his brow just a bit. The XO leaned back in his chair, as if noticing Steph's change of demeanor. It didn't take long for Steph to fully realize the irony of the situation.

He'll be remembered as a victim of an accident while I rot in a military prison. But… it's all fine. Chief and I are responsible for this mess, not the XO, not SEAL Team Four, and certainly not Chief's family. The LT might be partially responsible, but he did save my life. He finally just said, "Yes sir, sounds about right."

"Good. Lieutenant JG Walker is going to help guide you through some details this morning, and then get you right back to work, if you're up for it. We have a major situation brewing, so we need every able bodied

SEAL in a platoon and I need to get back to operations."

Steph thought he must have misheard him. "Sir, I don't understand."

"You don't understand what?"

"The... situation..." Steph still couldn't bring himself to say the assassination. "The... situation with Marcelos Quirános, sir."

"What about him?"

"His death, sir... I..."

Steph was just about to explain what happened in that room when the XO interrupted him. "Quirános isn't dead."

Steph just stared at him. The silence hung in the air for a few seconds, but felt like an eternity to Steph, an eternity that he should fill with words, until he remembered to be patient.

Keep your mouth shut.

The XO went on, "He almost forced all of you to stay in-country, claiming that somebody tried to kill him. We don't know exactly what happened, but we assumed... Chief Wendley had... We assume Chief Wendley tried to cover Dr. Lukely's tracks or that Quirános had something on Chief Wendley. It was tuck and go for a while, but we got you all out. Partially because of your medical condition." The XO leaned forward, genuine concern on his face. "Are you alright, Petty Officer Austin? You're white as a sheet."

"Yes, sir. Just a little... surprised."

"Well, we probably won't be training in Bolivia for a while, but that's okay. We have our hands full in Central America right now." The XO stood, clearly indicating the meeting was over. "I do want to talk more about some of your amazing abilities. Lieutenant Hensen thinks very highly of you and your skills as an intelligence rep, but we don't have time right now." He started walking toward the door, one hand on Steph's shoulder, encouraging and guiding him out. "Usually we'd give you some leave to recuperate, but we're desperate for men right now. So, unless you feel unable to perform your duty, we're keeping you in Alpha platoon. You seem to have a special knack for solving problems and observing and remembering details, skills all of us could improve upon, especially in this war."

"Which war is that, sir?"

"The war on drugs, the war against the cartels and dictators like Noriega." The Commodore looked at him carefully. "The fight for the American way of life."

Steph wasn't exactly sure what that meant in this moment, but he was willing to fight for it. He trusted the XO, and he needed to fight for something. "Yes, sir. I'm in."

"Good. Go find Mr. Walker, meet your new OIC, and get to the intel locker. We need smart guys like you in the field." He opened the door as he finished his sentence, and put out his hand.

Steph shook it firmly. "Thank you, sir. I appreciate the second chance. I won't let you down. But sir, you said new OIC. What happened to Lieutenant Hensen?"

"He requested and was awarded a transfer. You're dismissed."

Operations, including the XO and CO's offices, was separated from the rest of the team by the quarterdeck, a tall circular desk station where the duty officer checked people in and maintained the log. Steph asked the watch, "Hey, do you know where Mr. Walker is?"

The watch, a technician who worked in the dive locker, looked at Steph as if deciding whether or not to answer him. The guy was an E-4 Steph had never seen before today. He wasn't a SEAL, Steph probably outranked him by time in the Navy, certainly by status, and he was clearly being disrespectful. "Petty Officer whatever, did you hear me?"

"Yea, I heard you."

"Well, answer the question." Steph hadn't had time to think about the Team's reaction to Chief's death because it wouldn't matter in prison. He immediately realized the Team blamed him.

"I don't know. Maybe he's in the locker room."

Steph stared at him for a long moment, then walked off. He should have expected this. Chief Wendley had many friends, both SEALs and support personnel. SEALs are incredibly loyal and very emotional when it comes to the Brotherhood. Once again, Steph felt alone, like an outsider, where he once felt safe and at home.

He walked down the empty hall and into the empty locker room. It should have been called the locker hall because rows of lockers facing each other seemed to go on forever, more like a long wide hallway. Cruise boxes were neatly lined up under long benches dividing the two sides of the room. Each guy had two lockers and two or three cruise boxes holding all their extra individual gear. It was an awkward space with little room to maneuver and only two exit/entrances, one at each end of the long skinny room.

Steph looked down the aisles and then walked to the middle of the room and called out, "Mr. Walker?"

"He's not here." Breck stood quietly at the end of the row near the north exit, staring daggers at Steph.

Steph hadn't seen any of the boys from Alpha Platoon since the incident. At first he assumed they were prohibited from visiting him because of the court-martial, but now he knew they probably chose not to visit because they either didn't know what to say or blamed him for Chief's death. *I wonder if anyone knows what really happened?*

Steph didn't know what to say, so he said nothing, just faced Breck and waited, assuming the worst.

"Why are you looking for him?"

"None of your business, Breck." Steph swallowed instinctively, almost feeling Breck's forearm squeezing his throat, cutting off his air. He knew why Breck was here, and he didn't care. He just didn't care. He felt in his pocket, no knife. It wasn't part of the dress camo uniform.

"You're wrong, Austin. Again!" He almost spit the words across the room. "It is my business."

Steph could tell something had changed. Breck wasn't a bluffer, too arrogant for that. But he wasn't going to ask.

Breck slowly started walking toward him. "What are you doing here."

"What do you mean? I work here."

"They should have discharged you, out of the Teams and the Navy, dishonorably."

"Well, they didn't."

Breck stopped about fifteen feet from Steph. "No, they didn't." He pulled his box knife from his pocket, clicked it open, started cleaning his fingernails the way Chief always had, never veering his eyes away from Steph. And then he tapped his knife twice on the locker next to him.

Suddenly, Steph had a flashback. He was no longer only in the locker room, but also on the floor of a Bolivian barracks, tied to a chair. He could see LT and Chief at the same time. Even though he'd been blindfolded during the event, he knew where both Chief and the LT had stood and argued, could imagine them glaring at each other, Chief trying to manipulate the LT to do what was best for the Team, the LT silently raging at Chief for killing his friend, pointing his 9 mm Glock at everyone's mentor. He could imagine the two men trying to protect what they believed in. And although Steph couldn't see anything, he could hear a lot. He remembered the sound of Chief tapping his knife twice on the floor. He remembered the sound of Chief preparing the needle. He remembered the yelling and the sound of a large caliber bullet exploding, filling the room with deafening noise and smoke and the smell of gunpowder. Not the explosion a 9 mm bullet makes, but the explosion a much larger, more powerful 45 caliber bullet makes. Steph realized the explosion must have come from just behind the LT, not from in front of him, not from his gun.

Steph focused on Breck's eyes. "You."

"Shut up!" Breck stepped forward, pointing the knife at Steph's face.

"You did it."

Breck's face flashed red, his eyes almost swelled, showing his entire irises and dark, dark pupils. "I swear to God, I'll…"

"You saved me." Steph could see Breck slowly getting closer, but didn't register it. "The LT couldn't do it. But you could… You did… Holy shit…" Steph sank to a bench, rubbing his head in his hands. He sat for just a second, then stood back up and looked right at Breck. "Breck, I don't know how to say this, but…"

"Don't!" He was looming over Steph again, holding the knife near his face. "Don't say a fucking word! I should have ended you when I had the chance." He gritted his teeth for a moment, shaking his head. "Just so you know, clearly…" Breck was so angry it was difficult for him to speak. "…for the Teams, not you. I did it for the Teams, for the chain of command, for the military, for the Navy. Not your sorry fucking ass!" Breck's hatred seemed to seethe from every pore, almost coating him like sweat or the lather an overworked horse creates. "Chief was the best of men, better than you'll ever be… he just got in over his head."

Steph stared hard at Breck. They were less than a foot from each other. "You know, I didn't want this to happen. You think I wanted any of this to happen?"

"I don't give a rat's ass what you wanted."

"I didn't start this shit, or… or…"

"Or what? Cause it? Your entire life caused it, your entire life is shit, Austin! I don't even know who you are… or what you are. But I do know one thing. You don't belong here."

Steph wanted to say he did belong, that he was a part of the Team, a part of the Brotherhood, but he couldn't. Maybe because he wasn't sure that it was true, or maybe he wasn't sure how it was true, but he certainly knew he wanted it to be true.

Breck continued, "What are you doing here? Is this a game for you?"

Steph had had enough. "I know what I'm doing now, Breck. I know what I'm doing now, and I'm staying."

Breck smiled at him. "Well, be careful, Petty Officer Austin, or before you know it, your time will come." He looked down at his knife for a second. "Here, there. Who knows... But be careful... because you don't belong here."

"Why not?" Steph asked, starting to get angry. "Why the fuck not, Breck? I love my country, and my Brothers. I loved Chief. Do you think I wanted him to die? Do you think I wanted to lie underneath him, on the floor, waiting for a needle in my neck? Yea, I screwed up, but I didn't want any of this to happen. So why don't I deserve to be here?"

"You're too damn smart for your own good."

"It's bad to be smart? Is that what you're saying?"

"Yes! Sometimes. But that's not the real problem."

"What's the real problem, Breck?"

"The real problem, asshole, is that you think you're smarter than you are, and it's the wrong kind of smart. All this," He waved his hand at everything in the room. "it's not about you or answers or truth; it's about us, not you, but the guys next to you and at home, their wives and kids." Breck was too upset to say anything else. "It doesn't matter. You don't get it."

"You don't know shit, Breck! You don't know what I get."

"I know it'll work itself out. If not here, today, then soon."

"Is that a threat, Breck?"

They both knew they were done talking. Steph could see something in Breck's facial expressions, and then remembered the look in the parking lot and the feeling of Breck's forearm across his throat.

Never again. You will never again get my back. You can stab me in the face, but you'll never again get my back. Then he said aloud, "Never again, Breck."

They were so close to each other, there didn't seem to be any options. Steph knew he was already at a disadvantage because he was thinking through what should have been obvious: Attack! He knew Breck had his knife out, but he too had hesitated, so he just stood there, waiting for Breck to decide.

As they stood face to face, almost leaning into each other, newly promoted Lieutenant JG Walker walked around the corner of a locker. He stopped, saw the knife, and asked, "What's going on?"

"Nothing, sir." Breck said, keeping his eyes on Steph a little longer until he turned to face Mr. Walker, flipped the knife in the air and caught it with the blade toward himself.

"Why do you have your knife out, Petty Officer Breckendae?"

Breck smiled at him. "It's a box knife… Ensign Walker. You know, for cutting string and rigging." He spoke slowly, as if to a child, raising his eyebrows a little.

"First, it's Lieutenant Walker. Second, are you cutting string or rigging in here?" He took a step closer to Breck.

"No, sir. But you never know… we might rig for a rubber duck today. I think Charlie platoon is." Breck flipped the knife again, blade pointing toward Mr. Walker. "I was going to ask Austin if he wanted to help."

For a second, Steph wasn't sure Mr. Walker would hold up, but he stepped even closer, bringing the knife to his chest, and said, "Put it away. Now. And get to the platoon hut. The new LT wants to see everyone."

Breck smiled, "I thought you were the LT, sir."

"I'll be Alpha platoon's AOIC." Mr. Walker stepped back just enough to open a path for Breck to leave. "Close that, so nobody accidentally gets hurt. And get to the platoon hut."

"Yes, sir. On my way." He deftly closed the blade and slid it into his pocket. "And congratulations on your promotion, sir. After only a few weeks in the jungle, you're probably ready to be in charge of real men now." Breck brushed past him, saying over his shoulder, "Wow! That's great… sir!" The sarcasm dripped from every word as he left the locker room.

Mr. Walker turned to Steph, "Petty Officer Austin, what was that about? I mean, I can guess, but…"

Steph watched the door close and said, "Nothing for you to worry about, sir. Just different perspectives."

"Well, you two will have to work it out. You are both staying in Alpha platoon because we need every able body right now. And, as I said, I'll be Alpha's AOIC." He tried to stand a little taller as he said the next part. "I know I'm young, but I'm not going to put up with any of Breck's bullshit from Bolivia." He paused for a minute, as if preparing to either critique or encourage Steph. But he finally just said, "Get to medical. The LT wants you checked out this morning. When you're done, go straight to the platoon hut."

"I'll be ready, sir. I mean, I am ready. Physically and mentally." Steph thought that must have sounded bad.

"Good." He walked toward the door.

"I'm ready, sir. Don't worry about me." Steph wasn't sure it was true, but he knew he needed to say it. "Sir, the XO told me to go to the intel locker after checking in with you."

"Afterward. Medical first, then check in with the new LT." He walked to the door and opened it.

"Sir, you said it's heating up. What's heating up?"

Mr. Walker looked back from the door. "You're the intel rep, you should be able to tell me. As a matter of fact, I want an intel report on the situation by 1600 hours."

Steph asked again, "Yes, sir, but where are we going?"

Mr. Walker walked through the door, letting it swing closed behind him as he simply said, "Panama."

Steph waited, trying to lower his heart rate while secretly hoping Breck would come back, with or without his knife. He wished they could settle it one way or another right then, even though the odds were against him. He knew that in one sense Breck was right, but he didn't want to admit it, so he looked at his hands, wondering about Los Amazonas and El Madre de Dios, regretting Nicolás and Dr. Lukely, missing his Chief, questioning the possibility of justice, and doubting his own abilities. He balled his hands into fists and then opened them again, wondered whether pumas have memories, what they dream about after eating their kill, and why they were going to Panama.

The End

Keep reading for a sneak peek of the 2nd installment of the Steph Austin SEAL Stories Mystery series: A Just Cause. A riveting mystery that takes you into the heart of the tragic events of the invasion of Panama in 1989, through the dangerous and sensual streets of Panama City as Steph tries to save his closest enemy, and into the heart of a beautiful Panamanian police officer who might be even more determined to do good than Steph.

ABOUT BRETT HANSON

Author, teacher, mentor, father, and public speaker, Brett Hanson has taught English for almost twenty-five years in Montana, Oregon, and Wisconsin. Before graduating from The University of Montana with high honors, he served his country in the toughest military assignment in the world: The Navy SEAL Teams. His four years at SEAL Team Four taught him many things, including the importance of setting high goals, believing in oneself, intentionally developing physical and mental toughness, and turning spectacular failure into future success. But the first important lesson he learned is the primary American lesson: *You will succeed: Work hard.*

And that is exactly what he does now to teach and serve young adults in our public schools. In addition to writing his SEAL Stories series to entertain and motivate young people, Brett has started Hanson Education Services to share The Teacher's Promise podcast, celebrating, inspiring, and sharing the wonderful stories of compassionate teachers across the country; *Grammarology,* a music-based, dynamic 21st century curriculum of English grammar and mechanics that kids actually like doing because it's fun; and *Good Writing,* a simple-to-complex writing system focusing on growing anyone's writing skills from where they are toward excellence, one step at a time.. All this work can be explored at hansoneducationservices.com

A Just Cause

The 2ⁿᵈ Installment of the Steph Austin SEAL Stories Mysteries

Panama
1 - A Good Night

The PB's cut through the long, rolling waves like dark, silent knives, sleek black machines rising and falling on small mountains of water that had started their inevitable course toward this place in order to crash on this shore long before this awesome, dark night. The train of boats moved through the midnight waters of El Golfo de Panamá, along the dark shoreline of El Chorillo, past el Aeroporto Internacional, toward Punta Paitilla and the small cove that would ultimately allow them to officially invade Panama. They towed fourteen rubber zodiacs carrying three full SEAL platoons and approximately fifty support staff, SEAL operations command, a medical unit, a communications unit, and an Air Force liason team for Spectre gun support. The smaller rubber boats, being pulled behind the PB's, buoyed on the waves like streamlined corks; sometimes they rose above the PB's, like curious children peeking over fences they shouldn't cross, and other times they sank into the wells of the rolling waves, sitting precariously under the long, heavy swells. On this dark night, the water shined like an ancient pebble, pockmarked and chipped, and the only sounds were the low, throbbing pulses of the PB motors and the distant surf crashing on the shore. It was eerily quiet, especially considering all the tension built up in the city and along the Canal Zone after weeks of provocations. Clouds muffled most normal sounds and minimized both

273

moon and star light, intensifying the darkness. A few stars illuminated a few patches of clear sky far to the north, but the only real light came from Panama City. So, without any lights behind them, their shadowy forms blended into the dark Pacific Ocean that disappeared south all the way to Ecuador. From their perspective, it was a good night for war.

The SEALs had left the beach at Fort Kobbe long before midnight, waited approximately two kilometers offshore until 0000 hours, then slowly headed east. H-hour for the full Panama invasion had been set for 0100, and they were part of the first wave. But General Maxwell moved H-hour up fifteen minutes, so they sped up and adjusted their plans. Any changes in the well-rehearsed mission could cause minor issues that would later transform into bigger problems. The Ops officers made all these decisions from the safety of the PB's. Lieutenant Commander Townsend, the senior officer of the shore team, sat in the stern of the lead zodiac, towed behind the first PB, fully aware they were going faster than originally planned, calmly waiting next to his radioman for any updates before they detached from the PB's, which would rally offshore for extraction and support. The Op's officers must have known they were behind schedule now, with the new H-hour, but they could do nothing but adapt.

Almost everybody watched the shoreline and the city, illuminated like any other city of one million people, but so much quieter. Occasionally, a distant sound could be faintly heard, but for the most part, Panama City was muted. The Bridge of the Americas' lights, glowing like a Disney attraction, spread across the Canal, the gift that had brought so much wealth and so many problems to the tiny country. El Chorillo was sporadically lit up, with its large, boxy apartment buildings and low-level shanties housing the poor mestizos and laborers who couldn't afford an apartment. On any other night, before the troubles, the SEALs would have been driving over the bridge and past El Chorillo to get downtown, to go club hopping or enjoy the warm, late night patio breezes in one of the beautiful hotel bars. Before the troubles began, Panama City was a haven for young Americans who spoke even just a little Spanish. But all that had changed. What had been brewing for years, intensified quickly, scaring most people in the city. But this was the moment a handful of young men had been eagerly awaiting. Some of them gazed northeast, watching and listening for the faint sounds of aircraft that could just barely be heard over the PB's, far in the distance. Petty Officer 3rd class Steph Austin hoped that once his eyes were completely acclimated to the night darkness, he might be able to see the flicker of C-130 running lights, like faint, flying lighthouses in the sky.

That's stupid! he thought. *They'd be running dark, like us.*

He pushed his hat back a bit, cocked his head and listened more carefully, and then looked at the dark water flowing beneath the black zodiac.

What do I know? I'm not a pilot.

Petty Officer Steph Austin was in one of the last boats. His platoon, Alpha, was designated first support. As their intelligence rep, he knew more about the full mission than most of his platoon, except for maybe the LT. And because he couldn't stop his insatiable curiosity, he knew more about the entire situation, the history, politics, economics, and the probable consequences, than even most of the Ops officers. So, he knew that approximately two hundred high-tech, cutting edge aircraft, including the new stealth Nighthawk F117 bombers, the new Apache gunship helicopters, the reliable C130 Spectre gunships and transport UH-1 Huey's were navigating the dark night sky to converge on Panama City. He knew cargo planes would be unloading M113 APC's and M551 Sheridan tanks and jeeps and trucks and thousands more soldiers to back up the ten thousand paratroopers that would be parachuting into the city in the next few hours. He knew the sheer force of what was coming from the north, from California, Texas, Florida and Georgia. He knew the seriousness of the new, brutal technological war, a 21st Century war, and he knew that Panama would never be the same. He knew that computers and cameras and laser-targeting and data processing would change everything, that more than ever before, the world was watching. And he knew that he and his brothers would be there first, the tip of the sword.

The tip of the sword on a dark night in a dark boat is an exciting place to be. Steph had never been to war; most of the men in the boats hadn't either, so they were all excited, nervous, and a little scared, but in a good way. Their adrenaline levels were far higher than normal, but since they were still a long way from the insertion point and any real danger, they felt safe. The darkness was their friend, and they knew it. It hid them and dispersed the noises from the PB's. With all the light coming from Panama City, they felt safe and in command, until suddenly, Steph heard a deep, motor sound from the dark, seaward side, off to their right. He looked over his shoulder, toward the back of the boat where Lieutenant Walker sat with the radioman, waved his hand twice, pointed to his ear, and then toward the sound. The LT nodded his head and picked up the radio handset. Steph looked back toward the sound as the large silhouette of a boat running the opposite direction materialized out of the dark. Steph pointed his Car-15 toward the dark shape, waited for what seemed inevitable, and thought about how he wound up in this boat, how lucky he was to be included, to be a part of the Team again, and to not be in prison. He remembered everything that happened just a week ago, like a time-lapsed explanation of a person's life. And then he saw nothing but a world of bright, white, blinding light.

Made in the USA
Columbia, SC
15 August 2022

64958192R00169